Diana Palmer's heroes are compelling, vibrant and utterly impossible to resist, just like her novels!

DIANA PALMER

"Ms. Palmer masterfully weaves a tale that entices on many levels, blending adventure and strong human emotion into a great read."
—*RT Book Reviews*

"Nobody tops Diana Palmer when it comes to delivering pure, undiluted romance. I love her stories."
—*New York Times* bestselling author Jayne Ann Krentz

"Palmer knows how to make the sparks fly... heartwarming."
—*Publishers Weekly* on *Renegade*

"A compelling tale… [that packs] an emotional wallop."
—*Booklist* on *Lawman*

Bonus Book!

For your enjoyment, we've added in this volume *Passion Flower*, a classic, bestselling book by Diana Palmer!

Diana Palmer has a gift for telling the most sensual tales with charm and humor. With over forty million copies of her books in print, Diana Palmer is one of North America's most beloved authors and is considered one of the top ten romance authors in the U.S.

Diana's hobbies include gardening, archaeology, anthropology, iguanas, astronomy and music. She has been married to James Kyle for more than twenty-five years, and they have one son.

For news about Diana Palmer's latest releases please visit www.dianapalmer.com or www.eHarlequin.com.

DIANA PALMER

TOUGH TO *Tame*

TORONTO • NEW YORK • LONDON
AMSTERDAM • PARIS • SYDNEY • HAMBURG
STOCKHOLM • ATHENS • TOKYO • MILAN • MADRID
PRAGUE • WARSAW • BUDAPEST • AUCKLAND

Recycling programs
for this product may
not exist in your area.

ISBN-13: 978-0-373-83757-1

TOUGH TO TAME

Included in this volume is *Passion Flower,* originally published as a Silhouette Romance novel.

PASSION FLOWER

This edition published by arrangement with Harlequin Books S.A.

For questions and comments about the quality of this book please contact us at Customer_eCare@Harlequin.ca.

www.eHarlequin.com

Printed in U.S.A.

CONTENTS

TOUGH TO TAME 9

BONUS BOOK!
PASSION FLOWER 203

Dear Reader,

Dr. Bentley Rydel has had a special place in my heart ever since he showed up, surly and difficult, in *Heart of Stone.* I thought he deserved a book of his own, and here is the result.

Over the years, veterinarians have been my best friends. They've taken care of my sick pets, comforted me when I lost them, and generally made my life richer and happier. We take them for granted, and we shouldn't. I thank God for them every day of my life.

I am also a fan of veterinarian technicians—of which my niece, Amanda, is one—and groomers, who do a wonderful job of not only keeping our pets looking nice, but often finding conditions that we might miss, to the detriment of our furry friends.

I hope you enjoy Bentley's story.

As always, I am your fan,

Diana Palmer

TOUGH TO TAME

I dedicate this book to all the fine veterinarians, technicians, groomers and office workers who do so much every day to keep our furry friends healthy. Thanks!

CHAPTER ONE

CAPPIE DRAKE peered around a corner inside the veterinary practice where she worked, her soft gray eyes wide with apprehension. She was looking for the boss, Dr. Bentley Rydel. Just lately, he'd been on the warpath, and she'd been the target for most of the sarcasm and harassment. She was the newest employee in the practice. Her predecessor, Antonia, had resigned and run for the hills last month.

"He's gone to lunch," came an amused whisper from behind her.

Cappie jumped. Her colleague, Keely Welsh Sinclair, was grinning at her. The younger woman, nineteen to Cappie's twenty-three, was only recently married to dishy Boone Sinclair, but she'd kept her job at the veterinary clinic despite her lavish new lifestyle. She loved animals.

So did Cappie. But she'd been wondering if love of animals was enough to put up with Bentley Rydel.

"I lost the packing slip for the heartworm medicine,"

Cappie said with a grimace. "I know it's here somewhere, but he was yelling and I got flustered and couldn't find it. He said terrible things to me."

"It's autumn," Keely said.

Cappie frowned. "Excuse me?"

"It's autumn," she repeated.

The older woman was staring blankly at her.

Keely shrugged. "Every autumn, Dr. Rydel gets even more short-tempered than usual and he goes missing for a week. He doesn't leave a telephone number in case of emergencies, he doesn't call here and nobody knows where he is. When he comes back, he never says where he's been."

"He's been like this since I was hired," Cappie pointed out. "And I'm the fifth new vet tech this year, Dr. King said so. Dr. Rydel ran the others off."

"You have to yell back, or just smile when he gets wound up," Keely said in a kindly tone.

Cappie grimaced. "I never yell at anybody."

"This is a good time to learn. In fact..."

"Where the hell is my damned raincoat?!"

Cappie's face was a study in horror. "You said he went to lunch!"

"Obviously he came back," Keely replied, wincing, as the boss stormed into the waiting room where two shocked old ladies were sitting beside cat carriers.

Dr. Bentley Rydel was tall, over six feet, with pale blue eyes that took on the gleam of steel when he was angry. He had jet-black hair, thick and usually untidy because he ran his fingers through it in times of frustration. His feet were large, like his hands. His nose had been broken at some point, which only gave his angular face more character. He wasn't conventionally handsome, but women found him very attractive. He didn't find them attractive. If there was a more notorious woman hater than Bentley Rydel in all of Jacobs County, Texas, it would be hard to find him.

"My raincoat?" he repeated, glaring at Cappie as if it were her fault that he'd left without it.

Cappie drew herself up to her full height—the top of her head barely came to Bentley's shoulder—and took a deep breath. "Sir," she said smartly, "your raincoat is in the closet where you left it."

His dark eyebrows rose half a foot.

Cappie cleared her throat and shook her head as if to clear it. The motion dislodged her precariously placed barrette. Her long, thick blond hair shook free of it, swirling around her shoulders like a curtain of silk.

While she was debating her next, and possibly job-ending, comment, Bentley was staring at her hair. She always wore it on top of her head in that stupid ponytail. He hadn't realized it was so long. His pale eyes narrowed as he studied it.

Keely, fascinated, managed not to stare. She turned to the old ladies watching, spellbound. "Mrs. Ross, if you'll bring—" she looked at her clipboard "—Luvvy the cat on back, we'll see about her shots."

Mrs. Ross, a tiny little woman, smiled and pulled her

rolling cat carrier along with her, casting a wistful eye back at the tableau she was reluctantly foregoing.

"Dr. Rydel?" Cappie prompted, because he was really staring.

He scowled suddenly and blinked. "It's raining," he said shortly.

"Sir, that is not my fault," she returned. "I do not control the weather."

"A likely story," he huffed. He turned on his heel, went to the closet, jerked his coat out, displacing everybody else's, and stormed out the door into the pouring rain.

"And I hope you melt!" Cappie muttered under her breath.

"I heard that!" Bentley Rydel called without looking back.

Cappie flushed and moved back behind the counter, trying not to meet Gladys Hawkins's eyes, because the old lady was almost crying, she was laughing so hard.

"There, there," Dr. King, the long-married senior veterinarian, said with a gentle smile. She patted Cappie on the shoulder. "You've done well. By the time she'd been here a month, Antonia was crying in the bathroom at least twice a day, and she never talked back to Dr. Rydel."

"I've never worked in such a place," Cappie said blankly. "I mean, most veterinarians are like you—they're nice and professional, and they don't yell at the staff. And, of course, the staff doesn't yell…"

"Yes, they do," Keely piped in, chuckling. "My husband made the remark that I was a glorified groomer, and the next time he came in here, our groomer gave him an earful about just what a groomer does." She grinned. "Opened his eyes."

"They do a lot more than clip fur," Dr. King agreed. "They're our eyes and ears in between exams. Many times, our groomers have saved lives by noticing some small problem that could have turned fatal."

"Your husband is a dish," Cappie told Keely shyly.

Keely laughed. "Yes, he is, but he's opinionated, hardheaded and temperamental with it."

"He was a tough one to tame, I'll bet," Dr. King mused.

Keely leaned forward. "Not half as tough as Dr. Rydel is going to be."

"Amen. I pity the poor woman who takes him on."

"Trust me, she hasn't been born yet," Keely replied.

"He likes you," Cappie sighed.

"I don't challenge him," Keely said simply. "And I'm younger than most of the staff. He thinks of me as a child."

Cappie's eyes bulged.

Keely patted her on the shoulder. "Some people do." The smile faded. Keely was remembering her mother, who'd been killed by a friend of Keely's father. The whole town had been talking about it. Keely had landed well, though, in Boone Sinclair's strong arms.

"I'm sorry about your mother," Cappie said gently. "We all were."

"Thanks," Keely replied. "We were just getting to know one another when she was…killed. My father plea-bargained himself down to a short jail term, but I don't think he'll be back this way. He's too afraid of Sheriff Hayes."

"Now there's a real dish," Cappie said. "Handsome, brave…"

"…suicidal," Keely interjected.

"Excuse me?"

"He's been shot twice, walking into gun battles," Dr. King explained.

"No guts, no glory," Cappie said.

Her companions chuckled. The phone rang, another customer walked in and the conversation turned to business.

Cappie went home late. It was Friday and the place was packed with clients. Nobody escaped before six-thirty, not even the poor groomer who'd spent half a day on a Siberian husky. The animals had thick undercoats and it was a job to wash and brush them out. Dr. Rydel had been snippier than usual, too, glaring at Cappie as if she were responsible for the overflow of patients.

"Cappie, is that you?" her brother called from the bedroom.

"It's me, Kell," she called back. She put down her raincoat and purse and walked into the small, sparse bedroom where her older brother lay surrounded by magazines and books and a small laptop computer. He managed a smile for her.

"Bad day?" she asked gently, sitting down beside him on the bed, softly so that she didn't worsen the pain.

He only nodded. His face was taut, the only sign of the pain that ate him alive every hour of the day. A journalist, he'd been on overseas assignment for a magazine when he was caught in a firefight and wounded by shrapnel. It had lodged in his spine where it was too dangerous for even the most advanced surgery. The doctors said someday, the shrapnel might shift into a location where it would be operable. But until then, Kell was basically paralyzed from the waist down. Oddly, the magazine hadn't provided any sort of health care coverage for him, and equally oddly, he'd insisted that he wasn't going to court to force them to pay up. Cappie had wondered at her brother being in such a profession in the first place. He'd been in the army for several years. When he came out, he'd become a journalist. He made an extraordinary living from it. She'd mentioned that to a friend in the newspaper business who'd been astonished. Most magazines didn't pay that well, he'd noted, eyeing Kell's new Jaguar.

Well, at least they had Kell's savings to keep them going, even if it did so frugally now, after he paid the worst of the medical bills. Her meager salary, although good, barely kept the utilities turned on and food in the aging refrigerator.

"Taken your pain meds?" she added.

He nodded.

"Not helping?"

"Not a lot. Not today, anyway," he added with a forced grin. He was good-looking, with thick short hair even blonder than hers and those pale silvery-gray eyes. He was tall and muscular; or he had been, before he'd been wounded. He was in a wheelchair now.

"Someday they'll be able to operate," she said.

He sighed and managed a smile. "Before I die of old age, maybe."

"Stop that," she chided softly, and bent to kiss his forehead. "You have to have hope."

"I guess."

"Want something to eat?"

He shook his head. "Not hungry."

"I can make southwestern corn soup." It was his favorite.

He gave her a serious look. "I'm impacting your life. There are places for ex-military where I could stay…"

"No!" she exploded.

He winced. "Sis, it isn't right. You'll never find a man who'll take you on with all this baggage," he began.

"We've had this argument for several months already," she pointed out.

"Yes, since you gave up your job and moved back here with me, after I got…wounded. If our cousin hadn't died and left us this place, we wouldn't even have a roof over our heads, stark as it is. It's killing me, watching you try to cope."

"Don't be melodramatic," she chided. "Kell, all we have is each other," she added somberly. "Don't ask me to throw you out on the street so I can have a social life. I don't even like men much, don't you remember?"

His face hardened. "I remember why, mostly."

She flushed. "Now, Kell," she said. "We promised we wouldn't talk about that anymore."

"He could have killed you," he gritted. "I had to browbeat you just to make you press charges!"

She averted her eyes. Her one boyfriend in her adult life had turned out to be a homicidal maniac when he drank. The first time it happened, Frank Bartlett had grabbed Cappie's arm and left a black bruise. Kell advised her to get away from him, but she, infatuated and rationalizing, said that he hadn't meant it. Kell knew better, but he couldn't convince her. On their fourth date, the boy had taken her to a bar, had a few drinks, and when she gently tried to get him to stop, he'd dragged her outside and lit into her. The other patrons had come to her rescue and one of them had driven her home. The boy had come back, shamefaced and crying, begging for one more chance. Kell had put his foot down and said no, but Cappie was in love and wouldn't listen. They were watching a movie at the rented house, when she asked him about his drinking problem. He'd lost his temper and started hitting her, with hardly any provocation at all. Kell had managed to get into his wheelchair and into the living room. With nothing more than a lamp base as a weapon, he'd knocked the lunatic off Cappie and onto the floor. She was dazed and bleeding, but he'd told her how to tie the boy's thumbs together behind his back, which she'd done while Kell picked up his cell phone and called for law enforcement. Cappie had gone to the hospital and the boy had gone to jail for assault.

With her broken arm in a sling, Cappie had testified against him, with Kell beside her in court as moral support. The sentence, even so, hadn't been extreme. The boy drew six months' jail time and a year's probation. He also swore vengeance. Kell took the threat a great deal more seriously than Cappie had.

The brother and sister had a distant cousin who lived in Comanche Wells, Texas. He'd died a year ago, but the probation of the will had dragged on. Three months ago, Kell had a letter informing her that he and Cappie were inheriting a small house and a postage-stamp-size yard. But it was at least a place to live. Cappie had been uncertain about uprooting them from San Antonio, but Kell had been strangely insistent. He had a friend in nearby Jacobsville who was acquainted with a local veterinarian. Cappie could get a job there, working as a veterinary technician. So she'd given in.

She hadn't forgotten the boy. It had been a wrench, because he was her first real love. Fortunately for her, the relationship hadn't progressed past hot kisses and a little petting, although he'd wanted it to. That had been another sticking point: Cappie's impeccable morals. She was out of touch with the modern world, he'd accused, from living with her overprotective big brother for so long. She needed to loosen up. Easy to say, but Cappie didn't want a casual relationship and she said so. When he drank more than usual, he said it was her fault that he got drunk and hit her, because she kept him so frustrated.

Well, he was entitled to his opinion. Cappie didn't share it. He'd seemed like the nicest, gentlest sort of man when she'd first met him. His sister had brought her dog to the veterinary practice where Cappie worked. He'd been sitting in the truck, letting his sister wrangle a huge German shepherd dog back outside. When he'd seen Cappie, he'd jumped out and helped. His sister had seemed surprised. Cappie didn't notice.

After it was over, Cappie had found that at least two of her acquaintances had been subjected to the same sort of abuse by their own boyfriends. Some had been lucky, like Cappie, and disentangled themselves from the abusers. Others were trapped by fear into relationships they didn't even want. It was hard, she decided, telling by appearance what men would be like when they got you alone. At least Dr. Rydel was obviously violent and dangerous, she told herself. Not that she wanted anything to do with him socially.

"What was that?" Kell asked.

"Oh, I was thinking about one of my bosses," she

confided. "Dr. Rydel is a holy terror. I'm scared to death of him."

He scowled. "Surely he isn't like Frank Bartlett?"

"No," she said quickly. "I don't think he'd ever hit a woman. He really isn't the sort. He just blusters and rages and curses. He loves animals. He called the police on a man who brought in a little dog with cuts and bruises all over him. The man had beaten the dog and pretended it had fallen down stairs. Dr. Rydel knew better. He testified against the man and he went to jail."

"Good for Dr. Rydel." He smiled. "If he's that nice to animals, he isn't likely the sort of person who'd hit women," he had to agree. "I was told by my friend that Rydel was a good sort to work for." He frowned. "Your boyfriend kicked your cat on your first date."

She grimaced. "And I made excuses for him." Not long after that, her cat had vanished. She'd often wondered what had happened to him, but he returned after her boyfriend left. "Frank was so handsome, so…eligible," she added quietly. "I guess I was flattered that a man like that would look twice at me. I'm no beauty."

"You are. Inside."

"You're a nice brother. How about that soup?"

He sighed. "I'll eat it if you'll fix it. I'm sorry. About the way I am."

"Like you can help it," she muttered, and smiled. "I'll get it started."

He watched her walk away, thoughtful.

She brought in a tray and had her soup with him. There were just the two of them, all alone in the world. Their parents had died long ago, when she was ten. Kell, who'd been amazingly athletic and healthy in those days, had simply taken over and been a substitute parent to her. He'd been in the military, and they'd traveled all over the world. A good deal of her education had been completed through correspondent courses, although she'd seen a lot of the world. Now, Kell thought he was a burden, but what had she been for all those long years when he'd sacrificed his own social life to raise a heartbroken kid? She owed him a lot. She only wished she could do more for him.

She remembered him in his uniform, an officer, so dignified and commanding. Now, he was largely confined to bed or that wheelchair. It wasn't even a motorized one, because they couldn't afford it. He did continue to work, in his own fashion, at crafting a novel. It was an adventure, based on some knowledge he'd acquired from his military background and a few friends who worked, he said, in covert ops.

"How's the book coming?" she asked.

He laughed. "Actually I think it's going very well. I spoke to a buddy of mine in Washington about some new political strategies and robotic warfare innovations."

"You know everybody."

He made a face at her. "I know almost everybody." He sighed. "I'm afraid the phone bill will be out of sight again this month. Plus I had to order some more books on Africa for the research."

She gave him a look of pride. "I don't care. You accomplish so much," she said softly. "More than a lot of people in much better shape physically."

"I don't sleep as much as most people do," he said wryly. "So I can work longer hours."

"You need to talk to Dr. Coltrain about something to make you sleep."

He sighed. "I did. He gave me a prescription."

"Which you didn't get filled," she accused. "Connie, at the pharmacy, told on you."

"We don't have the money right now," he said gently. "I'll manage."

"It's always money," she said miserably. "I wish I was talented and smart, like you. Maybe I could get a better-paying job."

"You're good at what you do," he replied firmly. "And you love your work. Believe me, that's a lot more important than making a big paycheck. I should know."

She sighed as she sipped her soup. "I guess." She gave him a quick glance. "But it would help with the bills."

"My book is going to make us millions," he told her with a grin. "It will hit the top of the *New York Times* bestseller list, I'll be in demand for talk shows and we'll be able to buy a new car."

"Optimist," she accused.

"Hey, without hope, what have we got?" He looked

around with a grimace. "Unpainted walls, cracks in the paint, a car with two hundred thousand miles on it and a leaky roof."

"Oh, darn," she muttered, following his eyes to the yellow spot on the ceiling. "I'll bet another one of those stupid nails worked its way out of the tin. I wish we could have afforded a shingle roof."

"Well, tin is cheaper, and it looks nice."

She looked at him meaningfully.

"It's cheap, anyway," he persisted. "Don't you like the sound of rain on a tin roof? Just listen. It's like music."

It was like a tin drum, she pointed out, but he just laughed.

She smiled. "I guess you're right. It's better not to wish we had more than we do. We'll get by, Kell," she assured him. "We always do."

"At least we're in it together," he agreed. "But you should think about the military home."

"After I'm dead and buried, you can go into a home," she assured him. "For now, you just eat your soup and hush."

He smiled tenderly. "Okay."

She smiled back. He was the nicest big brother in the whole world, and she wasn't abandoning him while there was a breath in her body.

It had stopped raining when she got to work the next morning. She was glad. She hadn't wanted to get out of bed at all. There was something magical about lying in the bed with rain coming down, all safe and cozy and warm. But she wanted to keep her job. She couldn't do both.

She was putting her raincoat in the closet when a long arm presented itself over her shoulder and deposited a bigger raincoat there.

"Hang that up for me, please," Dr. Rydel said gruffly.

"Yes, sir."

She fumbled it onto a hanger. When she closed the door and turned, he was still standing there.

"Is something wrong, sir?" she asked formally.

He was frowning. "No."

But he looked as if he had the weight of the world on his shoulders. She knew how that felt, because she loved her brother and she couldn't help him. Her soft gray eyes looked up into his pale blue ones. "When life gives you lemons, make lemonade?" she ventured.

A laugh escaped his tight control. "What the hell would you know about lemons, at your age?" he asked.

"It isn't the age, Dr. Rydel," she said. "It's the mileage. If I were a car, they'd have to decorate me with solid gold accessories just to get me off the lot."

His eyes softened, just a little. "I suppose I'd be in a junkyard."

She laughed, quickly controlling it. "Sorry."

"Why?"

"You're sort of hard to talk to," she confessed.

He drew in a long breath. Just for a minute, he looked oddly vulnerable. "I'm not used to people. I deal with them in the practice, but I live alone. I have most of my life." He frowned. "Your brother lives with you, doesn't he? Why doesn't he work?"

She tightened up. "He was overseas covering a war and a bomb exploded nearby. He caught shrapnel in the spine and they can't operate. He's paralyzed from the waist down."

He grimaced. "That's a hell of a way to end up in a wheelchair."

"Tell me about it," she agreed quietly. "He was in the military for years, but he got tired of dragging me all over the world, so he mustered out and got a job working for this magazine. He said it would mean he wouldn't be gone so much." She sighed. "I guess he wasn't, but he's in a lot of pain and they can't do much for it." She looked up at him. "It's hard to watch."

For an instant, some fellow feeling flared in his eyes. "Yes. It's easier to hurt yourself than to watch someone you love battle pain." His face softened as he looked down at her. "You take care of him."

She smiled. "Yes. Well, as much as he'll let me, anyway. He took care of me from the age of ten, when our parents died in a wreck. He wants me to let him go into some sort of military home, but I'll never do that."

He looked very thoughtful. And sad. He looked as if he badly needed someone to talk to, but he had nobody. She knew the feeling.

"Life is hard," she said gently.

"Then you die," he added, and managed a smile.

"Back to work, Miss Drake." He hesitated. "Your name, Cappie. What's it short for?"

She hesitated. She bit her lower lip.

"Come on," he coaxed.

She drew in a breath. "Capella," she said.

His eyebrows shot up. "The star?"

She laughed, delighted. Most people had no idea what it meant. "Yes."

"One of your parents was an astronomy buff," he guessed.

"No. My mother was an astronomer, and my father was an astrophysicist," she corrected, beaming. "He worked for NASA for a while."

He pursed his lips. "Brainy people."

"Don't worry, it didn't rub off on me. Kell got all that talent. In fact, he's writing a book, an adventure novel." She smiled. "I just know it's going to be a blockbuster. He'll rake in the money, and then we won't have to worry about money for medicine and health care."

"Health care." He harrumphed. "It's a joke. People going without food to buy pills, without clothes to afford gas, having to choose between essentials and no help anywhere to change things."

She was surprised at his attitude. Most people seemed to think that health care was available to everybody. Actually she could only afford basic coverage for herself. If she ever had a major medical emergency, she'd have to beg for help from the state. She hoped she could even get it. It still amazed her that Kell's employers hadn't offered him health care benefits. "We don't live in a perfect society," she agreed.

"No. Nowhere near it."

She wanted to ask him why he was so outspoken on the issue, which hit home for her, too. But before she could overcome her shyness, the phones were suddenly ringing off the hook and three new four-legged patients walked in the door with their owners. One of them, a big Boxer, made a beeline for a small poodle whose owner had let it come in without a lead.

"Grab him!" Cappie called, diving after the Boxer.

Dr. Rydel followed her, gripping the Boxer's lead firmly. He pulled up on it just enough to establish control, and held it so that the dog's head was erect. "Down, sir!" he said in a commanding tone. "Sit!"

The Boxer sat down at once. So did all the pet owners. Cappie burst out laughing. Dr. Rydel gave her a speaking glance, turned, and led the Boxer back to the patient rooms without a single word.

CHAPTER TWO

WHEN SHE got home, Cappie told her brother about the struggle with the Boxer, and its result. He roared with laughter. It had been a long time since she'd seen him laugh.

"Well, at least he can control animals and people," he told her.

"Indeed he can." She picked up the dirty dishes and stacked them from their light supper. "You know, he's very adamant about health care. For people, I mean. I wonder if he has somebody who can't afford medicines or doctors or hospitals? He never talks about his private life."

"Neither do you," he pointed out dryly.

She made a face. "I'm not interesting. Nobody would want to know what I do at home. I just cook and clean and wash dishes. What's exciting about that? When you were in the army, you knew movie stars and sports legends."

"They're just like you and me," he told her. "Fame isn't a character reference. Neither is wealth."

"Well, I wouldn't mind being rich," she sighed. "We could fix the roof."

"One day," he promised her, "we'll get out of the hole."

"You think?"

"Miracles happen every day."

She wasn't touching that line with a pole. Just lately, she'd have given blood for a miracle that would treat her just to a new raincoat. The one she had, purchased for a dollar at a thrift shop, was worn and faded and missing buttons. She'd sewed others on, but none of them matched. It would be so nice to have one that came from a store, brand-new, with that smell that clothes had when nobody had ever worn them before.

"What are you thinking about?" Kell asked.

"New raincoats," she sighed. Then she saw his expression and grimaced. "Sorry. Just a stray thought. Don't mind me."

"Santa Claus might bring you one," he said.

She glowered at him on her way out the door. "Listen, Santa Claus couldn't find this place if he had GPS on his sleigh. And if he did, his reindeer would slide off the tin roof and fall to their doom, and we'd get sued."

He was still laughing when she got to the kitchen.

It was getting close to Christmas. Cappie dug out the old, faded artificial Christmas tree and put it up in the living room where Kell could see it from his hospital bed. She had one new string of minilights, all she could afford, and she put the old ornaments on it. Finally she plugged in the tree. It became a work of art, a magical thing, when she turned out the other lights and looked at it.

"Wow," Kell said in a soft tone.

She moved to the doorway and smiled at him. "Yeah. Wow." She sighed. "Well, at least it's a tree. I wish we could have a real one."

"Me, too, but you spent every Christmas sick in bed until we realized you were allergic to fir trees."

"Bummer."

He burst out laughing. "Now, all we have to do is decide what we're going to put under it."

"Artificial presents, I guess," she said quietly.

"Stop that. We're not destitute."

"Yet."

"What am I going to do with you? There is a Santa Claus, 'Virginia,'" he chided. "You just don't know it yet."

She turned the lights back on and smiled at him. "Okay. Have it your way."

"And we'll put presents under it."

Only if they come prepaid and already wrapped, she thought cynically, but she didn't say it. Life was hard, when you lived on the fringes of society. Kell had a much better attitude than she did. Her optimism was losing ground by the day.

The beginning of the week started out badly. Dr. Rydel and Dr. King had a very loud and disturbing argument over possible treatments for a beautiful black Persian male cat with advanced kidney failure.

"We can do dialysis," Dr. King argued.

Dr. Rydel's pale blue eyes threw off sparks. "Do you intend to contribute to the 'let's prolong Harry's suffering' fund?"

"Excuse me?"

"His owner is retired. All she has is her social security, because her pension plan crashed and burned during the economic downturn," he said hotly. "How the hell do you think she's going to afford dialysis for a cat who's got, at the most, a couple of weeks of acute suffering to go before he faces an end to the pain?"

Dr. King was giving him very odd looks. She didn't say anything.

"I can irrigate him and pump drugs into him and keep him alive for another month," he said through his teeth. "And he'll be in agony all that time. I can do dialysis and prolong it even more. Or do you think that animals don't really feel pain at all?"

She still hadn't spoken. She just looked at him.

"Dialysis!" he scoffed. "I love animals, too, Dr. King, and I'd never give up on one that had a ghost of a chance of a normal life. But this cat isn't having a normal life— he's going through hell on a daily basis. Or haven't you ever seen a human being in the final stages of kidney failure?" he demanded.

"No, I haven't," Dr. King said, in an unusually gentle tone.

"You can take it from me that it's the closest thing to hell on earth. And I am not, repeat not, putting the cat on dialysis and that's the advice I'm giving his owner."

"Okay."

He frowned. "Okay?"

She didn't smile. "It must have been very hard to watch," she added quietly.

His face, for an instant, betrayed the anguish of a personal loss of some magnitude. He turned away and went back into his office. He didn't even slam the door.

Cappie and Keely flanked Dr. King, all big eyes and unspoken questions.

"You don't know, do you?" she asked. She motioned them off into the chart room and closed the door. "You didn't hear me say this," she instructed, and waited until they both nodded. "His mother was sixty when they diagnosed her with kidney failure three years ago. They put her on dialysis and gave her medications to help put off the inevitable, but she lost the battle just a year later when they discovered an inoperable tumor in her bladder. She was in agony. All that time, she had only her social security and Medicaid to help. Her husband, Dr. Rydel's stepfather, wouldn't let him help at all. In fact, Dr. Rydel had to fight just to see his mother. He and his stepfather have been enemies for years, and it just got worse when his mother was so ill. His mother died and he blames his stepfather, first for not letting her go to a doctor for tests in the first place, and then for not letting him help with the costs afterward. She lived in terrible poverty. Her husband was too proud to accept a dime from any other source, and he worked as a night watchman in a manufacturing company."

No wonder Dr. Rydel was so adamant about health care, Cappie thought. She saw him through different eyes. She also understood his frustration.

"He's right, too, about Harry's owner," Dr. King added. "Mrs. Trammel doesn't have much left after she pays her own medicine bills and utilities and groceries. Certainly she doesn't have enough to afford expensive treatments for an elderly cat who doesn't have long to live no matter what we do." She grimaced. "It's wonderful that we have all these new treatments for our pets. But it's not good that we sometimes make decisions that aren't realistic. The cat is elderly and in constant pain. Are we doing it a favor to order thousands of dollars of treatments that its owner can't afford, just to prolong the suffering?"

Keely shrugged. "Bailey, Boone's German shepherd, would have died if Dr. Rydel hadn't operated on him when he got bloat," she ventured.

"Yes, and he's old, too," Dr. King agreed. "But Boone could afford it."

"Good point," Keely agreed.

"We do have medical insurance for pets now," Cappie pointed out.

"It's the same moral question, though," Dr. King

pointed out. "Should we do something just because we can do it?"

The phone rang, both lines at once, and a woman with a cat in a blanket and red, tear-filled eyes rushed in the door calling for help.

"It's going to be a long day," Dr. King sighed.

Cappie told her brother about Dr. Rydel's mother. "I guess we're not the only people who wish we had adequate health care," she said, smiling gently.

"I guess not. Poor guy." He frowned. "How do you make a decision like that for a pet?" he added.

"We didn't. We recommended what we thought best, but let Mrs. Trammel make the final decision. She was more philosophical than all of us put together. She said Harry had lived for nineteen good years, been spoiled rotten and shame on us for thinking death was a bitter end. She thinks cats go to a better place, too, and that they have green fields to run through and no cars to run over them." She smiled. "In the end, she decided that it was kinder to just let Dr. Rydel do what was necessary. Keely's barn cat has a new litter of kittens, solid white with blue eyes. She promised Mrs. Trammel one. Life goes on."

"Yes." He was somber. "It does."

She lifted her eyebrows. "Any day now, there's going to be a breakthrough in medical research and you're going to have an operation that will put you back on your feet and give you a new lease on life."

"After which I'll win the British Open, effect détente

with the eastern communists and perfect a cure for cancer," he added dryly.

"One miracle at a time," she interrupted. "And just how would you win the British Open? You don't even play tennis!"

"Don't confuse me with a bunch of irrelevant facts." He sank back into his pillows and grimaced. "Besides, the pain is going to kill me long before they find any miraculous surgical techniques." He closed his eyes with a long sigh. "One day without pain," he said quietly. "Just one day. I'd do almost anything for it."

She knew, as many other people didn't, that chronic pain brought on a kind of depression that was pervasive and dangerous. Even the drugs he took for pain only took the edge off. Nothing they'd ever given him had stopped it.

"What you need is a nice chocolate milkshake and some evil, fattening, oversalted French fries and a cholesterol-dripping hamburger," she said.

He made a tortured face. "Go ahead, torment me!"

She grinned. "I overpaid the hardware bill and got sent a ten-dollar refund," she said, reaching into her purse. "I'll go to the bank, cash it and we'll eat out tonight!"

"You beauty!" he exclaimed.

She curtsied. "I'll be back before you know it." She glanced at her watch. "Oops, better hurry or the bank will be closed!"

She grabbed her old denim jacket and her purse and ran out the door.

The ancient car was temperamental. It had over two hundred thousand miles on it, and it looked like a piece of junk. She coaxed it into life and grimaced as she read the gas gauge. She had a fourth of a tank left. Well, it was only a five-minute drive to Jacobsville from Comanche Wells. She'd have enough to get her to work and back for one more day. Then she'd worry about gas. The ten-dollar check would have come in handy for that, but Kell needed cheering up more. These spells of depression were very bad for him, and they were becoming more frequent. She'd have done anything to keep him optimistic. Even walking to work.

She cashed the check with two minutes to spare before the bank closed. Then she drove to the local fast-food joint and ordered burgers and fries and milkshakes. She paid for them—had five cents left over—and pulled out into the road. Then two things went wrong at once. The engine quit and a car flew out of a side road and right into the passenger side of her car.

She sat, shaking, amid the ruins of her car, with chocolate milkshake all over her jeans and jacket, and pieces of hamburgers on the dirty floorboard. It was quite an impact. She couldn't move for a minute. She sat, staring at the dash, wondering how she'd manage without a car, because her insurance only covered liability. She had nothing that would even pay to repair the car, if it could be repaired.

She turned her head in slow motion and looked at

the car that had hit her. The driver got out, staggering. He laughed. That explained why he'd shot through a stop sign without braking. He leaned against his ruined fender and laughed some more.

Cappie wondered if he had insurance. She also wondered if she didn't have a tire iron that she could get to, before the police came to save the man.

Her car door was jerked open. She looked up into a pair of steely ice-blue eyes.

"Are you all right?" he asked.

She blinked. Dr. Rydel. She wondered where he'd come from.

"Cappie, are you all right?" he repeated. His voice was very soft, nothing like the glitter in those pale eyes.

"I think so," she said. Time seemed to have slowed to a stop. She couldn't get her sluggish brain to work. "I was taking hamburgers and shakes home to Kell," she said. "He was so depressed. I thought it would cheer him up. I was worried about spending the money on treats instead of gas." She laughed dully. "I guess I won't need to worry about gas, now," she added, looking around at the damage.

"You're lucky you weren't in one of the newer little cars. You'd be dead."

She looked toward the other driver. "Dr. Rydel, do you have a tire tool I could borrow?" she asked conversationally.

He saw where she was looking. "You don't want to upset the police, Cappie."

"I won't tell if you won't."

Before he could reply, a Jacobsville police car roared up, lights flashing, and stopped. Obviously somebody in the fast-food place had called them.

Officer Kilraven climbed out of the police car and headed right for Cappie.

"Oh, good, it's him," Cappie said. "He'll scare the other driver to death."

Kilraven bent down on Cappie's side of the car. "You okay? Need an ambulance?"

"Heavens, no," she said quickly. As if she could afford to pay for that! "I'm fine. Just shaken up." She nodded toward the giggling driver who'd hit her. "Dr. Rydel won't loan me a tire iron, so could you shoot that man in the foot for me, please? I don't even have collision insurance and it wasn't my fault. I'll be walking to work on account of him."

"I can't shoot him," Kilraven said with a twinkle in his silver eyes. "But if he tries to hit me, I'll take him to detention in the trunk of my car. Okay?"

She brightened. "Okay!"

He straightened and said something to Dr. Rydel. A minute later, he marched over to the drunk man, smelled his breath, made a face and asked him to perform a sobriety test, which the subject refused. That would mean a blood test at the hospital, which Kilraven was fairly certain the man would fail. He told him he was under arrest and cuffed him. Cappie vaguely heard him calling for a wrecker and backup.

"A wrecker?" She groaned. "I can't afford a wrecker."

"Just don't worry about it right now. Come on. I'll drive you home."

He helped her out of the car. She retrieved her purse, wincing. "I hope he has a Texas-size hangover when he wakes up tomorrow," she said coldly, watching Kilraven putting the prisoner in the back of his squad car. The man was still laughing.

"Oh, I hope he gets pregnant," Dr. Rydel mused, "and it's twins."

She laughed huskily. "Even better. Thanks."

He put her into his big Land Rover. "Wait here. I'll just be a minute."

She sat quietly, fascinated with the interior of the vehicle. It conjured up visions of the African veldt, of elephants and giraffes and wildebeest. She wished she could afford even a twenty-year-old version of this beast. She'd never have to worry about bad roads again.

He was back shortly with a bag and a cup carrier. He put them in her lap. "Two hamburgers and fries and two chocolate shakes."

"How…?"

"Well, it's easier to tell when you're wearing parts of them," he pointed out, indicating chocolate milk stains and mustard and catsup and pieces of food all over her clothes. "Fasten your seat belt."

She did. "I'll pay you back," she said firmly.

He grinned. "Whatever."

He started the engine and drove her out of town. "You'll have to direct me. I don't know where you live."

She named the road, and then the street. They didn't talk. He pulled up in the front yard of the dinky little house, with its peeling paint and rickety steps and sagging eaves.

He grimaced.

"Hey, don't knock it," she said. "It's got a pretty good roof and big rooms and it's paid for. A distant cousin willed it to us."

"Nice of him. Do you have any other cousins?"

"No. It's just me and Kell."

"No other siblings?"

She shook her head. "We don't have any family left."

He gave the house a speaking look.

"If we had the money to fix it up, it would look terrific," she said.

He helped her out of the car and onto the porch. He hesitated about handing her the bag with the food and the carrier of milkshakes.

"Would you like to come in and meet Kell?" she ventured. "Only if you want to," she added quickly.

"Yes, I would."

She unlocked the door and motioned him in. "Kell, I'm home!" she called. "I brought company."

"If it's wearing lipstick and has a good sense of humor, bring it in here quick!" he quipped.

Dr. Rydel burst out laughing. "Sorry, I don't wear lipstick," he called back.

"Oops."

Cappie laughed and walked toward the room a little unsteadily, motioning the vet to follow her.

Kell was propped up in bed with the old laptop. He paused, eyebrows arched, as they walked in. "We should have ordered more food," he said with a grin.

Cappie winced. "Well, see, the food is the problem. I was pulling out of the parking lot and the engine died. A drunk man ran into the car and pretty much killed it."

"Luckily he didn't kill you," Kell said, frowning. "Are you all right?"

"Just bruised a little. Dr. Rydel was kind enough to bring me home. Dr. Rydel, this is my brother, Kell," she began.

"You're the veterinarian?" Kell asked, and his silvery-gray eyes twinkled. "I thought you had fangs and a pointed tail…"

"Kell!" she burst out, horrified.

Dr. Rydel chuckled. "Only during office hours," he returned.

"I'll kill you!" she told her brother.

"Now, now," Dr. Rydel said complacently. "We all know I'm a horror to work for. He's just saying what you aren't comfortable telling me."

"And he does have a sense of humor," Kell said. "Thanks for bringing her home," he added, and the smile faded. "My driving days are apparently over."

"There are vehicles with hand controls now," Dr. Rydel pointed out.

"We're ordering one of those as soon as we get our new yacht paid off," Kell replied with a serious expression.

Cappie burst out laughing. "And our dandy indoor swimming pool."

Dr. Rydel smiled. "At least you still have a sense of humor."

"It's the only part of me that works," Kell replied. "I've offered to check myself into a military home, but she won't hear of it."

"Over my dead body," she reiterated, and glared at him.

He sighed. "It's nice to be loved, but you can take family feeling over the cliff with you, darlin'," he reminded her.

"Sink or swim, we're a matched set," she said stubbornly. "I'm not putting you out on the street."

"Military homes can be very nice," Kell began.

Cappie grimaced. "Your milkshake is getting warm," she interrupted. She took the carrier from Dr. Rydel and handed one to Kell, along with a straw. "There's your burger and fries," she said. "Working?"

"Taking a short break to play mah-jongg," he replied. "I'm actually winning, too."

"I play Sudoku," Dr. Rydel commented.

Kell groaned. "I can't do numbers. I tried that game and thought I'd go nuts. I couldn't even get one column to line up. How do you do it?"

"I'm left-brained," the other man said simply. "Numbers and science. I'd have loved to be a writer, but I'm spelling-challenged."

Kell laughed. "I'm left-brained, too, but I can't handle Sudoku. I can spell, however," he added, tongue in cheek.

"That's why we have a bookkeeper," Dr. Rydel said. "I think people would have issues if their names and animal conditions were constantly misspelled. I had a time in college."

"So did I," Kell confessed. "College trigonometry almost kept me from getting my degree in the first place. I also had a bad time with biology," he added pointedly.

Dr. Rydel grinned. "My best subject. All A's."

"I'll bet the biology-challenged loved you," Cappie said with a chuckle. "Blew the curve every time, didn't you?"

He nodded. "I bought pizzas for my classmates every Saturday night to make it up to them."

"Pizza," Cappie mused. "I remember what that tastes like. I think."

"I don't want to talk about pizza," Kell said and sipped his milkshake. "You and your mushrooms!"

"He hates mushrooms, and I hate Italian sausage," Cappie commented. "I love mushrooms."

"Yuuuuck," Kell commented.

She smiled. "We'll leave you to your supper. If you need anything, call me, okay?"

"Sure. What would you like to be called?"

She wrinkled her nose at him and went out the door.

"Nice to have met you," Kell told the vet.

"Same here," Dr. Rydel said.

He followed Cappie out into the living room. "You'd better eat your own burger and fries before they're cold," he said. "They don't reheat well."

She smiled shyly. "Thanks again for bringing me home, and for the food." She wondered how she was going to get to work the following Monday, but she knew she'd come up with something. She could always beg one of the other vet techs for a ride.

"You're welcome." He stared down at her quietly, frowning. "You sure you're all right?"

She nodded. "I'm wobbly. That's because I was scared to death. I'll be fine. It's just a little bruising. Honest."

"Would you tell me if it was more?" he asked.

She grinned.

"Well, if you think you need to go to the doctor later, you call me. Call the office," he added. "They'll take a message and page me, wherever I am."

"That's very nice of you. Thanks."

He drew in a long breath. His blue eyes narrowed on her face. "You've got a lot on your shoulders for a woman your age," he said quietly.

"Some people have a lot more," she replied. "I love my brother."

He smiled. "I noticed that."

She studied him curiously. "Do you have family?"

His face tautened. "Not anymore."

"I'm sorry."

"People get old. They die." He became distant. "We'll talk another time. Good evening."

"Good evening. Thanks."

He shrugged. "No problem."

She watched him go with a strange sense of loss. He was in many ways the saddest person she'd ever known.

She finished her supper and went to collect her brother's food containers.

"Your boss is nice," he said. "Not what I expected."

"How could you tell him what I said about him, you horrible man?" she asked with mock anger.

"He's one of those rare souls who never lie," he said simply. "He comes at you head-on, not from ambush."

"How do you know that?"

"It's in his manner," he said simply. He smiled. "I'm that way myself. It does take one to know one. Now come here and sit down and tell me what happened."

She drew in a deep breath and sat down in the chair beside the bed. She hated having to tell him the whole truth. It wasn't going to be pretty.

CHAPTER THREE

CAPPIE HITCHED a ride to work with Keely, promising not to make a regular thing of it.

"I'll just have to get another car," she said, as if all that required was a trip to a car lot. In fact, she had no idea what she was going to do.

"My brother is best friends with Sheriff Hayes Carson," Keely reminded her, "and Hayes knows Kilraven. He told him the particulars, and Kilraven had a talk with the driver's insurance company." She chuckled. "I understand some interesting what-ifs were mentioned. The upshot is that the driver's insurance is going to pay to fix your car."

"What?"

"Well, he was drunk, Cappie. In fact, he's occupying a cell at the county detention center as we speak. You could sue his insurance company for enough to buy a new Jaguar like my brother's got."

She didn't mention that Kell had owned a Jaguar, and not too long ago. Those days seemed very far away now. "Wow. I've never sued anybody, you know."

Keely laughed. "Me, neither. But you could. Once the insurance people were reminded of that, they didn't seem to think fixing an old car was an extravagant use of funds."

"It's really nice of them," Cappie said, stunned. It was like a miracle. "I didn't know what I was going to do. My brother is an invalid, and the only money we've got is his savings and what I bring home. That's not a whole lot."

"Before I married Boone, I had to count pennies," the other girl said. "I know what it's like to have very little. I think you do very well."

"Thanks." She sighed. "You know, Kell was in the military for years and years. He went into all sorts of dangerous situations, but he never got hurt. Then he left the army and went to work for this magazine, went to Africa to cover a story and got hit with shrapnel from an exploding shell. Go figure."

Keely frowned. "Didn't he have insurance? Most magazines have it for their employees, I'm sure."

"Well, no, he didn't. Odd, isn't it?"

"They sent him to Africa to do a story," Keely added. "What sort of story? A news story?"

Cappie blinked. "You know, I never asked him. I only knew he was leaving the country. Then I got a call from him, saying he was in the hospital with some injuries and he'd be home when he could get here. He wouldn't even let me visit him. An ambulance brought him to our rented house in San Antonio."

Keely didn't say what she was thinking. But she almost had to bite her tongue.

Cappie stared at her. "That's a very strange story, even if I'm the one telling it," she said slowly.

"Maybe it's the truth," Keely said comfortingly. "After all, it's very often stranger than fiction."

"I guess so." She let it drop. But she did intend to talk it over with Kell that night.

When she got home, there was a big SUV parked in the driveway. She frowned at it as she went up the steps and into the house. The door was unlocked.

She heard laughter coming from Kell's room.

"I'm home!" she called.

"Come on in here," Kell called back. "I've got company."

She took off her coat and moved into the bedroom. Kell's visitor was very tall and lean, with faint silvering at the temples of his black hair. He had green eyes and a somber face, and one of his hands seemed to be burned. He moved it unobtrusively into his pocket when he saw her eyes drawn to it.

"This is an old friend of mine," Kell said. "My sister, Cappie. This is Cy Parks. He owns a ranch in Jacobsville."

Cappie held out her hand, smiling, and shook the one offered. "Nice to meet you."

"Same here. You'll have to bring Kell over to the ranch to see us," he added. "I have a terrific wife and two little boys. I'd love for you to meet them."

"You, with a wife and kids," Kell said, shaking his head. "I'd never have imagined it in my wildest dreams."

"Oh, it comes to all of us, sooner or later," Cy replied lazily. He pursed his lips. "So you work for Bentley Rydel, do you?"

She nodded.

"Does he really carry a pitchfork, or is that just malicious gossip?" Cy added, tongue in cheek.

She flushed. "Kell…!" she muttered at her brother.

He held up both hands and laughed. "I didn't tell him what you said. Honest."

"He didn't," Cy agreed. "Actually Bentley makes a lot of calls at my place during calving season. He's our vet. Good man."

"Yes, he is," Cappie said. "He brought me home after a drunk ran into my car."

Cy's expression darkened. "I heard about that. Tough break."

"Well, the man's insurance company is going to fix our car," Cappie added with a laugh. "It seems they were worried that we might sue."

"We would have," Kell said, and he wasn't smiling. "You could have been killed."

"I just got bruised a little," she said, smiling. "Nice of you to worry, though."

Kell grinned. "It's a hobby of mine."

"You need to get out more," Cy told the man in the bed. "I know you've got pain issues, but staying cooped up in here is just going to make things worse. Believe me, I know."

Kell's eyes darkened. "I guess you're right. But I do have something to do. I'm working on a novel. One about Africa."

Cy Parks's face grew hard. "That place has made its mark on several of us," he said enigmatically.

"It's still making marks on other men," Kell said.

"The Latin American drug cartels are moving in there as well," Cy replied. "Hell of a thing, as if Africa didn't have enough internal problems as it is."

"As long as power-hungry tyrants can amass fortunes by oppressing other men, it won't lower the casualty rates for any combatants working there," Kell muttered.

"Combatants?" Cappie asked curiously.

"Two groups of people are fighting for supremacy," Kell told her.

"One good, one evil," she guessed.

"No. As far as African internal politics go, both sides have positive arguments. The outsiders are the ones causing the big problems. Their type of diplomacy is most often practiced with rapid-firing automatic weapons and various incendiary devices."

"And IEDs," Cy added.

Cappie blinked. "Excuse me?"

"Improvised explosive devices," Kell translated.

"Were you in the military, too, Mr. Parks?" Cappie asked.

Cy hesitated. “Sort of. Look at the time,” he remarked, glancing at his watch. “Lisa wants me to go with her to pick out a new playpen for our youngest son,” he added with a grin. “Our toddler more or less trashed the first one.”

“Strong kid,” Kell noted.

“Yes. Bullheaded, too.”

“I wonder where he gets that from,” Kell wondered aloud, with twinkling eyes.

“I am not bullheaded,” Cy said complacently. “I simply have a resistance to stupid ideas.”

“Same difference.”

Cy made a face. “I’ll come back and check on you later in the week. If you need anything…”

Kell smiled. “Thanks, Cy.”

“I’d have come with Eb and Micah when they dropped by,” Cy added, “but we were out of town with the kids. It’s good to see you again.”

“Same here,” Kell said. “I owe you.”

“For what?” Cy shrugged. “Friends help friends.”

“They do.”

Cappie stared at her brother with a blank expression. A whole conversation seemed to be going on under her nose that she didn’t comprehend.

“I’ll see you,” Cy said. “Nice to have met you, Miss Drake,” he added, smiling.

“You, too,” she replied.

Cy left without a backward glance.

After he drove away, Cappie was still staring at her

brother. "You didn't say you had friends here. Why haven't I seen them?"

"They came while you were at work," he said. "Several times."

"Oh."

He averted his eyes. "I met them when I was in the service," he said. "They're fine men. A little unorthodox, but good people."

"Oh!" She relaxed. "Mr. Parks has an injury."

"Yes. He was badly burned trying to save his wife and child from a fire. He was the only one who got out. It turned him mean. But now he's remarried and has two sons, and he seems to have put the past behind him."

"Poor guy." She grimaced. "No wonder he was mean. Who were the other men he mentioned?"

"Other friends. Eb Scott and Micah Steele. Micah's a doctor in Jacobsville. Eb Scott has a sort of training center for paramilitary units."

She blinked. "You do seem to attract the oddest friends."

"Men with guns." He nodded. He grinned.

She laughed. "Okay. I'm stonewalled. What do you want for supper?"

"Nothing heavy," he said. "I had a big lunch."

"You did?" She didn't recall leaving anything out for him except sandwiches in a Baggie.

"Cy brought a whole menu full of stuff from the local Chinese restaurant," he said. "The remains are in the fridge. I wouldn't mind having some of them for supper."

"Chinese food? Real Chinese food, from a real restaurant, that I don't have to cook?" She felt her forehead. "Maybe I'm delusional."

He chuckled. "It does sound like that, doesn't it? Go dig in. Bring me some of the pork and noodles, if you will. There's sticky rice and mangoes for dessert, too."

"I have died and am now in heaven," she said in a haunted tone.

"Me, too. Get cracking. I'm on the fourth chapter of this book already!"

"You are?" She laughed. He looked so much more cheerful. More than he'd been in weeks. "Okay, then."

He pulled the laptop back into place.

"Do I get to read it?"

He nodded. "When it's done."

"That's a deal." She went into the kitchen and got out the boxes of Chinese food. It was all she could do to keep back the tears. Cy Parks was a nice man. A very nice man. Except for their splurged hamburgers and milkshakes, for which she still owed Dr. Rydel she reminded herself, there hadn't been any convenience food for a long time. This was a feast. She put some of it in the freezer for hard times and heated up the rest. Her day was already getting better.

It got even better than that. A tall man with sandy hair and blue eyes came driving up in Cappie's own car two days later. The big SUV was following close behind.

Cappie gaped at the sight. Her old car had been refurbished, its dents beaten out and the whole thing repainted and repaired. There were even seat covers and floor mats. She stared at it helplessly surprised.

Cy Parks got out of the SUV and followed the sandy-haired man up onto the porch. "I hope you like blue," he told Cappie. "There was a paint sale."

She could barely manage words. "Mr. Parks, I don't even know what to say…" She burst into tears. "It's so kind!"

He patted her awkwardly on the shoulder. "There, there, it's just one of those random acts of kindness we're supposed to pass around. You can do the same thing for somebody else one day."

She dabbed at her eyes. "When I strike it rich, I swear I will!"

He chuckled. "Harley Fowler, here," he introduced his companion, "is as good a mechanic as he is a ranch foreman. I had him supervise the work on your car. The insurance company paid for it all," he added when she started to protest. He grinned. "We get things done here in Jacobsville. The insurance agent locally is the sister-in-law of my top wrangler."

"Well, thank you both," she said huskily. "Thank you so much. I was almost ashamed to ask Keely for rides. She's so nice, but it was an imposition. I live five miles out of her way."

"You're very welcome."

The front door opened and Kell wheeled himself

out onto the porch. He whistled when he saw the car. "Good grief, that was quick work," he said.

Cy grinned. "You might remember that I always did know how to cut through the red tape."

"Thanks," Kell told him. "From both of us. If I can ever do anything for you…"

"You've done enough," Cy returned quietly. His green eyes twinkled. "But you could always put me in that novel you're writing. I'd like to be twenty-seven, drop-dead handsome and a linguist."

Kell rolled his eyes. "You can barely speak English," he pointed out.

Cy glared at him. "You take that back, or I'll have Harley shoot all the tires out on this car."

Kell held up both hands, his silver eyes twinkling. "Okay, you could get work as a translator at the U.N. any day. Honest."

Cy sighed. "Don't I wish." He frowned. "Do you still speak Farsi?"

Kell nodded, smiling.

"I've got a friend who's applying for a job with the company. Think you could tutor him? He's well-off, and he'd pay you for your time."

Kell frowned.

"It's not charity," Cy muttered, glowering at him. "This is a legitimate need. The guy wants to work overseas, but he'll never get the job unless he can perfect his accent."

Kell relaxed. "All right, then. I'll take him on. And thanks."

Cy smiled. "Thank you," he replied. "He's a nice guy. You'll like him." He glanced at Cappie, who was wondering what sort of company Cy's friend worked for. "You won't," he assured her. "I used to be a woman hater, but this guy makes me look civilized. He'll need to come over when you're at work."

Cappie was curious. "Why does he hate women?"

"I think he was married to one," Cy mused.

"Well, that certainly explains that," Kell chuckled.

"Thank you very much for fixing up my car," Cappie told Cy. "I won't forget it."

"No problem. We were glad to help. Oh, mustn't forget the keys, Harley!"

Harley handed the keys to her as Cy headed back and got into the other vehicle. "She purrs like a kitten now," Harley told her. "She drives good."

"The car is a girl?" she asked.

"Only when a guy is driving it," Kell told her with a wicked grin.

"Amen," Harley told him.

"Come on, Harley," Cy called from the SUV.

"Yes, sir." He grinned at the brother and sister and jumped into the passenger seat in Cy's SUV.

"What a nice man," Cappie said. "Just look, Kell!" She walked out to the car, opened the door and gasped. "They oiled the hinges! It doesn't squeak anymore. And look, they fixed the broken dash and replaced the radio that didn't work…" She started crying again.

"Don't do that," Kell said gently. "You'll have me wailing, too."

She made a face at him. "You have nice friends."

"I do, don't I?" He smiled. "Now you won't have to beg rides."

"It will be a relief, although Keely's been wonderful about it." She glanced at her brother. "I don't think the insurance paid for all this."

"Yes, it did," he said firmly. "Period."

She smiled at him. "Okay. You really do have nice friends."

"You don't know how nice," he told her. "But I may tell you one day. Now let's get back inside. It's cold out here today."

"It is a bit nippy." She turned and followed him inside.

The week went by fast. She got her paycheck on Friday and went shopping early Saturday morning in Jacobsville. Kell had said he'd love a new bathrobe for Christmas, so she went to the department store looking.

It was a surprise when she bumped into Dr. Rydel in the men's department. He gave her a curious look. She didn't realize why until she recalled that she'd left her hair long around her shoulders instead of putting it up. He seemed to find it fascinating.

"Shopping for anything particular?" he asked.

"Yes. Kell wants a bathrobe."

"Christmas shopping," he guessed, and smiled.

"Yes."

"I'm replacing a jacket," he sighed. "I made the mistake of going straight from church on a large animal call. A longhorn bull objected to being used as a pin-cushion and ripped out the sleeve."

She laughed softly. "Occupational hazard," she said.

He nodded. "Your car looks nice."

"Thanks," she said. She could imagine how her old wreck, even repainted, looked to a man who drove a new Land Rover, but she didn't say so. "Mr. Parks had his foreman supervise the work. The insurance company paid for it."

"Nice of him. He knows your brother?"

"They're friends." She frowned. "Mr. Parks doesn't look like a rancher," she blurted out.

"Excuse me?"

"There's something, I don't know, dangerous about him," she said, searching for the right word. "He's very nice, but I wouldn't want him mad at me."

He grinned. "A few drug dealers in prison could attest to the truth of that statement," he said.

"What?"

"You don't know?"

"Know what?"

"Cy Parks is a retired mercenary," he told her. "He was in some bloody firefights in Africa some years back. More recently, he and two other friends and Harley Fowler shut down a drug distribution center here. There was a gunfight."

"In Jacobsville, Texas?" she exclaimed.

"Yep. Parks is one of the most dangerous men I've ever met. Kind to people he likes. But there aren't many of those."

She felt odd. She wondered how it was that her brother had come to know such a man, because he and Cy seemed to be old friends.

"Where do you go from here?" Dr. Rydel asked suddenly.

She blinked. "I don't know," she blurted out, flushing. "I mean, I thought I might, well, stop by the game store in the strip mall."

He stared at her blankly. "Game store?"

She cleared her throat. "There's this new video game. 'Halo…'"

"'…ODST,'" he said, with evident surprise. "You're a gamer?"

She cleared her throat again. "Well…yes."

He said something unprintable.

She glared at him. "Dr. Rydel!" she exclaimed. "It's not a vice, you know, playing video games. They release tension and they're fun," she argued.

He chuckled. "I have all three Halo games from Bungie, plus the campaigns," he confessed, naming the famous company whose amazing staff had engineered one of the most exciting video game series of all time. "And the new one that just came out."

Now her jaw fell open. "You do?"

"Yes. I have 'Halo: ODST,'" he said, pursing his lips. "Do you game online?"

She didn't want to confess that she couldn't afford the fees. "I like playing by myself," she said. "Or with Kell. He's crazy about the Halo series."

"So am I," Dr. Rydel told her. His blue eyes twinkled. "Maybe we could play split screen sometime, when we're both free."

She gave him a wicked look. "I can put down Hunters with a .45 automatic." Hunters were some of the most formidable of the alien Covenant bad guys, fearsome to engage in the Halo game because they were huge and it took a dead shot to hit them in their very few vulnerable places.

He whistled. "Not bad, Miss Drake!"

"Have you been a gamer for a long time?" she asked.

"Since college," he replied, smiling. "You?"

"Since high school. Kell was in the military and a bunch of guys in his unit would come over to the house when they were off duty and play war-game videos. We lived off base." She pursed her lips and her eyes twinkled. "I not only learned how to use tactics and weapons, I also learned a lot of very interesting and useful words to employ when I got killed in the games."

"Bad girl," he chided.

She laughed.

"I'll probably see you in the video store," he added.

She beamed. "You probably will."

He grinned and went back to the suits.

Fifteen minutes later, she parked in front of the video store and went inside. It was full of teenage boys mostly, but there were two men standing in front of a rack with the newest sword and sorcery and combat games. One of them was Dr. Rydel. The other, surprisingly, was Officer Kilraven.

Dr. Rydel looked up and smiled when he saw her coming. Kilraven's silver eyes cut around to follow his companion's gaze. His black eyebrows arched.

"She's Christmas shopping," Dr. Rydel announced.

"Buying video games for a relative?" Kilraven wondered aloud.

Dr. Rydel chuckled. "She's a gamer," he confided. "She can take down Hunters with a .45 auto."

Kilraven whistled through his teeth. "Impressive," he said. "I usually do that with a sniper rifle."

"I can use those, too," she said. "But the .45 works just as well, thanks to that magnified sight."

"Have you played all the Halo series?" Kilraven asked.

She nodded. "Now I'm shopping for ODST," she said. "Kell, my brother, likes it, too. He taught me how to play."

Kilraven frowned. "Kell Drake?"

"Yes..."

"I know him," Kilraven replied quietly. "Good man."

"Were you in the army?" she asked innocently.

Kilraven chuckled. "Once, a long time ago."

"Kell only got out a year ago," she said. "He was freelancing for a magazine in Africa and got hit by flying shrapnel. He's paralyzed from the waist down—

at least until the shrapnel shifts enough so that they can operate."

Kilraven blinked. "He got hit by flying…he was working for a magazine?" He seemed incredulous. "Doing what?"

"Writing stories."

"Writing stories? Kell can write?"

"He has very good English skills," she began defensively.

"I never," Kilraven said in an odd tone. "Why did he get out of the army?" he wanted to know.

She blinked. "Well, I'm not really sure…" she began.

"Look at this one," Dr. Rydel interrupted helpfully, holding up a game. "Have you ever played this?"

Kilraven was diverted. He took the green case and stared at the description. He grinned. "Have I ever! 'Elder Scrolls IV, Oblivion,'" he murmured. "This is great! You don't have to do the main quest, if you don't want to. There are dozens of other quests. You can even design your own character's appearance, name him, choose from several races…ever played it?" he asked Cappie.

She chuckled. "Actually it's sort of my favorite. I love 'Halo,' but I like using a two-handed sword as well."

"Vicious girl," Kilraven mused, smiling at her.

Dr. Rydel unobtrusively moved closer to Cappie and cleared his throat. "You shopping or working today?" he asked Kilraven.

The other man looked from Cappie to Dr. Rydel and his silver eyes twinkled. "If you notice, I'm wearing a real uniform," he pointed out. "I even carry a real gun. Now would I be doing that if it was my day off?"

Dr. Rydel smiled back at him. "Would you be shopping for video games on city time?"

Kilraven glared at him. "For your information, I am here detecting crime."

"You are?"

"Absolutely. I have it on good authority that there might be an attempted shoplifting case going on here right now." He raised his voice as he said it and a young boy cleared his throat and eased a game out from under his jacket and back on the shelf. With flaming cheeks he gave Kilraven a hopeful smile and moved quickly to the door.

"If you'll excuse me," Kilraven murmured, "I'm going to have a few helpful words of advice for that young man."

"How did he know?" Cappie asked, stunned, as she watched the tall officer walk out the door and call to the departing teen.

"Beats me, but I've heard he does things like that." He smiled. "He's on his lunch hour, in case you wondered. I was just ribbing him. I like Kilraven."

She gave him a wry glance. "Sharks like other sharks, do they?" she asked wickedly.

CHAPTER FOUR

AT FIRST, Bentley wasn't sure he'd heard her right. Then he saw the demure grin and burst out laughing. She'd compared him to a shark. He was impressed.

"I wondered if you were ever going to learn how to talk to me without getting behind a door first," he mused.

"You're hard going," she confessed. "But so is Kell, to other people. He just walks right over people who don't talk back."

"Exactly," he returned. He shrugged his broad shoulders. "I don't know how to get along with people," he confessed. "My social skills are sparse."

"You're wonderful with animals," she replied.

His eyebrows arched and he smiled. "Thanks."

"Did you always like them?" she wondered.

His eyes had a faraway look. He averted them. "Yes. But my father didn't. It wasn't until after he died that I indulged my affection for them. It was just my mother and me until I was in high school. That's when she met my stepfather." His expression hardened.

"It must have been very difficult for you," she said quietly, "getting used to another man in your house."

He frowned as he looked down at her. "Yes."

"Oh, I'm remarkably perceptive," she said with amusement in her eyes. "I also suffer from extreme modesty about my other equally remarkable attributes." She grinned.

He laughed again.

Kilraven came back, looking smug.

"You look like a man with a mission," Bentley mused.

"Just finished one. That young man will never want to lift a video game again."

"Good for you. Didn't arrest him?"

Kilraven arched an eyebrow. "Actually he knows some cheat codes for 'Call of Duty' that even I haven't worked out. So I called our police chief."

"Cheat codes are against the law?" Cappie asked, puzzled.

Kilraven chuckled. "No. Cash has a young brother-in-law, Rory, who's nuts about 'Call of Duty,' so our potential shoplifter is going to go over to Cash's house later and teach them to him. Cash may have a few words to add to the ones I gave him."

"Neat strategy," Bentley said.

Kilraven shrugged. "The boy loves gaming but he lives with a widowed mother who works two jobs just to keep food on the table. He wanted 'Call of Duty,' but he didn't have any money. If he and Rory hit it off, and

I think they might, he'll get to play the game and learn model citizen habits on the side."

"Good psychology," Bentley told him.

Kilraven sighed. "It's tough on kids, having an economy like this. Gaming is a way of life for the younger generation, but those game consoles and games for them are expensive."

"That's why we have a whole table of used games that are more affordable," the owner of the store, overhearing them, commented with a grin. "Thanks, Kilraven."

The officer shrugged. "I spend so much time in here that I feel obliged to protect the merchandise," he commented.

The store owner patted him on the back. "Good man. I might give you a discount on your next sale."

Kilraven glared at him. "Attempting to bribe a police officer…"

The owner held up both hands. "I never!" he exclaimed. "I said 'might'!"

Kilraven grinned. "Thanks, though. It was a nice thought. You wouldn't have any games based on Scottish history?" he added.

The store owner, a tall, handsome young man, gave him a pitying look. "Listen, you're the only customer I've ever had who likes sixteenth-century Scottish history. And I'll tell you again that most historians think James Hepburn got what he deserved."

"He did not," Kilraven muttered. "Lord Bothwell

was led astray by that French-thinking queen. Her wiles did him in."

"Wiles?" Cappie asked, wide-eyed. "What are wiles?"

"If you have to ask, you don't have any," Bentley said helpfully.

She laughed. "Okay. Fair enough."

Kilraven shook his head. "Bothwell had admirable qualities," he insisted, staring at the shop owner. "He was utterly fearless, could read and write and speak French, and even his worst enemies said that he was incapable of being bribed."

"Which may be, but still doesn't provide grounds for a video game," the manager replied.

Kilraven pointed a finger at him. "Just because you're a partisan of Mary, Queen of Scots, is no reason to take issue with her Lord High Admiral. And I should point out that there's no video game about her, either!"

"Hooray," the manager murmured dryly. "Oh, look, a customer!" He took the opportunity to vanish toward the counter.

Kilraven's two companions were giving him odd looks.

"Entertainment should be educational," he defended himself.

"It is," Bentley pointed out. "In this game—" he held up a Star Trek one "—you can learn how to shoot down enemy ships. And in this one—" he held up a comical one about aliens "—you can learn to use a death ray and blow up buildings."

"You have no appreciation of true history," Kilraven sighed. "I should have taught it in grammar school."

"I can see you now, standing in front of the school board, explaining why the kids were having nightmares about sixteenth-century interrogation techniques," Bentley mused.

Kilraven pursed his lips. "I myself have been accused of using those," he said. "Can you believe it? I mean, I'm such a law-abiding citizen and all."

"I can think of at least one potential kidnapper who might disagree," Bentley commented.

"Lies. Vicious lies," he said defensively. "He got those bruises from trying to squeeze through a car window."

"While it was going sixty miles an hour, I believe?" the other man queried.

"Hey, it's not my fault he didn't want to wait for the arraignment."

"Good thing you noticed the window was cracked in time."

"Yes," Kilraven sighed. "Sad, though, that I didn't realize he had a blackjack. He gave it to me very politely, though."

Bentley glanced at Cappie. "Was it a sprained wrist or a fractured one?" he wondered.

Kilraven gave him a cold glare. "It was a figment."

"A what?"

"Of his imagination," Kilraven assured him. He

chuckled. "Anyway, he's going to be in jail for a long time. The resisting arrest charge, added to assault on a police officer, makes two felony charges in addition to the kidnapping ones."

"I hope you never get mad at me," Bentley said.

"I'd worry more about the chief," Kilraven replied. "He fed a guy a soapy sponge in front of the whole neighborhood."

"He was provoked, I hear," Bentley said.

"A felon verbally assaulted him in his own yard while he was washing his car. Of course, Cash has mellowed since his marriage."

"Not much," Bentley said. "And he's still pretty good with a sniper kit. Saved Colby Lane's little girl when she was kidnapped."

"He practices on Eb Scott's firing range," Kilraven said. "We all do. He lets us use it free. State-of-the-art stuff, computers and everything."

"Eb Scott?" Cappie asked.

"Eb was a merc," Kilraven told her. "He and Cy Parks and Micah Steele fought in some of the bloodiest wars in Africa a few years back. They're all married and somewhat settled. But like Cash Grier, they're not really tame."

Cappie only nodded. She was recalling what her brother had said about Cy Parks.

Kilraven cleared his throat. "Oops, lunchtime is over. I've got to go. See you."

"You didn't have lunch," Bentley observed.

"I had a big breakfast," Kilraven replied. "Can't waste my lunch hour eating," he added with a grin. "See you."

"Imagine him, a gamer," Cappie commented. "I'd never have thought it."

"A lot of military men keep their hand-eye coordination skills sharp playing them," he said.

"Were you in the military?" Cappie wanted to know.

He smiled and nodded. "I have it on good authority that it's all that saved me from a life of crime. I got picked up for hanging around with a couple of bad kids who knocked over a drugstore. I was just in the car with them, but I got charged with a felony." He sighed. "My mother went to the judge and promised him her next child if he'd let me join the army instead of standing trial. He agreed." He glanced down at her with a smile. "He's in his seventies now, but I still send him a Christmas present every year. I owe him."

"That was nice."

"I thought so, too."

"Kell got into some trouble in his senior year of high school. I don't remember it, I was so young, but he told me about it. He was hanging out with one of the inner-city gangs and there was a firefight. He didn't get shot, but one of the boys in the gang was killed. Kell got arrested right along with them. He drew a female judge who had grown up in gang territory and lost a brother to the violence. She gave him a choice of facing trial or going into the service and making something of his life. He took her at her word, and made her proud." She sighed. "It was tragic, about her. She was shot and killed in her own living room during a drug deal shootout next door."

"Life is dangerous," Bentley remarked.

She nodded. "Unpredictable and dangerous." She looked up at him. "I guess maybe that's why I like playing video games. They give me something that I can control. Life is never that way."

He smiled. "No. It isn't." He watched as she took a copy of "Halo: ODST" off the shelf. "Going to make him wait until Christmas to play it?"

"Yes."

His eyes twinkled. "I could bring my copy over. Let you get a taste of it before the fact."

She looked fascinated. "You could?"

"Ask Kell." He hesitated. "I could bring a pizza with me. And some beer."

She pursed her lips. "I'm already drooling." She grimaced. "I could cook something…"

"Not fair. You shouldn't have to provide for guests. Besides, I haven't had a decent pizza in weeks. I'll be on call tonight, but we might get lucky."

Her eyes brightened. "That would be nice. I'm sure Kell would enjoy it. We don't get much company."

"About six?"

Her heart jumped. "Yes. About six would be fine."

"It's a date."

"I'll see you then."

He nodded.

She walked, a little wobbly, to the counter and paid for her game. Her life had just changed in a heartbeat. She didn't know where it would lead, and she was a little nervous about getting involved with her boss. But he was very nice-looking and he had qualities that she admired. Besides, she thought, it was just a night of gaming. Nothing suspect about that.

She told Kell the minute she got home.

He laughed. "Don't look so guilty," he chided. "I like your boss. Besides, it's neat to see the game I might get for Christmas." He smiled angelically.

"You might get it," she said, "and you might not."

"You might get a new raincoat," he mused.

She grinned. "Wow."

He looked at her fondly. "It's hard, living like this, I know. We were better off in San Antonio. But I didn't want us to be around when Frank got out of jail." His face hardened.

Her heart jumped. She hadn't thought about Frank for several days in a row. But now the trial and his fury came back, full force. "It was almost six months ago that he was arrested, and three months until the trial. He got credit for time served. We've been here just about three months." She bit her lower lip. "Oh, dear. They'll let him out pretty soon."

His pale eyes were cold. "It should have been a tougher sentence. But despite his past, it was the first time he was ever charged with battery, and they couldn't get more jail time for him on a first offense. The public defender in his case was pretty talented as well."

She drew in a long breath. "I'm glad we're out of the city."

"So am I. He lived barely a block from us. We're not as easy to get to, here."

She stared at him closely. "You believe the threats he made," she murmured. "Don't you?"

"He's the sort of man who gets even," he told her. "I'm not the man I was, or we'd never have left town on the chance he might come after you. But here, I have friends. If he comes down here looking for trouble, he'll find some."

She felt a little better. "I didn't want to have him arrested again."

"It wouldn't have mattered," he told her. "The fact that you stood up to him was enough. He was used to women being afraid of him. His own sister sat in the back of the courtroom during the trial. She was afraid to get near him, because she hadn't lied for him when the police came."

"What makes a man like that?" she asked sadly. "What makes him so hard that he has to beat up a woman to make him feel strong?"

"I don't know, sis," Kell told her gently. "Honestly I don't think the man has feelings for anybody or anything. His sister told you that he threw her dog off a bridge when they were kids. He laughed about it."

Her face grew sad. "I thought he was such a gentleman. He was so sweet to me, bringing me flowers and candy at work, writing me love letters. Then he came over to our house and the first thing he did was kick my cat when it spit at him."

"The cat was a good judge of character," Kell remarked.

"When I protested, he said that animals didn't feel pain and I shouldn't get so worked up over a stupid cat. I should have realized then what sort of person he was."

"People in love are neither sane nor responsible," Kell replied flatly. "You were so crazy about him that I think you could have forgiven murder."

She nodded sadly. "I learned the hard way that looks and acts are no measure of a man. I should have run for my life the first time he phoned me at work just to talk."

"You didn't know. How could you? He was a stranger."

"You knew," she said.

He nodded. "I've known men like him in the service," he said. "They're good in combat, because they aren't bothered by the carnage. But that trait serves them poorly in civilian life."

She cocked her head at him. "Kilraven said that Eb Scott lets law enforcement use his gun range for free. Don't you know him, too?"

"Yes."

"And Micah Steele."

"Yes."

She hesitated. "They're all retired mercenaries, Kell."

"So they are."

"Were they involved with the military?" she persisted.

"The military uses contract personnel," he said evasively. "People with necessary skills for certain jobs."

"Like combat."

"Exactly," he replied. "We used certain firms to supplement our troops overseas in the Middle East. They're used in Africa for certain covert operations."

"So much secrecy," she complained.

"Well, you don't advertise something that might get you sued or cause a diplomatic upheaval," he pointed out. "Covert ops have always been a part of the military. Even what they call transparency in government is never going to threaten that. As long as we have renegade states that threaten our sovereignty, we'll have black ops." He glanced at the clock. "Shouldn't you warm up the game system?" he asked. "It's five-thirty."

"Already?" she exclaimed. "Goodness, I need to tidy up the living room! And the kitchen. He's bringing pizza and beer!"

"You don't drink," he said.

"Well, no, but you like a beer now and then. I expect somebody told him." She flushed.

"I do like a glass of beer." He smiled. "It's also nice to have friends who provide food."

"Like your friend Cy and the Chinese stuff. I'll get spoiled."

"Maybe that's the idea. Your boss likes you."

She'd gotten that idea, herself. "Don't mention horns, pitchforks or breathing fire while he's here," she said firmly.

He saluted her.

She made a face at him and went to do her chores.

"That's not fair!" Cappie burst out when she'd "died" for the tenth time trying to take out one of the Hunters in the Halo game.

"Don't throw the controller," Kell said firmly.

She had it by one lobe, gripped tightly. She grimaced and slowly lowered it. "Okay," she said. "But they do bounce, and they're almost shockproof."

"She ought to know," Kell told an amused Bentley Rydel. "She's bounced it off the walls several times in recent weeks."

"Well, they keep killing me!" she burst out. "It's not my fault! These Hunters aren't like the ones in 'Halo 3…' they're almost invincible, and there are so many of them…!"

"I'd worry more about the alien grunts that keep taking you out with sticky grenades," Bentley pointed out. "While you're trying to snipe the Hunters, the little guys are blowing you up right and left."

"I want a flame thrower," she wailed. "Or a rocket launcher! Why can't I find a rocket launcher?"

"We wouldn't want to make it too easy, now would we?" Bentley chided. He smiled at her fury. "Patience.

You have to go slow and take them on one at a time, so they don't flank you."

She gave her boss a speaking look, turned back to the screen and tried again.

It was late when he left. The three of them had taken turns on the controller. Bentley and Kell had wanted to try the split screen, but that would have put Cappie right out of the competition, because she was only comfortable playing by herself.

She walked Bentley outside. "Thanks for bringing the pizza and beer," she said. "Some other time, I'd like to have you over for supper, if you'd like. I can cook."

He smiled. "I'll take you up on that. I can cook, too, but I only know how to do a few things from scratch. It gets tiresome after a while."

"Thanks for bringing the game over, too," she added. "It's really good. Kell is going to love it."

"What did we all do for entertainment before video games?" he wondered aloud as they reached his car.

"I used to watch game shows," she said. "Kell liked police dramas and old movies."

"I like some of the forensic shows, but I almost never get to see a whole one," he sighed. "There's always an emergency. It's always a large animal call. And since I'm the only vet on staff who does large animal calls, it's always me."

"Yes, but you never complain, not even if it's sleeting out," she said gently.

He smiled. "I like my clients."

"They like you, too." She shook her head. "Amazing, isn't it?"

"Excuse me?"

She flushed. "Oh, no, not because of…I mean…" She grimaced. "I meant it's amazing that you never get tired of large animal calls when the weather's awful."

He chuckled. "You really have got to take an assertiveness course," he said, and not unkindly.

"It's hard to be assertive when you're shy," she argued.

"It's impossible not to be when you have a job like mine and people don't want to do what you tell them to," he returned. "Some animals would die if I couldn't outargue their owners."

"Point taken."

"If it's any consolation," he said, "when I was your age, I had the same problem."

"How did you overcome it?"

"My stepfather decided that my mother wasn't going to the doctor for a urinary tract infection. I was already in veterinary school, and I knew what happened when animals weren't treated for it. I told him. He told me he was the man of the house and he'd decide what my mother did." He smiled, remembering. "So I had a choice—either back down, or let my mother risk permanent damage to her health, even death. I told him she was going to the doctor, I put her in the car and drove her there myself."

"What did your stepfather do?" she asked, aghast.

"There wasn't much that he could do, since I paid the doctor." His face hardened. "And it wasn't the first disagreement we'd had. He was poor and proud with it. He'd have let her suffer rather than admit he couldn't afford a doctor visit or medicine." He looked down at her. "It's a hell of a world, when people have to choose between food and medicine and doctors. Or between heated houses and medicine."

"Tell me about it," she replied. She colored a little, and hoped he didn't notice. "Kell and I do all right," she said quickly. "But he'll go without medicine sometimes if I don't put my foot down. You'd think I'd be tough as nails, because I stand up to him."

"He's not a mean person."

"He could be, I think," she said. She hesitated. "There was a man I dated, briefly, in San Antonio." She hesitated again. Perhaps it was too soon for this.

He stepped closer. "A man."

His voice was very soft. Quiet. Comforting. She wrapped her arms around her chest. She had on a sweater, but it was chilly outside. The memories were just as chilling. She was recalling it, her face betraying her inner turmoil. He'd hit her. The first time, he said it was because he'd had a drink, and he cried, and she went back to him. But the second time, he'd have probably killed her if Kell hadn't heard her scream and come to save her. As it was, he'd fractured her arm when he threw her over the couch. Kell had knocked

Frank out with a lamp, from his wheelchair, and made her call the police. He made her testify, too. She held her arms around herself, chilled by the memory.

"What happened?"

She looked up at him, wanting to tell him, but afraid to. Frank got a six-month sentence, but he'd already served three months and he was out. Would he come after her now? Would he be crazy enough to do that? And would Bentley believe her, if she told him? They barely knew each other. It was too soon, she thought. Much too soon, to drag out her past and show it to him. There was no reason to tell him anyway. Frank wouldn't come down here and risk being sent back to jail. Bentley might think less of her if she told him, might think it was her own fault. Besides, she didn't want to tell him yet.

"He was a mean sort of person, that's all," she hedged. "He kicked my cat. I thought it was terrible. He just laughed."

His blue eyes narrowed. "A man who'll kick a cat will kick a human being."

"You're probably right," she admitted, and then she smiled. "Well, I only dated him for a little while. He wasn't the sort of person I like to be around. Kell didn't like him, either."

"I like your brother."

She smiled. "I like him, too. He was just going downhill with depression in San Antonio. We were over our ears in debt, from all the hospital bills. It's lucky our cousin died and left us this place," she added.

Bentley's eyebrows lifted. "This place belonged to Harry Farley. He got killed overseas in the military about six months ago. He didn't have any relatives at all. The county buried him, out of respect for his military service."

"But Kell said…" she blurted out.

Her expression made Bentley hesitate. "Oh. Wait a minute," Bentley said at once. "That's right, I did hear that he had a distant cousin or two."

She laughed. "That's us."

"My mistake. I wasn't thinking." He studied her quietly. "Well, I guess I'd better go. This is the first Saturday night I can remember when I didn't get called out," he added with a smile. "Pure dumb luck, I guess."

"Law of averages," she countered. "You have to get lucky sooner or later."

"I guess. I'll see you Monday."

"Thanks again for the pizza."

He opened the door of the Land Rover. "I'll take you up on the offer of supper," he said. "When we set a date, you can tell me what you want to fix and I'll bring the raw ingredients." He held up a hand when she started to protest. "It does no good to argue with me. You can't win. Just ask Keely. Better yet, ask Dr. King," he chuckled.

She laughed, too. "Okay, then."

"Good night."

"Good night."

He closed the door behind him. Cappie went back up on the porch and watched him throw up a hand as he drove away. She stood there for several seconds before she realized that the wind was chilling her. She went in, feeling happier than she had in a long time.

CHAPTER FIVE

CAPPIE FELT awkward with Bentley the following Monday. She wasn't sure if she should mention that he'd been to her house over the weekend. Her coworkers were very nice, but she was nervous when she thought they might tease her about the doctor. That would never do. She didn't want to make him feel uncomfortable in his own office.

Having lived so long in San Antonio, she didn't know about life in small towns. It hadn't occurred to her that nothing that happened could be kept secret.

"How was the pizza?" Dr. King asked her.

Cappie stared at her in horror.

Dr. King grinned. "My cousin works at the pizza place. Dr. Rydel mentioned where he was taking it. And she's best friends with Art, who runs the software store, so she knew he was taking the game over to play with you and your brother."

"Oh, dear," Cappie said worriedly.

Dr. King patted her on the back. "There, there," she

said in a comforting tone. "You'll get used to it. We're like a big family in Jacobs County, because most of us have lived here all our lives, and our families have lived here for generations, mostly. We know everything that's going on. We only read the newspaper to find out who got caught doing it."

"Oh, dear," Cappie said again.

"Hi," Keely said, removing her coat as she joined them. "How was the game Saturday?" she added.

Cappie looked close to tears.

Dr. King gave Keely a speaking glance. "She's not used to small towns yet," she explained.

"Not to worry," Keely told her. "Dr. Rydel certainly is." She laughed at Cappie's tormented expression. "If he was worried about gossip, you'd better believe he'd never have put a foot inside your door."

"She thinks we'll tease her," Dr. King said.

"Not a chance," Keely added. "We were all dating somebody once." She flushed. "Especially me, and very recently." She meant her husband, Boone, of course.

"And nobody teased her," Dr. King added. "Well," she qualified it, "not where Boone could hear it, anyway," she added, and chuckled.

"Thanks," she said.

Dr. King just smiled. "You know, Bentley hates most women. One of our younger clients made a play for him one day. She wore suggestive clothing and a lot of makeup and when he leaned over to examine her dog, she kissed him."

Cappie's eyes widened. "What did he do?"

"He left the room, dragged me in there and told the young lady that he was indisposed and Dr. King would be handling the case."

"What did the young lady do?" Cappie asked.

"Turned red as a beet, picked up her dog and left the building. It turns out," Dr. King added with a grin, "that the dog was in excellent health. She only used it as an excuse to get Dr. Rydel in there with her."

"Did she come back?"

"Oh, yes, she was an extremely persistent young woman. The third time she showed up here, she insisted on seeing Dr. Rydel. He called Cash Grier, our police chief, and had him come in and explain the legal ramifications of sexual harassment to the young lady. He didn't smile while he was speaking. And when he finished talking, the young lady took her animal, went home and subsequently moved back to Dallas."

"Well!" Cappie exclaimed.

"So you see, Dr. Rydel is quite capable of deterring unwanted interest." She leaned closer. "I understand that you like to play video games?"

Cappie laughed. "Yes, I do."

"My husband has a score of over 16,000 on Xbox LIVE," she said, and wiggled her eyebrows.

Keely was staring at her, uncomprehending.

"My scores are around 4,000," Cappie said helpfully. "And my brother's are about 15,000." She chuckled.

"The higher the score, the better the player. Also, the more often the playing."

"I guess my score would be around 200," Dr. King sighed. "You see, I get called in a lot for emergencies when Dr. Rydel is out on large animal calls. So I start a lot of games that my husband gets to finish."

"Kell had buddies in the army who could outdo even those scores. Those guys were great!" Cappie said. "They'd hang out with us when they were off duty. Kell always had nice video gaming equipment. Some of them did, too, but we always had a full fridge. Boy, could those guys eat!"

"You lived overseas a lot, didn't you?" Keely asked.

"Yes. I've seen a lot of exotic places."

"What was your favorite?"

"Japan," Cappie replied at once, smiling. "We went there when Kell was stationed in Korea. Not that Korea isn't a beautiful country. But I really loved Japan. You should see the gaming equipment they've got. And the cell phone technology." She shook her head. "They're really a long way ahead of us in technology."

"Did you get to ride the bullet train?" Keely asked.

"Yes. It's as fast as they say it is. I loved the train station. I loved everything! Kyoto was like a living painting. So many gardens and trees and temples."

"I'd love to see any city in Japan, but especially Kyoto," Keely said. "Judd Dunn's wife, Christabel, went over there with him to buy beef. She said Kyoto was just unbelievable. So much history, and so beautiful."

"It is," Cappie replied. "We got to visit a temple. The Zen garden was so stark, and so lovely. It's just sand and rocks, you know. The sand is raked into patterns like water. The rocks are situated like land. All around were Japanese black pine trees and bamboo trees as tall as the pines, with huge trunks. There was a bamboo forest, all green, and a huge pond full of Japanese Koi fish." She shook her head. "You know, I could live there. Kell said it was his favorite, too, of all the places we lived."

"Are we going to work today, or travel around the world?" came a deep, curt voice from behind them.

Everybody jumped. "Sorry, Dr. Rydel," Keely said at once.

"Me, too," Cappie seconded.

"Nihongo no daisuki desu," Dr. Rydel said, and made a polite bow.

Cappie burst out smiling. *"Nihon no tomodachi desu. Konichi wa, Rydel sama,"* she replied, and bowed back.

Keely and Dr. King stared at them, fascinated.

"I said that I liked Japanese language," Dr. Rydel translated.

"And I said that I was a friend of Japan. I also told him hello," Cappie seconded. "You speak Japanese!" she exclaimed to Bentley.

"Just enough to get me arrested in Tokyo," Bentley told her, smiling. "I was stationed in Okinawa when I was in the service. I spent my liberties in Tokyo."

"Well, isn't it a small world?" Dr. King wondered.

"Small, and very crowded," Bentley told her. He gave her a meaningful look. "If you don't believe me, you could look at the mob in the waiting room, glaring at the empty reception counter and pointedly staring at their watches."

"Oops!" Dr. King ran for it.

So did Keely and Cappie, laughing all the way.

There was a new rapport between Dr. Rydel and Cappie. He was no longer antagonistic toward her, and she wasn't afraid of him anymore. Their working relationship became cordial, almost friendly.

Then he came to supper the following Saturday, and she found herself dropping pots and pans and getting tongue-tied at the table while the three of them ate the meal she'd painstakingly prepared.

"You're a very good cook," Bentley told her, smiling.

"Thanks," she replied, flushing even more.

Kell, watching her, was amused and indulgent. "She could cook even when she was in her early teens," he told Bentley. "Of course, that was desperation," he added with a sigh.

She laughed. "He can burn water," she pointed out. "I had so much carbon in my diet that I felt like a fire drill. I borrowed a cookbook from the wife of one of his buddies and started practicing. She felt sorry for me and gave me lessons."

"They were delicious lessons," Kell recalled with a smile. "The woman was a *cordon bleu* cook and she could make French pastries. I gained ten pounds. Then her husband was reassigned and the lessons stopped."

"Hey, a new family moved in," she argued. "It was a company commander, and she could make these terrific vegan dishes."

Kell glared at her. "I hate vegetables."

"Different strokes for different folks," she shot back. "Besides, there's nothing wrong with a good squash casserole."

Kell and Bentley exchanged horrified looks.

"What is it with men and squash?" she exclaimed, throwing up her hands. "I have never met a man who would eat squash in any form. It's a perfectly respectable vegetable. You can make all sorts of things with it."

Bentley pursed his lips. "Door props, paperweights…"

"Food things!" she returned.

"Hey, I don't eat paperweights," Bentley pointed out.

She shook her head.

"Why don't you bring in that terrific dessert you made?" Kell prompted.

"I guess I could do that," she told him. She got up and started gathering plates. Bentley got up and helped, as naturally as if he'd done it all his life.

She gave him an odd look.

"I live alone." He shrugged. "I'm used to clearing the

table." He frowned. "Well, throwing away plastic plates, anyway. I eat a lot of TV dinners."

She made a face.

"There is nothing wrong with a TV dinner," Kell added. "I've eaten my share of them."

"Only when I was working late and it was all you could get," Cappie laughed. "And mostly, I left you things that you could just microwave."

"Point conceded." Kell grinned.

"What sort of dessert did you make?" Bentley asked.

She laughed. "A pound cake."

He whistled. "I haven't tasted one of those in years. My mother used to make them." His pleasant expression drained away for a few seconds.

Cappie knew he was remembering his mother's death. "It's a chocolate pound cake," she said, smiling, as she tried to draw him out of the past.

"Even better," he said, smiling. "Those are rare. Barbara sells slices of one sometimes at her café, but not too often."

"A lot of people can't eat chocolate, on account of allergies," she said.

"I don't have allergies," Bentley assured her. "And I do hope it's a large pound cake. If you offered to send a slice home with me, I might let you come in an hour late one day next week."

"Why, Dr. Rydel, that sounds suspiciously like a bribe," she exclaimed.

He grinned. "It is."

"In that case, you can take home two slices," she said.

He chuckled.

Watching them head into the kitchen, Kell smiled to himself. Cappie had been afraid of men just after her bad experience with the date from hell. It was good to see her comfortable in a man's company. Bentley might be just the man to heal her emotional scars.

"Where do you want these?" Bentley asked when he'd scraped the plates.

"Just put them in the sink. I'll clean up in here later."

He looked around quietly. The kitchen was bare bones. There was an older microwave oven, an old stove and refrigerator, a table and chairs that looked as if they'd come from a yard sale. The coffeepot and Crock-Pot on the counter had seen better days.

She noticed his interest and smiled sadly. "We didn't bring a lot of stuff with us when we moved back to San Antonio. We sold a lot of things to other servicemen so we wouldn't have to pay the moving costs. Then, after Kell got wounded, we sold more stuff so we could afford to pay the rent."

"Didn't he have any medical insurance?"

She shook her head. "He said there was some sort of mix-up with the magazine's insurer, and he got left out in the cold." She removed the cover from the cake pan and got out cake plates to serve it on. Her mother's small china service had been one thing she'd managed to salvage. She loved the pretty rose pattern.

"That's too bad," Bentley murmured. But he was

frowning behind her, his keen mind on some things he recalled about her mysterious brother. If Kell was friendly with the local mercs, it was unlikely he'd gotten to know them in the military. They were too old to have served anytime recently. But he did know that they'd been in Africa in recent years. So had Kell. That was more than a coincidence, he was almost sure.

His silence made her curious. She turned around, her soft eyes wide and searching.

His own pale blue eyes narrowed on her pretty face in its frame of long blond hair. She had a pert little figure, enhanced by the white sweater and blue jeans she was wearing. Her breasts were firm and small, just right for her build. He felt his whole body clench at the way she was looking at him.

He wasn't handsome, she was thinking, but he had a killer physique, from his powerful long legs in blue jeans to his broad chest outlined under the knit shirt. Beige suited his coloring, made his tan look bronzed, the turtleneck enhancing his strong throat.

"You're staring," he pointed out huskily.

She searched for the right words. Her mouth was dry. "Your ears have very nice lobes."

He blinked. "Excuse me?"

She flushed to her hairline. "Oh, good heavens!" She fumbled with the cake knife and it started to fall. He stepped forward and caught it halfway to the floor, just as she dived for it. They collided.

His arm slid around her to prevent her from going

headlong into the counter and pulled her up short, right against him. Her intake of breath was audible as she clung to him to keep her footing.

She felt his chin against her temple, heard his breath coming out raggedly. His arm contracted.

"Th...thanks," she managed to say against his throat. "I'm just so clumsy sometimes!"

"Nobody's perfect."

She laughed nervously. "Certainly not me. Thanks for saving the cake knife."

"My pleasure."

His voice was almost a purr, deep and soft and slow. He lifted his head very slowly, so that his eyes were suddenly looking right into hers. She felt his chest rise and fall against her breasts in an intimacy that grew more smoldering by the second. She looked up, but her eyes stopped at his chiseled mouth. It was very sensuous. She'd never really paid it much attention, until now. And she couldn't quite stop looking at it.

She felt his fingers curling into her long hair, as if he loved the feel of it.

"I love long hair," he said softly. "Yours is beautiful."

"Thanks," she whispered.

"Soft hair. Pretty mouth." He bent and his nose slid against hers as his mouth poised over her parted lips. "Very pretty mouth."

She stood very still, waiting, hoping that he wasn't going to draw back. She loved the way his body felt, so close to hers. She loved his strength, his height, the spicy scent of his cologne. She hung there, at his lips, her eyes half closed, waiting, waiting…

"Where's that cake?" came a plaintive cry from the living room. "I'm starving!"

They jumped apart so quickly that Cappie almost fell. "Coming right up!" Heavens, was that her voice? It sounded almost artificial!

"I'll take the coffeepot into the living room for you," Bentley said. His own voice was oddly hoarse and deep, and he didn't look at her as he went out of the room.

Cappie cut the cake, forcing her mind to ignore what had almost happened. She had so many complications in her life right now that she didn't really need another one. But she did wonder if it was possible to put this particular genie back in its bottle.

And, in fact, it wasn't. When they finished the cake and a few more minutes of conversation, Bentley got a call from his answering service and hung up with a grimace.

"One of Cy Parks's purebred heifers is calving for the first time. I'll have to go. Sorry. I really enjoyed the meal, and the cake."

"So did we," Cappie said.

"We'll have to do this again," Kell added, grinning.

"Next time, I'll take the two of you out to a nice restaurant," Bentley said.

"Well…" Cappie hesitated.

"Walk me out," Bentley told her, and he didn't smile.

Cappie looked toward Kell to save her, but he only grinned. She turned and followed Bentley out the door.

He paused at the steps, looking down at her with a long, unblinking stare in the faint light that shone out from the windows.

She bit her lower lip and searched for something to say. Her mind wouldn't cooperate.

He couldn't seem to find anything to say, either. They just stared at each other.

"I hate women," he bit off.

She faltered. "I'm sorry," she said.

"Oh, what the hell. Come here."

He scooped her up against him, bent his head and kissed her with such immediate passion that she couldn't even think. Her arms went around his neck as she warmed to the hard, insistent pressure of his mouth as it parted her lips and invaded the soft, secret warmth of her mouth. It was too much, too soon, but she couldn't say that. He didn't leave her enough breath to say anything, and the pleasure throbbing through her body robbed her mind of the words, anyway.

Seconds later, he put her back on her feet and moved away. "Well!" he said huskily.

She stared up at him with her mouth open.

His eyebrows arched.

She tried to speak, but she couldn't manage a single word.

He let out a rough breath. "I really wish you wouldn't look at me in that tone of voice," he said.

"Wh…what?" she stammered.

He chuckled softly. "Well, I could say I'm flattered that I leave you speechless, but I won't embarrass you. See you Monday."

She nodded. "Monday."

"At the office."

She nodded again. "The office."

"Cappie?"

She was still staring at him. She nodded once more. "Cappie."

He burst out laughing. He bent and kissed her again. "And they say the way to a man's heart is through his stomach," he mused. "This is much quicker than food. See you."

He turned and went to his car. Cappie stood and watched him until he was all the way to the main highway. It wasn't until Kell called to her that she realized it was cold and she didn't even have on a coat.

After that, it was hard to work in the same office with Bentley without staring at him, starstruck, when she saw him in between patients. He noticed. He couldn't seem to stop smiling. But when Cappie started running into door facings looking at him, everybody else in the office started grinning, and that did inhibit her.

She forced herself to keep her mind on the animal patients, and not the tall man who was treating them.

Just before quitting time, a little boy came careening into the practice just ahead of a man. He was carrying a big dog, wrapped in a blanket, shivering and bleeding.

"Please, it's my dog, you have to help him!" the boy sobbed.

A worried man joined him. "He was hit by a car," the man said. "The so-and-so didn't even stop! He just kept going!"

Dr. Rydel came out of the back and took a quick look at the dog. "Bring him right back," he told the boy. He managed a smile. "We'll do everything we can. I promise."

"His name's Ben," the boy sobbed. "I've had him since I was little. He's my best friend."

Dr. Bentley helped the boy lift Ben onto the metal operating table. He didn't ask the boy to leave while he did the examination. He had Keely help him clean the wound and help restrain the dog while he assessed the damage. "We're going to need an X-ray. Get Billy to help you carry him," he told her with a smile.

"Yes, sir."

"Is he going to die?" the boy wailed.

Dr. Rydel put a kindly hand on his shoulder. "I don't see any evidence of internal damage or concussion. It looks like a fracture, but before I can reduce it, I'm going to need to do X-rays to see the extent of the damage. Then we'll do blood work to make sure it's safe to anesthetize him. I will have to operate. He has some skin and muscle damage in addition to the fracture."

The man with the boy looked worried. "Is this going to be expensive?" he asked worriedly.

The boy wailed.

"I lost my job last week," the man said heavily. "We've got a new baby."

"Don't worry about it," Dr. Rydel said in a reassuring tone. "We do some pro bono work here, and I'm overdue. We'll take care of it."

The man bit his lower lip, hard, and averted his eyes. "Thanks," he gritted.

"We all have rough patches," Dr. Rydel told him. "We get through them. It will get better."

"Thanks, Doc!" the boy burst out, reaching over to rub a worried hand over the old dog's head. "Thanks!"

"I like dogs, myself," the doctor chuckled. "Now this is going to take a while. Why don't you leave your phone number at the desk and I'll call you as soon as your dog's through surgery?"

"You'd do that?" the man asked, surprised.

"Of course. We always do that."

"His name's Ben," the boy said, sniffing. "He's had all his shots and stuff. We take him every year to the clinic at the animal shelter."

Which meant money was always tight, but they took care of the animal. Dr. Rydel was impressed.

"We'll give her our phone number. You're a good man," the boy's father said quietly.

"I like dogs," Dr. Rydel said again with a smile. "Go on home. We'll call you."

"You be good, Ben," the boy told his dog, petting him one last time. The dog wasn't even trying to bite anybody. He whined a little. "We'll come and get you just as soon as we can. Honest."

The man tugged the boy along with him, giving the vet one last grateful smile.

"I can take care of his bill," Keely volunteered.

Dr. Rydel shook his head. "I do it in extreme cases like this. It's no hardship."

"Yes, but..."

He leaned closer. "I drive a Land Rover. Want to price one?"

Keely burst out laughing. "Okay. I give up."

Billy, the vet tech, came to help Keely get Ben in to X-ray. Cappie came back after a minute. "I promised I'd make sure you knew that Ben likes peanut butter," she said. "Who's Ben?"

"Fractured leg, HBC," he abbreviated.

She smiled. "Hit by car," she translated. "The most frequent injury suffered by dogs. They know who hit him?"

"I wish," Dr. Rydel said fervently. "I'd call Cash Grier myself."

"They didn't stop?"

"No," he said shortly.

"I'd stop, if I hit somebody's pet," Cappie said gently. "I had a cat, when we lived in San Antonio, after Kell got out of the army. I had to give him away when we moved down here." She was remembering that Frank had kicked him, so hard that Cappie took him to work with her the next day, just to have him checked out. He had bruising, but, fortunately, no broken bones. Then the cat had run away, and returned after Frank was gone. She'd given the cat away before she and Kell left town, to make sure that Frank wouldn't send somebody to get even with her by hurting her cat. He was that sort of man.

"You're very pensive," he commented.

"I was missing my cat," she lied, smiling.

"We have lots of cats around here," he told her. "I think Keely has a whole family of them out in her barn and there are new kittens. She'd give you one, if you asked."

She hesitated. "I'm not sure if I could keep a cat," she replied. "Kell wouldn't be able to look out for him, you know. He has all he can do to take care of himself."

He didn't push. He just smiled. "One day, he'll meet some nice girl who'll want to take him home with her and spoil him rotten."

She blinked. "Kell?"

"Why not? He's only paralyzed, you know, not demented."

She laughed. "I guess not. He's pretty tough."

"And he's not a bad gamer, either," he pointed out.

"I noticed."

"Cappie, have you got the charges for Miss Dill's cat in here yet?" came a call from the front counter.

She grimaced. "No, sorry, Dr. King. I'll be right there."

She rushed back out, flustered. Dr. Rydel certainly had a way of looking at her that increased her heart rate. She liked it, too.

CHAPTER SIX

CAPPIE STAYED late to help with the overflow of patients, held up by the emergency surgery on the dog. The practice generally did its scheduled surgeries on Thursdays, but emergencies were always accommodated. In fact, there was a twenty-four-hour-a-day emergency service up in San Antonio, but the veterinarians at Dr. Rydel's practice would always come in if they were needed. In certain instances, the long drive to the big city would have meant the death of a furry patient. They were considering the addition of a fourth veterinarian to the practice, so that they could more easily accommodate those emergencies.

The dog, Ben, came out of surgery with a mended foreleg and was placed in a recovery cage to wait until the anesthetic wore off. The next day, if he presented no complications, he would be sent home with antibiotics, painkillers and detailed instructions on post-surgical care. Cappie was glad, for the boy's sake. She felt sorriest for the children whose pets were injured.

Not that grown-up people took those situations any easier. Pets were like part of the family. It was hard to see one hurt, or to lose one.

Kell was pensive when she got home. In fact, he looked broody. She put down her coat and purse. "What's the matter with you?" she asked with a grin.

He put his laptop computer aside with deliberation. "I had a call from an assistant district attorney's office in San Antonio, from the victim support people," he said quietly. "Frank Bartlett got out of jail today."

It was the day she'd been dreading. Her heart sank. He'd vowed revenge. He would make her pay, he said, for having him tried and convicted.

"Don't worry," he added gently. "We're among friends here. Frank would have to be crazy to come down here and make trouble. In addition to the jail time, he drew a year's probation. They'll check on him. He wouldn't want to risk having to go back to jail to finish his sentence."

"You think so?" she wondered. She recalled what a hardheaded man Frank was. He got even with people. She'd heard things from one of her coworkers in San Antonio at the animal clinic, one who was friends with Frank's sister. She'd said that Frank had run a man off the road who'd reported him for making threats at one of his jobs. The man was badly injured, but he could never prove it had been Frank who'd caused the accident. Cappie was sure, now, that there had probably been other incidents as well. Frank had admitted to her once that he'd spent time in juvenile hall as a youngster. He'd never said what for.

"He won't be able to get to you at home," Kell continued, "because I keep firearms and I know how to use them," he added grimly. "At work, I don't think he'd dare approach you. Dr. Rydel would likely propel him headfirst out the front door," he chuckled.

Cappie was reminded that Dr. Rydel had actually done that. Dr. King told her about it. A man had come in with a badly injured dog, one with multiple fractures, claiming that the animal had fallen down some steps. After examining the dog, Dr. Rydel knew better. He'd accused the man of abusing the dog, and the man had thrown a punch at him. Dr. Rydel had picked him up and literally thrown him out onto the front porch, while fascinated pet owners watched. Then he'd called the police and had the man arrested. There had been a conviction, too.

Cappie, remembering that, smiled. "Dr. Rydel gets very upset when people abuse animals," she told her brother.

"Obviously." He pursed his lips. "I wonder why he decided to become a veterinarian?"

"I'll have to ask him that."

"Yes, you will. I made macaroni and cheese for supper," he said, "when you called to say you'd be late."

She made a face before she could stop herself.

Kell just grinned. "It's frozen," he said. "I heated it up in the oven."

She sighed with relief. “Sorry. It’s just that I’ve had my carbon for today.”

He laughed. “I know I can’t cook. One day, though, I’ll learn how. Then watch out.”

“Some men are born to be chefs. You aren’t one of them. I’ll make a salad to go with the macaroni.”

“I did that already. It’s in the fridge.”

She went to kiss his cheek, bending over him in the wheelchair. “You’re the nicest brother in the whole world.”

“I could return the compliment.” He ruffled her hair. “Listen, kid, if the surly vet proposes, you take him up on it. I can take care of myself.”

“You can’t cook,” she wailed.

“I can buy nice frozen things to heat up,” he returned.

She sighed. “As if Dr. Rydel would ever propose,” she laughed. “He likes me, but that doesn’t mean he’ll want to marry me one day.”

“You need to invite him over again and make that shrimp and pasta dish you do so well. I have it from a spy that Dr. Rydel is partial to shrimp.”

“Really? Who knows that?”

“Cy Parks told me.”

She gave him a suspicious look. “Did you try to pump Cy Parks for inside information?”

Kell gave her his best angelic look. “I would never do such a sneaky thing.”

“Sure you would,” she retorted.

“Well, Dr. Rydel knew why Cy was asking him,

anyway. He just laughed and asked if there was any other inside information that Cy would like to have for us."

She flushed. "Oh, my."

"Cy said the good doctor talked more about you than he did about the heifer he was helping to deliver," Kell added. "It's well-known that Dr. Rydel can't abide women. People get curious when a notorious woman hater suddenly starts seeing a local woman."

"I wonder why he hates women?" she wondered aloud.

"Ask him. But for now, let's eat. I'm fairly empty."

"Goodness, yes, it's two hours past our usual suppertime," she agreed, moving into the kitchen. "I'm sorry I was late."

"How's the dog?" he asked, joining her at the table.

"He'll be fine, Dr. Rydel said. The poor boy was just devastated. I felt sorry for his dad. He'd just lost his job. You could see he was torn between getting the dog treated and taking care of his family. There's a new baby. Dr. Rydel didn't charge him a penny."

"Heart of gold," Kell said gently.

"We were going to take up a collection, when Dr. Rydel reminded us that he drove a Land Rover," she laughed. "He inherited money from his grandmother, Dr. King said, and he makes a good living as a vet."

"That means he'll be able to take care of you when you get married."

She made a face. "Horses before carts, not carts before horses."

"You wait and see," he replied. "That's a man who's totally hooked. He just doesn't know it yet."

She smiled from ear to ear as she started putting food on the table. She'd already pushed her fears about Frank to the back of her mind. Kell was right. He surely wouldn't risk his freedom by making trouble for Cappie again.

Dr. Rydel took her to a carnival Friday night. She was shocked not only at the invitation, but at the choice of outings.

"You like carnivals?" she'd exclaimed.

"Sure! I love the rides and cotton candy." He'd smiled with reminiscence. "My grandmother used to save her egg money to take me to any carnival that came through Jacobsville when I was a kid. She'd even go on the rides with me. I get tickled even now when I hear somebody talk about grandmothers who bake cookies and knit and sit in rocking chairs. My grandmother was a newspaper reporter. She was a real firecracker."

She was remembering the conversation as they walked down the sawdust-covered aisles between booths where carnies were enticing customers to pitch pennies or throw baseballs to win prizes.

"What are you brooding about?" he teased.

She looked up, laughing. "Sorry. I was remembering what you said about your grandmother. Did you spend a lot of time with her?"

His face closed up.

"Sorry," she said again, flushing. "I shouldn't have asked something so personal."

He stopped in the aisle and looked down at her, enjoying the glow of her skin against the pale yellow sweater she was wearing with jeans, her blond hair long and soft around her shoulders.

His big, lean hand went to her hair and toyed with it, sending sweet chills down her spine when he moved a step closer. "She raised me," he said quietly. "My mother and father never got along. They separated two or three times a year, and then fought about who got to keep me. My mother loved me, but my father only wanted me to spite her." His face hardened. "When I made him mad, he took it out on my pets. He shot one of my dogs when I talked back to him. He wouldn't let me take the dog to a veterinarian, and I couldn't save it. That's why I decided to become a vet."

"I did wonder," she confessed. "You talk about your mother, but never about your father. Or your stepfather." Her hands went to his shirtfront. She could feel the warm muscle and hair under the soft cotton.

He sighed. His hand covered one of hers, smoothing over her fingernails. "My stepfather thought that being a vet was a sissy profession, and he said so, frequently. He didn't like animals, either."

"Some sissy profession," she scoffed. "I guess he never had to wrestle down a sick steer that weighed several hundred pounds."

He chuckled. "No, he never did. We got along

somewhat. But I don't miss seeing him. I had hard feelings against him for a long time, for letting my mother get so sick that medical science couldn't save her. But sometimes we blame people when it's just fate that bad things happen. Remember the old saying, 'man proposes and God disposes'? It's pretty much true."

"Ah, you advocate being a leaf on the river, grasshopper," she said in a heavily accented tone.

"You lunatic," he laughed, but he bent and kissed her nose. "Yes. I do advocate being a leaf on the river. Sometimes you have to trust that things will work out the way they're meant to, not the way you want them to."

"Why do you hate women?"

His eyebrows arched.

"Everybody knows that you do. You even told me so." She flushed a little as she remembered when he'd told her so; the first time he'd kissed her.

"Remember that, do you?" he teased softly. "You don't know a lot about kissing," he added.

She moved restlessly. "I don't get in much practice."

"Oh, I think I can help you with that," he said in a deep, husky tone. "And for the record, I don't hate you."

"Thank you very much," she said demurely, and peered up at him through her lashes.

He bent slowly to her mouth. "You're very welcome," he whispered. His lips teased just above hers, coaxing her to lift her chin, so that he had better access to her mouth.

Before he could kiss her, a deep voice mused from behind him, "Lewd behavior in public will get you arrested."

"Kilraven," Bentley groaned, turning to face the man. "What are you doing here?"

Kilraven, in full uniform, grinned at the discomfort in their faces as he moved closer and lowered his voice. "I'm investigating possible cotton candy fraud."

"Excuse me?" Cappie said.

"I'm going to taste the cotton candy, and the candy apples, and make sure they're not using illegal counterfeit sugar."

They both stared at him as if he'd gone mad.

He shrugged. "I'm really off duty, I just haven't gone home to change. I like carnivals," he added, laughing. "Jon, my brother, and I used to go to them when we were kids. It brings back happy memories."

"They have a sharpshooting target," Bentley told him.

"I don't waste my unbelievable talent on games," Kilraven scoffed.

"I am in awe of your modesty," Bentley said.

"Why, thank you," Kilraven replied. "I consider it one of my best traits, and I do have quite a few of them." He peered past them. Winnie Sinclair, in jeans and a pretty pink sweater and matching denim jacket, was walking around the penny-pitching booth with her brother, Boone Sinclair, and his wife, Cappie's coworker, Keely. Kilraven looked decidedly uneasy. "I'll see you around," he added.

But instead of going to the cotton candy booth, he turned on his heel and walked right out of the carnival.

"How odd," Cappie murmured, watching him leave.

"Not so odd," Bentley replied. His eyes were on Winnie Sinclair, who'd just seen Kilraven glare in her direction and then walk away. She looked devastated. "Winnie Sinclair is sweet on him," he explained, "and he's even a worse woman hater than I am."

Cappie followed his glance. Keely smiled and waved. She waved back. Winnie Sinclair smiled wanly, and turned back to the booth. "Poor thing," she murmured. "She's so rich, and so unhappy."

"Money doesn't make you happy," Bentley pointed out.

"Well, the lack of it can make you pretty miserable," she said absently.

His hand reached down and locked in to hers, bringing her surprised eyes back up to meet his.

She was hesitant, because Keely was grinning in their direction.

"I don't care about public opinion," Bentley pointed out, "and she wouldn't dare tease me in my own practice," he added with a grin.

Cappie laughed. "Okay. I won't care, either."

His strong fingers linked with hers, while he held her gaze. "I can't remember the last time I smiled so much," he said. "I like being with you, Cappie."

She smiled. "I like being with you, too."

They were still smiling at each other when two running children bumped into them and broke the spell.

Bentley drove her home, but he didn't move to open the door after he cut off the lights and the engine. He unfastened her seat belt, and his own, and pulled her across the seat and into his lap. Before she could speak, his mouth was hard on hers, grinding into it, and his fingers were lazily searching under the soft hem of her sweater.

She wanted to protest. It was too soon. But he found the hooks on her bra and loosened them with one quick motion of his hand. Then he found soft flesh and teased around it with such expertise that she squirmed backward to give him access.

"Too quick?" he whispered against her mouth.

"No," she bit off, and arched her back.

He smiled as his mouth covered hers once more, and his hand settled directly over the hard little nub that raised against his palm.

After a few minutes, kissing was no longer enough. His hand moved in at the base of her spine and half lifted her against him, so that her belly ground against his in the rapt silence of the vehicle, broken only by the force of their audible breaths, and her soft moan. She could feel him wanting her. It had been exciting with Frank, but not like this. She wanted what Bentley wanted. She was on fire for him.

He unfastened the buttons on his shirt and pulled her against him, so that her soft breasts ground against the hair-roughened muscles of his chest. His hand moved her hips against his in a slow, anguished rotation that made her moan louder.

"Oh, God," he bit off, shivering. "Cappie!"

Her nails were scoring his back as she held on for dear life and began to shudder. "Don't stop," she whimpered. "Don't stop!"

"I've…got to!"

He moved abruptly, pushing her back into her seat. He opened the door and got out of the Land Rover, standing with his back to her as he sucked in deep breaths and tried to regain the control he'd almost lost.

Embarrassed, Cappie fumbled her bra closures into place and pulled her sweater down. She was still shaky. It had been a near thing. Thank goodness they were parked in her driveway instead of on some lonely road where there might not have been as much incentive to stop. Despite her passionate response to him, Cappie didn't move with the times. Did he know that? Was he hoping for some brief fling? She couldn't. She just couldn't. Now, she reasoned with something like panic, he wouldn't want to see her again, not if she said no. And either way, how was it going to affect her job? There was only one veterinary clinic in Jacobs County, and she worked for it. If she lost her job, she couldn't get another, not in her field.

While she was torturing herself with such thoughts, the door suddenly opened.

"I know," Bentley said in a strangely calm and amused tone, "you're kicking yourself mentally for taking advantage of me in a weak moment. But it's okay. I'm used to women trying to ravish me."

She stared up at him wide-eyed and speechless. Of all the things she expected he might say, that was the last.

"Come on, come on, you're not going to get a second shot at me in the same night," he teased. "I have my reputation to think of!"

Her mind started working again, and she laughed with relief. She picked up her purse and scrambled out the door, her discarded coat over one arm.

"Listen," he said gently, "don't start brooding. We got a little too involved, too quickly, but we'll deal with it."

She hesitated. "I'm not, well, modern," she blurted out.

"Neither am I, honey," he said softly.

She could have melted into the ground at the husky endearment. She blushed.

He bent and kissed her with tender respect. "I know what sort of woman you are," he said gently. "I'm not going to push you into something you don't want."

"Thanks."

"On the other hand, you have to make me a similar promise," he pointed out. "I'm not going to keep dating you if I have to worry about being ravished every time I bring you home. I'm not that sort of man,' he added haughtily.

She grinned from ear to ear. "Okay."

He walked her to the door, smiling complacently. "I'll see you at work Monday," he said. He framed her face in his hands and looked at her for a long time. "Just when you think you're safe," he mused, "you jump headfirst into the tiger trap."

"You know, I was just thinking the same thing," she said facetiously.

He chuckled as he bent to kiss her again. "We'll take it at a nice, easy pace," he whispered. "But I know already how it's going to end up. We're good together. And I'm tired of living alone."

Her heart almost burst with joy. "I…I don't think I could just live with someone," she blurted out, still a little worried.

He kissed her eyes shut. "Neither could I, Cappie," he whispered. "We can talk about licenses and rings." He lifted his head. His eyes were soft with feeling. "But not tonight. We have all the time in the world."

"Yes," she whispered. Her eyes were bright with the force of her emotions. "It's happening so fast."

He nodded. "Like lightning striking."

She felt her heart racing. But in the back of her mind, there was a sudden fear, a foreboding. She bit her lower lip. "You don't really know much about me," she began. "You see, when I lived in San Antonio, there was this man I dated…"

Before she could tell him about Frank, his phone rang. He jerked it out and answered it. "Rydel," he said. He listened, grimaced. "I'll be in the office in ten minutes. Bring the cat right in, I'll see it. Yes. Yes. You're welcome." He hung up. "I have to go."

"Be careful," she said.

He smiled. "I will. Good night."

"Good night, Dr. Rydel."

"Bentley."

She laughed. "Bentley."

He ran back to the Land Rover, started it and drove away with a wave of his hand. Cappie watched him go, then walked into her house, feeling as if she could have floated all the way.

Monday morning, Cappie still felt light-headed and ecstatic. She'd half expected Bentley to phone her Saturday or Sunday, considering how involved they'd gotten when he brought her home from the carnival on Friday night. But maybe he'd had emergencies. She hoped he hadn't had second thoughts. She was so crazy about him that she couldn't bear to even think about having him reconsider what he'd said. But she knew that wasn't going to happen. They were already so close that she knew it was going to be forever.

So it came as a shock when she walked in the office and Dr. Rydel met her beaming smile with a cold glare that sent chills down her spine.

"You're late, Miss Drake," he said curtly. "Please try to be on time in the future."

She looked as if she'd been hit in the head by a brick. Keely, at the counter, gave her a sympathetic look.

"I'm...I'm sorry, sir," she stammered.

"I need you to help Keely with an X-ray," he said, and turned away abruptly.

"Right away." She put up her coat and purse and rushed to join Keely, who was going in the room where they kept the medical cages. She took a hair band out of her pocket and scrunched her thick hair into a ponytail with it. Inside, she felt numb.

"It's Mrs. Johnson's cat," Keely explained, wary of being overheard by the vet, who was just going into a treatment room. "She stepped on his paw. It's swollen, and Dr. Rydel is afraid it may be broken. Mrs. Johnson is no lightweight," she added with a grin.

"Yes, I know."

"She had to leave him with us while she went to see her heart doctor. She was very upset. She's just getting over a heart attack, and she's worried about her cat!" she said, smiling. Keely opened the cage and Cappie lifted the old cat. It just purred. It didn't even offer to bite her, although it was obvious that it was in pain.

"What a sweet old fellow," Cappie murmured as they went toward the X-ray room. "I thought he might want to bite us."

"He's a sweetheart all right. Here." Keely motioned

to the X-ray table and closed the door behind them. "What in the world is wrong with Dr. Rydel?" she whispered. "He came in looking like a thundercloud."

"I don't know," Cappie said. "We went to the carnival Friday night and he was happy and laughing..."

"You didn't have a fight?" Keely persisted.

"No!" She wanted to add that they'd talked about rings, but this wasn't a good time. The tall man who met her at the door didn't look as if he'd ever said any such thing to her.

"I wonder what happened."

"So do I," Cappie said miserably.

They got the X-ray and Cappie took the old cat back to his cage while Keely developed it. Dr. King gave her a worried look, but she was too busy to say much. Cappie felt sick. She couldn't imagine what had turned Dr. Rydel into an enemy.

She waited and worried all day through two dozen patients and one long emergency. Mrs. Johnson came to pick up her cat, his paw in a neat cast, crying buckets because she'd been so worried about him. Cappie helped her out the door, smiling even though she didn't feel like it. Earlier, she'd thought maybe Dr. Rydel would say something to her, explain, anything. But he didn't. He treated her just as he had when she first joined the practice, courteous but cold.

At the end of the day, she wanted to wait around and see if she could get him to talk to her, but a large animal call took him out the door just minutes before the staff went home. She drove to her house with her heart in her shoes.

"You look like the end of the world," Kell remarked when she walked in. "What happened?"

"I don't know," she said sadly. "Dr. Rydel looked at me as if I had some contagious disease and he didn't say one kind word all day. It was business as usual. He was just like he was when I first went to work for him."

"He seemed pleasant enough when he picked you up Friday night," he remarked.

"And when he brought me home," she added. "Maybe he got cold feet."

Kell studied her sad face. "Maybe he did. Everybody says he was the biggest woman hater around town. But if that's the case, he might warm up again when he's had time to think about it. If he's really interested, Cappie, he's not going away."

"You think so?" she asked, hopeful.

"I know so. Men who act like he did when he came to supper don't suddenly turn ice-cold for no reason. Maybe he just had a rough weekend."

Which was no reason for him to take it out on Cappie. On the other hand, she didn't really know him that well.

"Maybe I can get him to talk to me tomorrow," she said.

He smiled. "Maybe you can."

She nodded. "I'll go make supper."

"Try not to worry."

"Of course."

But she did worry, and she didn't sleep. She went in to work the next morning with a feeling of foreboding.

Dr. Rydel was at the counter when she came in.

"I'm five minutes early," she said abruptly when he glared at her.

"Come into my office, please," he said.

She brightened. At last, he was going to explain. Surely it was something that didn't have anything to do with her.

He let her in and closed the door behind her. He didn't offer her a seat. He perched on the edge of his desk and stared at her coldly. "I had a visitor Saturday morning."

"You did?" An ex-girlfriend, she was thinking, and he wanted her back, was that it?

"Yes," he replied curtly. "Your boyfriend."

"My what?"

"Your boyfriend, Frank Bartlett," he said coldly.

She felt sick all the way to her toes. Frank had come down here! He'd come to Jacobsville! She held on to a chair. She should have told Bentley about him. She shouldn't have waited. "He's my ex-boyfriend," she began.

He laughed coldly. "Is he, really? Now that's not what he said."

CHAPTER SEVEN

CAPPIE COULD almost imagine what sort of story Frank had told Bentley. But now she understood his anger.

"I can explain," she began.

"You told me Friday night that you had an ex-boyfriend," he said icily. "I didn't get to hear the rest of the story, but Bartlett was kind enough to fill me in. You accused him of assaulting you and had him arrested. He actually spent time in jail and now he has a felony record because of you."

Her eyes widened. "Yes, but that isn't what happened…!"

"I know all about women who like to play with men," he interrupted. "When I was in my early twenties, I worked for a veterinarian while I was in college. It supplemented my grants and scholarships. He had a vet tech who was very pretty, but never got dates. I felt sorry for her. She could only work for him part-time, because I had the full-time position. She stayed late one weekend and teased me into kissing her. Then she very calmly tore her shirt, messed up her hair and phoned the police."

Cappie felt her face go pale.

"She wanted my job," Bentley continued cynically. "I dipped into my savings to hire a private detective, who discovered that it wasn't the first time she'd pulled that stunt. She was arrested and my record was cleared. The vet hired me back in a heartbeat and spent years trying to make it up to me."

"I had no idea," she whispered.

"Of course not, or you wouldn't have tried the same stunt on me."

She blinked in disbelief. "What?"

"You were always talking about what you'd do if you had money. You knew I was well-to-do. When were you going to accuse me of assaulting you? Have you got a lawyer waiting in the wings to sue me?"

She couldn't believe her ears. He actually thought she was playing him for cash. Frank had lied to him, and with his background, Bentley had fallen for the tall tale.

"I've never accused anyone falsely," she defended herself.

"Only Frank Bartlett?"

She swallowed, hard. "He broke my arm," she said with quiet dignity. "It wasn't the first time he hit me, either."

"He told me you'd say that," he replied. "Poor guy. You ruined his life. Well, you aren't going to get the chance to ruin mine. You can work your two weeks' notice." He got to his feet.

"You're firing me?" she asked weakly.

"No, you're quitting," he returned coldly. "That way, you won't be able to let the state support you with unemployment insurance, or sue me for unlawful termination of employment."

"I see."

"Women," he muttered coldly. "You'd think I'd already learned my lesson. You all look so innocent. And you all lie."

He opened the door. "Back to work, Miss Drake," he said in a formal tone. "It's going to be a long day."

She worked mechanically, even managed to smile at old Mr. Smith's jokes and Dr. King's bland comments. Keely was looking at her oddly, but nobody else seemed to find her behavior out of the ordinary.

At the end of the day, she went to her car almost gratefully. She still couldn't believe that Dr. Rydel had fallen for Frank's lies. But she was going to do something about it. She just didn't know what. Yet.

She pulled up in the front yard, puzzled at the colorful cloth piled at the foot of the steps. Was Kell cleaning house…?

She slammed on the brakes, cut off the engine and ran as fast as she could to the front door. That wasn't a bundle of cloth, it was Kell. Kell! He was unconscious, lying beside the wreck of his wheelchair and he was bleeding from half a dozen cuts. She felt for a pulse and, thank God, found one! At least he was still alive.

She saw the front door standing open and didn't dare go inside, for fear someone might be waiting there. She ran back to her car, jerked out her cell phone and punched in 911. Then she ran back to Kell and waited.

The next hour was a blur of ambulance sirens, police sirens, blue uniforms, tan uniforms and abject terror.

She waited for Dr. Micah Steele to come out and tell her what Kell's condition was. She was sick and chilled to the bone. If Kell died, she'd have nobody.

He came back out to the waiting room a few minutes after Kell was brought in, tall and blond and somber.

"How is he?" she asked frantically.

"Badly beaten," he told her, "which you already know. His back is one long bruise. We're still doing tests, but he has some feeling in his legs, which indicates that the shrapnel in his back may have shifted. If the tests verify that, I'm having him transported to the medical center in San Antonio. I have a friend who's an orthopedic surgeon there. He'll operate."

"You mean, Kell could walk again?" she asked, excited.

He smiled. "Yes." The smile faded. "But that's not my immediate concern. He said there were three men. One of them was a man you've had dealings with, I understand. Frank Bartlett."

"Beating up a paralyzed man, with a mob," she gritted. "What a brave little worm he is!"

"Sheriff's got an all-points bulletin out for him and his friends," Micah told her. "But you're in danger until they're found. You can't stay out there at the house by yourself."

"If you send Kell to San Antonio," she said, "I'll call a friend who works for the same veterinary practice that employed me until I moved here. She'll let me stay with her."

"You'll have to be in protective custody," Micah said firmly.

She smiled. "Her brother is a Texas Ranger. He lives with her."

"Well!"

"I'll call her as soon as I see Kell."

"That will be another twenty minutes," he said. "We have to finish the tests first. But he's going to be fine."

"Okay. Thanks, Dr. Steele."

He smiled. "Glad I can help. I like Kell."

"I do, too."

She phoned Brenda Banks in San Antonio. Brenda's brother, Colter, was a Texas Ranger. He'd been based out of Houston until his best friend, a Houston police officer named Mike Johns, was killed trying to stop a bank robbery. Colter had asked for reassignment to Company D of the Texas Rangers, based in Bexar County, and moved in with his sister. Since Company

D now had an official Cold Case sergeant, Colter applied for and obtained the job. Brenda said he loved solving old cases.

She tried the apartment, first, and sure enough, Brenda was at home and not at work. "How do you like your new job?" Brenda asked when she heard Cappie's voice.

"I like it a lot. Do you still have a spare bedroom, and is there a job opening there at the vet clinic?"

"Oh, dear."

"Yes, well, things didn't work out as well as I hoped," Cappie said quietly. "Frank and a couple of friends came down and almost beat Kell to death. He's on his way up to San Antonio for back surgery and I need a place to stay, just until after the surgery. They wanted me in protective custody, but I told them Colter lived with you…"

"You poor kid! You can come and stay as long as you like," Brenda said at once. "But Colter's out of the country on a case. He has an apartment of his own now. What's that about Kell?" she asked worriedly. "Is he going to be all right?"

"He's just banged up, mostly," Cappie said, "but the shrapnel in his back has shifted and he has feeling in his legs. They may be able to operate."

"What a blessing in disguise," the other woman said quietly. "But what about you? Don't tell me Frank went to your house just to beat up your brother."

"He was probably looking for me," she confessed.

"But he'd already done enough damage to my working relationship with my new boss. I don't have a job anymore, either."

"I'll ask Dr. Lammers about something part-time," she said immediately. "I know they'd love to have you back. The new tech doesn't have the dedication to the job that you had, and doesn't show up for work half the time, either. I'll phone her right now. Meanwhile, you come on up here. You know where the spare key's kept."

"Thanks a million, Brenda." Her voice was breaking, despite her efforts to control it.

"Honey, I'm so sorry," Brenda said gently. "If there's anything I can do, anything at all, you just tell me."

Cappie swallowed. "I've missed you."

"I've missed you, too. You just hang on. Get Kell up here and then come on yourself. We'll handle it. Okay?"

"Okay."

"I'll phone Dr. Lammers right now." She hung up.

Cappie went back to the waiting room and sat, sad and somber, while she waited for the test results and a chance to talk to Kell.

Dr. Steele was smiling when he came back. "I think it's operable," he said. "I'm going to send Kell to San Antonio by chopper. It's quicker and it will be easier on his back. We don't want that shrapnel to shift again. You can see him, just for a minute. Want to fly up with him?"

"Yes, if I can," she said.

He nodded toward Kell's room. "Cash Grier is in there with him. He wants a word with you, too."

"Okay. Thanks, Dr. Steele."

She opened the door and walked in. Cash Grier was leaning against the windowsill, very somber. Kell looked terrible, but he smiled when she bent over to kiss him.

"Dr. Steele thinks they may be able to operate," she told him.

"So I heard." He smiled. "I don't know how I'll afford it, but maybe they take IOUs."

"You get better before you worry about money," she said firmly. "We can always sell the car."

"Sure, that will pay for my aspirin," Kell chuckled.

"Stop that. It's going to work out," she said firmly. "Hi, Chief," she greeted Cash.

"Hi, yourself. Your ex-boyfriend was after you," he said without preamble. "He won't quit. He knows he'll go back to jail for what he did to Kell. He'll get you, if he can, before we catch him."

"I'm going to fly up to San Antonio with Kell," she said slowly, "and I'll be staying with my best friend. Her brother's a Texas Ranger." She didn't add that he was out of town. After all, Cash wouldn't know. But would she be putting Brenda in danger, just by being there?

"Colter's out of the country, and Brenda doesn't own a weapon," Cash said, stone-faced. He nodded when she gasped. "I know Colter. I used to be a Texas Ranger, too. We've kept in touch. You don't want to put Brenda in the line of fire."

"I was just worrying about that." She bit her lower lip. "Then what do we do?"

"You stay in a hotel near the hospital," he said. "We're sending security up to watch you."

"Police officers from here?" she wondered.

"Not really," Cash said slowly. "Actually Eb Scott is detailing two of his men to stay with you. One is just back from the Middle East, and the other is waiting for an assignment."

"Mercenaries," she said softly.

"Exactly."

She looked worried.

"They're not the sort you see in movies," Kell assured her. "These guys have morals and they only work for good causes, not just for money."

"Do you know the men?" she asked him.

He hesitated.

"I know them," Cash said at once. "And you can trust them. They'll take care of you. Just go with Kell to the hospital and they'll meet you there."

She frowned. "I'll have to phone somebody at my office, to tell them what's happened."

"Everybody at your office already knows what happened," Cash told her. "Well, except your boss," he added, just when her heart had skipped two beats. "He had to fly to Denver on some sort of personal business. Something to do with his stepfather."

"Oh." It was just as well, she thought. Now she wouldn't have to see him again. Kell didn't know Dr. Rydel had fired her, but this wasn't really the time to tell him. It could wait. "What about our house?"

"Kell gave me the key," he said. "I'll get it to Keely. She'll make sure the lights are off and everything's locked up and the fridge is cleaned out."

"I don't want to live there anymore," she told Kell in a subdued tone.

"We don't have to make decisions right now," he replied, wincing as he moved. "Hell, I think it was better when I couldn't feel my legs!"

"You'll enjoy walking again," Cappie said gently. "Kell, it would be like a miracle. At least some good would have come out of all this."

"Just what I was thinking." He smiled at her. "Now don't worry. It's going to work out."

"Yes, it is," Cash agreed. "Rick Marquez is going to make sure every cop in San Antonio has a personal description of Frank Bartlett, and he's talked to a reporter he knows at one of the news stations. Your nemesis Frank is going to be so famous that if he walks into a convenience store, ten people are going to tackle him and yell for the police."

"Really? But why?"

"Did I mention that there's a reward for his capture?" Cash added. "We took up a little collection."

"How kind!"

"You should stay here," Cash said seriously. "It's a good town. Good people."

Her face closed up. "I'm not living in any town that also houses Dr. Rydel."

Cash and Kell exchanged a long look.

"But Kell might like to stay," she added.

Kell wondered what was going on. Cappie had been crazy about her boss until today. "I think we need to have a talk about why you're down on your boss," he told her.

"Tomorrow," she said. "First thing."

"I'll probably be in surgery tomorrow, first thing," Kell replied.

She smiled wanly. "Then I'll tell you while you're unconscious. When do we leave?" she added.

Kell wanted to argue, but they'd given him something for pain, and he was already drooping. "As soon as the helicopter gets here. Need anything from the house? I'm sure Cash would run you over there."

She shook her head. "I've got my purse and my phone. Oh, here's the house key," she added, pulling it off her key ring and handing it to Cash. "I know you gave Kell's to Keely, but you may need mine. Thanks a lot."

"If you need anything, you can call Keely. She'll run it up to you, or her husband or her sister-in-law will."

"I'll do that."

"And try not to worry," Cash added, moving away from the window. "Things always seem darkest before the dawn. Believe me, I should know," he added with a smile. "I've seen my share of darkness."

"You're a wonderful police chief," she told him.

"Another good reason to stay in Jacobs County," he advised.

"We can agree to disagree on that point," she replied. "I might reconsider if you'd lock Dr. Rydel up and throw away the key."

"Can't do that. He's the best veterinarian around."

"I guess he is, at that."

Cash wisely didn't add to his former statement.

The trip in the helicopter was fascinating to Cappie, who'd never flown in one, despite Kell's years in the military. She'd had the opportunity, but she was afraid of the machines. Now, knowing that it was helping to save Kell's legs, she changed her opinion of them.

She sat quietly in her seat, smiling at the med techs, but not talking to them. She'd had just about all she could stand of men, she decided, for at least the next twenty years. She only hoped and prayed that Kell would be able to walk again. And that somebody would find Frank Bartlett before he came back to finish what he'd started.

Bentley Rydel walked into his office three days later, out of sorts and even more irritable than he'd been when he left. His stepfather had suffered a stroke. It hadn't killed him, but he was temporarily paralyzed on one side and in a nursing home for the foreseeable future. Bentley had tracked down the man's younger brother and made arrangements to fly him to Denver to look after his sibling. All that had taken time. He didn't begrudge giving help, but he was still upset about

Cappie. Why had he been stupid enough to get involved with her? Hadn't he learned his lesson about women by now?

The office hadn't officially opened for business; it was ten minutes until it did. He found every employee in the place standing behind the counter glaring at him as if he'd invented disease.

His eyebrows arched. "What's going on?" His face tautened. "Cappie's suing me for asking her to quit, is she?" he asked with cold sarcasm.

Dr. King glared back. "Cappie's in San Antonio with her brother," she said. "Her ex-boyfriend and two of his friends beat Kell within an inch of his life."

He felt the blood drain out of his face. "What?"

"They've got Cappie surrounded by police and volunteers, trying to keep the same thing from happening to her," Keely added curtly. "Sheriff Carson checked into Frank Bartlett's background and found several priors for battery against women, but nobody was willing to press charges until Cappie did. She wasn't exactly willing at that—her brother forced her to, when she got out of the hospital. Bartlett beat her bloody and broke her arm. She said that she'd probably be dead if Kell hadn't managed to knock out Bartlett in time."

He felt as if his throat had been cut. He'd believed the man. How could he have done that to Cappie? How could he have suspected her of such deceit? She'd been the victim. Bentley had believed the lying ex-boyfriend and fired Cappie. Now she was in danger and it was his fault.

"Where is she?" he asked heavily.

"She told us not to tell you," Dr. King said quietly. "She doesn't want to see you again. In fact, she's got her old job back in San Antonio and she's going to live there."

He felt sick all over. No, she wouldn't want to stay in Jacobs County now. Not after the job Bentley had done on her self-esteem. It had probably been hard for her to trust a man again, having been physically assaulted. She'd trusted Bentley. She'd been kind and sweet and trusting. And he'd kicked her in the teeth.

He didn't answer Dr. King. He looked at his watch. "Get to work, people," he said in a subdued tone.

Nobody answered him. They went to work. He went into his office, closed the door and picked up the telephone.

"Yes?" Cy Parks answered.

"Where's Cappie?" he asked quietly.

"If I tell you, I'll have to change my name and move to a foreign country," Cy replied dryly.

"Tell me anyway. I'll buy you a fake mustache."

Cy chuckled. "Okay. But you can't tell her I sold her out."

"Fair enough."

Cappie was worn-out. She'd been in the waiting room around the clock until Kell was through surgery, and it had taken a long time. The chairs must have been selected for their comfort level, she decided, to make sure nobody wanted to stay in them longer than a few minutes. It was impossible to sleep in one, or even to doze. Her back was killing her. She needed sleep, but she couldn't leave the hospital until she knew Kell was out of the recovery room.

Beside her, two tall, somber men sat waiting also. One of them was dark-eyed and dark-headed, and he never seemed to smile. The other one had long blond hair in a ponytail and one pale brown eye and an eye-patch on the other. He was good-natured about his disability and referred to himself as Dead-Eye. He chuckled as he said it. She didn't know their names.

Detective Sergeant Rick Marquez had dropped by earlier in the day to talk to her about Frank Bartlett's family and friends. She did know about Frank's sister, but she hadn't met any of his friends. Detective Marquez was, she thought, really good-looking. She wondered why he didn't have a steady girlfriend.

Marquez had assured her that he was doing everything possible to track down Frank Bartlett, and that a friend of his who was a news anchor was going to broadcast a description of Bartlett and ask for help from the public to apprehend him. There was a two-thousand-dollar reward being offered for information leading to his arrest and conviction.

Brenda came with her to the hospital and stayed until she was called into her own office for an emergency surgery on a dog patient. She'd promised to return as soon as she could. She was upset that Cappie wasn't going to stay with her. She could borrow a gun, she muttered, and shoot that two-legged snake if he came near the apartment. But Cappie smiled and said she hadn't been thinking straight when she'd called and asked for a place to stay. She wasn't risking Brenda. Besides, she had security. Brenda gave the two men a long, curious glance. She did mention that she wouldn't want to mess with them, if she was a bad man. The one with the ponytail grinned at her.

After Brenda left, Cappie sat with her two somber male attachments while people came and went in the waiting room. She drank endless cups of black coffee and tried not to dwell on her fears. If Kell could just walk again, she told herself, the misery of the past few days would be worth it. If only!

Finally the surgeon on Kell's case came out to speak with her, smiling in his surgical greens.

"We removed the shrapnel," he told her. "I'm confident that we got it all. Now we wait for results, once your brother has time to heal. But I'm cautiously optimistic that he'll walk again."

"Oh, thank God," she breathed, giving way to tears. "Thank God!"

"Now, will you please go and get some sleep?" he asked. "You look like death walking."

"I'll do that. Thank you, Dr. Sims. Thank you so much!"

"You're very welcome. Leave your cell phone number at the nurses' desk and they'll phone you if they need you."

"I'll do that right now."

She went to the nurses' desk with her two companions flanking her and looking all around them covertly.

"I'm Kell Drake's sister," she told a nurse. "I want to give you my cell phone number in case you need to get in touch with me."

"Certainly," a little brunette replied, smiling. She pulled a pad over to her and held a pen poised over it. "Go ahead."

Cappie gave the number to her. "I'll always have it with me, and I won't turn it off."

The brunette looked from one man to the other curiously.

"They're with me," Cappie told her. She leaned over the counter. "You see, they're in terrible danger and I have to protect them."

The two men gave her a simultaneous glare that could have stopped traffic. The brunette managed to smother a giggle.

"Okay, guys, I'm ready whenever you are," she told them.

The one with the eye-patch pursed his lips. "Want a head start?" he asked pointedly.

She grinned up at him. "You want one?" she countered.

He chuckled, and indicated that she could go first. He turned and winked at the little brunette, who flushed with pleasure. He was whistling as he followed Cappie out through the waiting room.

"You, protect us," the other man scoffed. "From what…bug bites?"

"Keep that up," Cappie told him, "and I'll show you a bite."

"Now, now, let's try to get along," Dead-Eye murmured as they waited for the elevator to come back up.

"I'm getting along. She's the one with the attitude problem," the other man muttered.

"Says you," Cappie told him.

He stared at Dead-Eye and pointed at Cappie.

"I never take sides in family squabbles," Dead-Eye told him.

"She is not a member of my family!" the other man said.

"A likely story," Dead-Eye said. "Anyway, how can you be sure? Have you had your DNA compared to hers?"

"I know I'm not related to you," the man told Dead-Eye.

"How do you know that?" came the dry retort.

"Because you're too ugly to be any kin to me."

"Well, I never," Dead-Eye harrumphed. "Look who's calling who *ugly*."

"Your mother dresses you funny, too."

Cappie was already light-headed with relief. These two were setting off her quirky sense of humor. "I can't take the two of you anywhere," she complained. "You embarrass me to tears."

"Can I help it if he's ugly?" the second man said. "I was only stating a fact."

"He's not ugly," Cappie defended Dead-Eye. "He's just unique."

Dead-Eye grinned at her. "We can get married first thing in the morning," he said. "I've been keeping a wedding ring in my chest of drawers for just such an emergency."

Cappie shook her head. "Sorry. I can't marry you tomorrow."

"Why not?"

"My brother won't let me date ugly men."

"You just said I wasn't ugly!" he protested.

"I lied."

"I can have my nose fixed."

She frowned. It was a very nice nose.

"I can alter it for you with my fist," the other man volunteered.

"I can alter you first," Dead-Eye informed him.

"No fighting," Cappie protested. "We'll all end up in jail."

"Some of us have probably escaped from one recently," the other man said with a pointed look at Dead-Eye.

"I didn't have to escape. They let me out on account of my extreme good looks," Dead-Eye scoffed.

"Your looks are extreme," came the reply. "Just not good."

"If you two don't stop arguing, I'm going to have my best friend come over to spend the night with us, and you two will be sharing the sofa," she assured them.

"Just shoot me now," Dead-Eye muttered, "and be

done with it. I'm not sharing anything with him. Not unless he's got proof he isn't rabid."

The elevator door had opened while they were arguing. Dr. Bentley Rydel stepped off it and stared at the younger man while Cappie gaped at his sudden appearance.

"He isn't rabid," Bentley assured Dead-Eye.

"And how would you know?" Dead-Eye asked.

"I'm a veterinarian," Bentley replied curtly.

"We should go," Cappie said, avoiding Bentley's eyes.

"We?" he asked, scowling.

"These are my two new boyfriends," Cappie told him with a cold scowl. "We're sharing a room."

He knew she wasn't involved with two strangers. He had a pretty good idea of who they were and why she was with them. She probably expected him to believe the bald statement, with his track record.

"I heard about Kell," he said quietly. "How is he?"

"Out of surgery and resting comfortably, thank you," she said formally. "We have to go."

"Can we talk?" Bentley asked somberly.

"If you can get them," she indicated her companions, "to tie me up and gag me, sure. Let's go, guys."

She walked into the elevator and stood with her back to the door until she heard it close.

CHAPTER EIGHT

CAPPIE DIDN'T sleep, of course. She was replaying the last forty-eight hours in her mind all night, sick with worry about Kell. It was her fault that Frank Bartlett had ever gotten near them. If only she hadn't been so flattered by his attention, so crazy about him that she ignored Kell's warnings. If only she hadn't gone out with him at all.

Pity, she thought, that people couldn't set the clock backward and erase all the stupid things they did. Like getting involved with Dr. Bentley Rydel, for example, she told herself. It had surprised her to find him at the hospital. Somebody in Jacobsville must have told him what had happened, and he felt sorry for her. Maybe he was willing to overlook her smarmy past long enough to check on her brother's condition. That didn't mean he believed her innocence or wanted to get involved with her again. Which was just as well, she told herself, because she certainly wanted nothing more to do with him!

She got up and dressed…in the same clothes she'd worn the day before. She hadn't packed anything. She'd have to call Keely and ask her to go to the house and pack a few items of clothing for her and Kell. But she'd make sure Keely got an armed person to go with her, in case Frank was waiting around to see if Cappie turned back up.

When she opened her bedroom door, the two men were arguing over the coffee in the tiny little coffeepot that came, with coffee, as a perk for staying in the hotel.

"There's not enough for three people," Dead-Eye was muttering, refusing to let go of the pot.

"Then you can get yours at a café, because I'm having mine here," the other man said coldly.

"We're all having ours at the hospital, because I'm leaving right now," Cappie informed them, starting for the door.

"See what you get for starting a fight? Now neither of us is having coffee," Dead-Eye scoffed as he turned off the coffeepot and put the little carafe back in it.

"You started it first," the other man said coolly.

Cappie ignored the banter and opened the door.

"Hold it right there."

Dead-Eye was in front of her in a heartbeat, his hand under his jacket as a tall man walked into view in the hall. He stood immobile, waiting.

But it wasn't Frank. It was another man, and a woman and child suddenly appeared behind him and started talking to him.

"Nice day," Dead-Eye told them with a smile.

"Huh? Oh. Yeah." The man smiled back and herded his family ahead of him down the hall.

Dead-Eye stood aside to let Cappie out. "Wait until one of us makes sure it's safe," he told her in a kind tone. "Men who commit battery without fear of arrest are usually not planning to go back in prison, if you get my drift. He might decide a bullet is better than a fist."

"Sorry," she said. "I didn't think."

"That's what we're here for," the other man said, following her out the door and closing it. "We'll think for you."

"Were you thinking, just then?" Dead-Eye grinned.

The other man indicated his sleeve. The hilt of a large knife was in his palm. He flexed his hand and snapped it back in place. "Learned that from Cy Parks," he said. "He taught me everything I know."

"Then what are you doing with Eb?"

"Learning…diplomacy." He said it through gritted teeth. "They say my attitude needs work."

Dead-Eye opened his mouth to speak.

Cappie beat him to it. "And you think I need an attitude adjustment?" she exclaimed.

The other man shifted restlessly. "We should get to the hospital."

Cappie just smiled. So did Dead-Eye.

When they got to the hospital cafeteria, it was already full. One of the tables was occupied by a somber Dr.

Rydel, moving eggs around on a plate as if he couldn't decide between eating them or throwing them.

Cappie's traitorous heart jumped at the sight of him, but she didn't let her pleasure show. She was still fuming about his assumption of her guilt, without any proof except the word of a man who was a stranger.

He looked up and saw her and grimaced.

"Want me to frisk him for you?" Dead-Eye asked pleasantly. "I can do it discreetly."

"Yeah, like you discreetly frisked that guy at the airport," the dark-eyed man muttered. "Isn't he suing?"

"I apologized," Dead-Eye retorted.

"Before or after airport security showed up?"

"Well, after, but he said he understood how I might have mistaken him for an international terrorist."

"He was wearing a Hawaiian shirt and flip-flops!"

"The best disguise on earth for a spy, and I ought to know. I used to live in Fiji."

"Did you, really?" Cappie asked, fascinated. "I've always wanted to go there."

"Have you?" Dead-Eye looked past her to Bentley, who had gotten up from the table and was moving toward them. "Now might not be a bad time," he advised.

Bentley had dark circles under his eyes from lack of sleep. But he was just as arrogant as ever. He stopped in front of Cappie.

"I'd like to talk to you for a minute."

She didn't want to talk to him, and almost repeated her words of the night before. But she was tired and worried and a little afraid of Frank. It didn't matter now, anyway. Her life in Jacobsville was already over. She and Kell would start over again, here in San Antonio, once the threat was over.

"All right," she said wearily. "I'll only be a minute, guys," she told Dead-Eye and his partner. "You can get coffee."

"Finally," Dead-Eye groaned. "I'm having caffeine withdrawal."

"Is that why you look so ugly?" the other man taunted.

They moved off, still fencing verbally.

"Who are they?" Bentley asked as he seated her at his table.

"Bodyguards," she said. "Eb Scott loaned them to me."

"Want coffee?"

"Please."

He went to the counter, got coffee and a sweet roll and put them in front of her. "You have to eat," he said when she started to argue. "I know you like those. You bring them to work in the morning sometimes when you have to eat on the run."

She shrugged. "Thanks."

He pushed sugar and cream to her side of the table.

"I phoned the nurses' desk on the way here, on my cell phone," she said wearily. "They said Kell's having his bath and then breakfast, so I'd have time to eat before I went up to see him."

"I talked to him briefly last night," he said.

She lifted her eyebrows. "It's family only. They posted it on the door!"

"Oh, that. I told them I was his brother-in-law."

She glared at him over her coffee as she added cream.

"Well, they let me in," he said.

She lifted the cup and sipped the hot coffee, with an expression of absolute delight on her face.

"He was about as friendly as you are," he sighed. "I screwed up."

She nodded. "With a vengeance," she added, still glaring.

He pushed his plate of cold scrambled eggs to one side. His pale blue eyes were intent on her gray ones. "After what happened to me, I was down on women for a long time. When I finally got to the stage where I thought I might be able to trust one again, I found out that she was a lot more interested in what I could give her than what I was." His face tautened. "You get gun-shy, after a while. And I didn't know you, Cappie. We had supper a few times, and I took you to a carnival, but that didn't mean we were close."

She stared at the roll and took a bite of it. It was delicious. She chewed and swallowed and sipped coffee, all without answering. She'd thought they were getting to be close. How dumb could she be?

He drew in a long breath and sipped his own coffee. "Maybe we were getting close," he admitted. "But trust comes hard to me."

She put down the cup and met his eyes evenly. "How hard do you think it comes to me?" she asked baldly. "Frank beat me up. He broke my arm. I spent three days in the hospital. Then at the trial, his defense attorney tried his best to make it look as if I deliberately provoked poor Frank by refusing to go to bed with him! Apparently that was enough to justify the assault, in his mind."

He scowled. "You didn't sleep with him?"

The glare took on sparks. "No. I think people should get married first."

He looked stunned.

She flushed and averted her eyes. "So I live in the past," she muttered. "Kell and I had deeply religious parents. I don't think he took any of it to heart, but I did."

"You don't have to justify yourself to me," he said quietly. "My mother was like you."

"I'm not trying to justify myself. I'm saying that I have an idealistic attitude toward marriage. Frank thought I owed him sex for a nice meal and got furious when I wouldn't cooperate. And for the record, I didn't even really provoke him. He beat me up because I suggested that he needed to drink a little less beer. That was all it took. Kell barely got to me in time."

He let out a long breath. "My stepfather hit my mother once, for burning the bacon, when they were first married. I was fifteen."

"What did she do?" she asked.

"She told me. I took him out back and knocked him around the yard for five minutes, and told him if he did it again, I'd load my shotgun and we'd have another, shorter, conversation. He never touched her again. He also stopped drinking."

"I don't think that would have worked with Frank."

"I rather doubt it." He studied her wan, drawn face. "You've been through hell, and I haven't helped. For what it's worth, I'm sorry. I know that won't erase what I said. But maybe it will help a little."

"Thanks." She finished her roll and coffee. But when she got through, she put two dollar bills on the table and pushed them toward him.

"No!" he exclaimed, his high cheekbones flushing as he recalled with painful clarity his opinion of her as a gold digger.

"I pay my own way, despite what you think of me," she said with quiet pride. She stood up. "Money doesn't mean so much to me. I'm happy if I can pay bills. I'm sorry I gave you the impression that I'd do anything for it. I won't."

She turned and left him sitting there, with his own harsh words echoing in his mind.

Kell was lying on his stomach in bed. His bruises were much more obvious now, and he was pale and weak from the surgery. She sat down beside him in a chair and smiled.

"How's it going?" she asked gently.

"Badly," he said with a long sigh. "Hurts like hell. But they think I might be able to walk again. They have to wait until I start healing and the bruising abates before they'll know for sure. But I can wiggle my toes." He smiled. "I'm not going to prove it, because it hurts. You can take my word for it."

"Deal." She brushed back his unkempt hair.

"Your old boss came by last night," he said coldly. "He explained what happened. I gave him an earful."

"So did I. He's back."

"I'm not surprised. He was pretty contrite."

"It won't do any good," she said sadly. "I won't forget what he said to me. He didn't believe me."

"Apparently he's had some hard knocks of his own."

"Yes, that explains it, but it doesn't excuse it."

"Point taken." He glanced past her toward the door. "You've got bodyguards."

"Yes. Some of Eb Scott's guys. They don't like each other."

"Chet has a chip on his shoulder, and Rourke likes to take potshots at it."

"Which is which?" she asked.

"Rourke lost an eye overseas."

"Oh. Dead-Eye."

He chuckled and then winced. "That's what he calls himself. He's got quite a history. He worked for the CIA over in the South Pacific for several years. Now he's trying to get back in. His language skills are rusty, and he's not up on the latest communications protocols, so he's studying with Eb. Chet, on the other hand, is trying to land a job doing private security for overseas embassies. He has anger issues."

"Anger issues?"

"He tends to slug people who make him angry. Doesn't go over well in embassies."

"I can understand that." She frowned. "How do you know them?"

He sighed. "That's a long story. We'll have to talk about it when I get out of here."

She was adding up things and getting uncomfortable totals. "Kell, you weren't working for a magazine when you went to Africa, were you?" she asked.

He hesitated. "That's one of the things we'll talk about. But not now. Okay?"

She relented. He did look very rocky. "Okay." She laid a gentle hand on his muscular arm. "You're my brother and I love you. That won't change, even if you tell me blatant lies and think I'll never know about them."

"You're too sharp for your own good."

"I've been told that."

"Don't stray from your bodyguards," he cautioned. "I have to agree with them. I think Frank's not planning to go back to jail. He'll do whatever it takes to get even with you, and then he'll try suicide-by-cop."

"Jail would be better than dead, certainly?"

"Frank has anger issues, too."

She flexed the arm he'd broken. "I noticed."

"Don't take chances. Promise me."

"I promise. Please get well. Being an orphan is bad enough. I can't lose you, too."

He smiled. "I'm not going anywhere. After all, I've got a book to finish. I have to get well in order to do that."

She hesitated. "Kell, he wouldn't come here, and try to finish the job he did on you?" she asked worriedly.

"I have company."

"You do?"

"Move it, you military rejects," came a deep voice from the door. A tall, familiar-looking man with silver eyes and jet-black hair moved into the room, dressed in boots and jeans and a chambray shirt, carrying a foam cup of coffee.

"Kilraven?" she asked, surprised. "Aren't you working?"

He shook his head. "Not tonight," he said. "I had a couple of vacation days I was owed, so I'm babysitting your brother."

"Thanks," she said with a broad grin.

"I'm getting something out of it," he chuckled. "I'm stuck on the middle level of a video game, and Kell knows how to crack it."

"Is it 'Halo: ODST'?" Dead-Eye asked. "I beat it."

"Yeah, on the 'easy' level, I'll bet," Chet chided.

"I did it on 'normal,' for your information," he huffed.

"Well, I did it on Legendary," Kell murmured, "so

shut up and take care of my sister, or I'll wipe the floor with you when I get back on my feet."

Dead-Eye gave him a neat salute. Chet shrugged.

"See you later," Cappie said, kissing her brother's cheek again.

"Where are you going?" he asked.

"On a job interview," she said gently. "Brenda's boss might have something part-time."

"Are you sure you want to move back here?" Kell asked.

"Yes," she lied.

"Good luck, then."

"Thanks. See you, Kilraven. Thank you, too."

He grinned. "Keep your gunpowder dry."

"Tell them." She pointed to her two companions. "I hate guns."

"Bite your tongue!" Kilraven said in mock horror.

She made a face and went out the door, her two companions right behind her.

Bentley met them at the elevator. "Where are you going now?" he asked her.

She hesitated.

"Job interview," Rourke said for her.

"You can't leave the clinic," Bentley said curtly. "I don't have anybody to replace you yet!"

"That's your problem," she shot back. "I don't want to work for you anymore!"

He looked hunted.

"Besides, Kell and I are moving back to San Antonio as soon as he heals," she said stubbornly. "It's too far to commute."

Bentley looked even more worried. He didn't say anything.

"Aren't you supposed to be at work?" she added.

"Dr. King's filling in for me," he said.

"Until when?"

His pale eyes glittered. "Until I can convince you to come home where you belong."

"Please. Hold your breath." She walked around him and into the next open elevator. She didn't even look to see which direction it was going.

It was going up. She was stuck between two oversize men and two perfume-soaked women. She started to cough before the women got off. The men left two floors later and the elevator slowly started down.

"Wasn't that heaven?" Rourke said with a dreamy smile, inhaling the air. "I love perfume."

"It makes me sick," Chet muttered, sniffing.

"It makes me cough," Cappie agreed.

"Well, obviously, you two don't like women as much as I do," Rourke scoffed.

They both glared at him.

He raised both hands, palms-out, in defense and grinned.

The elevator stopped at the cafeteria again and Bentley was still there, smoldering.

Cappie glared at him. It didn't help. He got on the elevator and pressed the down button.

"Where do you think you're going?" Cappie asked him.

"On a job interview," he said gruffly. "Maybe they need an extra veterinarian where you're applying."

"Does this mean that you're not marrying me?" Rourke wailed in mock misery.

Bentley gaped. "You're marrying him?" he exclaimed.

"I am not marrying anybody!" Cappie muttered.

Bentley shifted restlessly. "You could marry me," he said without looking at her. "I'm established in a profession and I don't carry a gun," he added, looking pointedly at the butt of Rourke's big .45 auto nestled under his armpit.

"So am I, established in a profession," Rourke argued. "And knowing how to use a gun isn't a bad thing."

"Diplomats don't think so," Chet muttered.

"That's only until other people start shooting at them, and you save their butts," Rourke told him.

Chet brightened. "I hadn't thought of it like that."

"Come on," Cappie groaned when the elevator stopped. "I swear, I feel like I'm leading a parade!"

"Anybody got a trombone?" Rourke asked the people waiting around the elevator.

Cappie caught his arm and dragged him along with her.

They took a cab to the veterinarian's office. The car was full. The men were having a conversation about video games, but they left Cappie behind when they mentioned innovations they'd found on the Internet, about how to do impossible things with the equipment in the Halo series.

"Using grenades to blow a Scorpion up onto a mountain?" she exclaimed.

"Hey, whatever works," Rourke argued.

"Yeah, but you have to shoot your buddies to get enough grenades," Chet said. "That's not ethical."

"This, from a guy who lifted a policeman's riot gun right out of the trunk of his car!" Rourke said.

"I never lifted it, I borrowed it! Anyway, everybody was shooting rifles or shotguns and I only had a .45," he scoffed.

"Everybody else's was bigger than his," Rourke translated with an angelic pose.

Chet hit his arm. "Stop that!"

"See why he can't get a job with diplomats?" Rourke quipped, holding his arm in mock pain.

"I'm amazed that either of you can get a job," Cappie commented. "You really need to work on your social skills."

"I'm trying to, but you won't marry me," Rourke grumbled.

"Of course she won't, she's marrying me," Bentley said smugly.

"I am not!" Cappie exclaimed.

"No woman is going to marry a veterinarian when she can have a dashing spy," Rourke commented.

"Do you know one?" Bentley asked calmly.

Rourke glared at him. "I can be dashing when I want to, and I used to work for the CIA."

"Yes, but does sweeping floors count as a real job?" Chet wanted to know.

"You ought to know," Rourke told the other man. "Isn't that what you did in Manila?"

"I was the president's bodyguard!"

"And didn't he end up in the hospital?"

"We're here!" Cappie said loudly, indicating where the cab was stopping. "And the ride is Dutch treat," she added. "I'm not paying cab fare for bodyguards and stubborn hangers-on."

"Who's a hanger-on?" Rourke asked.

But Cappie was already out of the cab. The three men followed her when they settled their part of the fare.

She walked into the veterinarian's front office, where Kate Snow was still holding down the job of receptionist. She was twenty-four, tall, brunette and had soft green eyes and a pleasant rather than pretty face. She smiled.

"Hi, Cappie," she greeted. "Come to visit your old stomping grounds?"

"Actually I'm here to apply for something part-time," she replied.

"Brenda said that, but I didn't believe her," Kate replied, stunned. "You just moved to Jacobsville."

"Well, I'm moving back."

"I'll buzz Dr. Lammers," she said, and pressed a button on the phone. She spoke into the receiver, nodded, spoke again and hung up. "He's with a patient, but he'll be out in a minute." She looked past Cappie. "Can I help you?" she asked the three men.

"I'm with her," Rourke said.

"Me, too," Chet seconded.

"I'm applying for a job, too," Bentley said. "I thought you might need an extra vet." He smiled.

"Who are you?" Kate asked, surprised.

"He's my ex-boss," Cappie muttered.

"You're Dr. Rydel?" Kate exclaimed. "But you have your own practice in Jacobsville!"

"I do, but if Cappie moves here, I move here," he said stubbornly.

"We might move here, too," Rourke interrupted. "I can interview for a job here, too. I can type."

"Liar," Chet said. "He can't type."

"I can learn!"

"All you know how to do is shoot people," Chet scoffed.

"Sir, it's illegal to carry a concealed weapon," Kate began nervously.

Rourke gave her his most charming smile. "I'm a professional bodyguard, and I have a permit. If you'd like to see it, I'll take you to this lovely little French bistro downtown and you can look at it while we eat."

Kate stared at him as if he'd grown horns.

"There's a guy stalking her," Chet told her. "We're

going to catch him if he tries anything and turn him over to local law enforcement."

"Stalking you?" Kate stammered.

Cappie glared at the two men. "Thank you so much for making me an employment liability!"

Rourke made her a bow. Chet just glowered. Bentley beamed.

"I don't mind employing you. Not one bit," Bentley said. "These two can work for the groomer and we'll protect you."

"I'm not grooming anything," Chet told him bluntly.

"Okay. Then you can deal with surly clients," Bentley compromised.

Chet gave him an appreciative look.

"Actually I know how to groom things," Rourke said. "I once shaved a monkey."

Cappie hit him.

"There you are!" Brenda exclaimed, coming out of the back in a green-and-blue polka-dotted lab coat. "I talked to Dr. Lammers, but he said we've already got more part-timers than we can spare. I'm so sorry," she added miserably.

"What's your address?" Bentley asked. "I'll send you flowers."

"I thought you wanted to marry her," Chet pointed at Cappie.

Brenda's eyes widened. "Who are you?" she asked the dark-eyed man.

"I'm a hired…"

"…assassin," Rourke finished for him.

"I don't kill people, I just shoot them!" Chet growled.

"I only wound them," Rourke added. "Are we going back to Jacobsville, then?"

"Who are these men?" Brenda asked again.

"Well, these two are my bodyguards—" she indicated them "—and that's my ex-boss."

"Why is your ex-boss here?" she asked, all at sea.

"He was going to get a job here, too, but there are no openings for part-timers or vets, so I guess we're all going back to Jacobsville," Cappie said miserably. "That is, if Frank doesn't shoot me first."

"Nobody's shooting you," Rourke assured her.

"You can bet on that," Chet said.

Brenda smiled at them. "Thanks. She's my best friend."

Cappie hugged her. "Thanks anyway, for trying. I'll call you. See you, Kate!"

Kate waved as she picked up the ringing telephone. Her eyes were still on Rourke, who grinned at her.

"Come on, let's go," Cappie told the men.

"How's Kell?" Brenda asked, walking them out.

"He's going to make it. We won't know if he can walk for several days, though."

"If you have to go home, I'll visit him for you."

"I can't leave just yet," Cappie said. "Not until we find Frank."

Brenda stared at Bentley, who was all smiles. "Aren't you going back to your practice?"

"When we find Frank," he commented pleasantly.

"You're not part of this bodyguard unit," Chet reminded him.

"I am now," Bentley assured him. His eyes smoothed over Cappie. "I'm in it until the end."

Cappie hated the rush of pleasure that comment gave her. So she disguised it by hugging Brenda and promising to keep in touch.

CHAPTER NINE

BENTLEY WENT with them back to the hotel where Cappie was staying. He left them at the desk to get a room for himself. He managed one on the same floor, two doors down, and then went back to the other hotel where he'd been staying to pack his bags and check out.

"Great," Cappie muttered when they were back in her suite. "Now we're really going to be a parade."

"He likes you," Rourke pointed out. "And at this point, the more eyes, the better. He might see something we'd miss. After all, he knows what Frank looks like. We only have a mug shot. And you said it didn't really look much like him," he added, because he'd shown it to her earlier.

"All right," she sighed. She moved to the window and looked down at the busy street. "At least Kell's in good hands. I wouldn't want to walk in on Kilraven, even if he was in a good mood, with evil intent."

"There's an odd bird," Rourke commented. "We can't even find out which branch of the government he really works for, and we've tried. His brother works for the FBI, but Kilraven's true affiliations are less obvious."

She turned to him. "Is he CIA?"

"If he was, he wouldn't say so. And just for the record," he added with a grin, "no CIA office address is ever listed, in any city where we have offices. We don't even mention which cities those are."

"What a shadowy bunch you are," she commented.

He just grinned. "That's why we're so good at what we do."

"What we *do*?" she asked, hitting on the obvious assumption.

"I didn't say I was still with them," he pointed out.

"You didn't say you weren't, either," she replied.

He made a face at her.

"At least my job is up-front and everybody knows what it is," Chet said.

They both looked at him with wide eyes.

He glared at them. "I'm a bodyguard!"

"Well, so am I, right now," Rourke said. "But it's not what I do full-time." He gave the other man a narrow-eyed appraisal. "And it isn't what you do full-time, either."

Chet looked uncomfortable.

"What does he do full-time?" Cappie asked, curious.

"It involves long-range rifles and black ops."

"It does not," Chet muttered.

"It used to."

"Well, after I broke my leg, I was less enthusiastic about jumping out of Blackhawks," he muttered.

"You broke both legs, I heard."

Chet sighed. "And an arm. Breaks never heal properly, even with good medical care." He sighed again. "You try getting good medical care in…" He caught himself and closed his mouth.

"I wasn't going to say a word," Rourke told him.

"Well, don't. I'm out of cigarettes. I'm going down the street and see if I can find anybody in the mob to sell me a pack under the table, if the police aren't looking."

"Smoking's not illegal, is it?" Cappie asked.

"Any day now, it probably will be," Chet said despondently. "Can't spit without a federal permit these days," he said, and kept muttering all the way out the door.

"Quick, tell me," Cappie said to Rourke, "was he a sniper?"

"I've never been sure," he told her with a grin. "But he and Cash Grier are pretty chummy."

"Should that mean something?"

"Grier was a high-level government assassin in his younger days, but I didn't tell you that," he said firmly. "Some secrets have to be kept to save one's skin."

"Well!" she exclaimed. "I'd never have guessed."

"Neither would most other people. I'm going down the hall to loiter and see if I see anybody I recognize. Keep the door locked and don't answer it unless you recognize my voice, or Chet's. Got that?"

She nodded. "Thanks."

"When I do a job, I do a job," he told her. He closed the door behind him when he left.

She was jumpy. With her protection, she shouldn't have been, but she kept remembering her last sight of Frank Bartlett, cursing her for all he was worth when the judge announced his sentence. He'd been yelling vengeance at the top of his lungs, and he'd almost managed to get away from the sheriff's deputy who had him in handcuffs. It had been a scary moment. Almost as scary as the memory of the night he'd beaten her.

She wrapped her arms around her rib cage and closed her eyes. She did hope they'd catch him before he got to her. Surely the job he'd done on Kell would guarantee him some quality prison time. But what if he got out again, after that? Would she have to live her entire life being afraid of Frank? After all, he could get out on good behavior, no matter how long his sentence was. Or he could hang a jury at his next trial. Or he could break out of prison. There were plenty of horrible possibilities, all of which would leave Cappie hiding behind locked doors as long as she lived. It wasn't a possibility she looked forward to.

The sudden knock on the door brought a cry of panic to her lips. She moved toward the door, but she didn't touch the knob. "Who…is it?" she called.

"Room service. We're checking to see if your veterinarian has been delivered yet."

She burst out laughing. She knew that curt voice, as well as she knew her own. "Bentley!" She moved closer to the door. "I don't recall ordering a veterinarian."

"Well, we're delivering one to you anyway, just in case you regret not ordering him later," he drawled.

She unlocked the door and gave him a droll look. "Nice tactics."

He shrugged. "I'm desperate. You wouldn't let me in if I just asked." He looked behind her and the smile faded. "Where are your bodyguards?"

"Chet went looking for cigarettes and Rourke is down the hall checking for intruders."

"And you're in here alone."

"Well, the door was locked until you asked to come in," she pointed out.

"Fair enough. Want to come downstairs and have coffee and pie with me? Then we can go to see Kell."

"I guess that would be okay. But I have to tell Rourke where I'm going..."

"He already knows," came an amused voice from the general direction of her purse.

"How did you get in here?" she asked, lifting the purse.

"I hid a microphone in there earlier, in case you escaped."

"I'm going downstairs to have coffee and pie, then Bentley and I are going to see Kell."

"Okay. I'll be around. Have fun. And don't hit him with the pie. You will be going to a hospital."

"On your way to a hospital is the best time to hit people with things," she retorted. "There are doctors there."

"Yes, I know," Bentley spoke into her purse. "I am one."

"You're a veterinarian," Rourke shot back.

"I can treat injuries if I want to."

"Try not to let her give you any."

"You stop that," Cappie told her purse. Nobody answered. "Hello?" she said, looking inside it.

"Don't do that in public, okay?" Bentley asked as they walked to the door. "There are probably psychiatrists around the hospital, too."

She rolled her eyes and went out into the hall just ahead of him.

The hospital cafeteria was crowded. They found a table, but they had to share it with an elderly couple who'd come all the way from the Mexican border to visit their daughter, who'd just had a baby. They had photographs, and showed every single one to Bentley and Cappie, who made the correct responses between sips of coffee and bites of apple pie.

Finally the elderly couple finished their soft drinks and went off toward the elevator.

"Alone at last," Bentley teased.

"One more photograph would have done me in," she confessed. "I swear, if I ever have a grandchild…"

"…you'll have even more photos than they did, and show them to total strangers, too," he chuckled.

She shrugged and smiled. "Yes. I guess I would."

"Babies are nice. I used to think I'd like one or two, myself."

"You don't anymore?" she asked.

He moved his coffee mug around on the table. "I sort of gave up hope. Until you came along." He didn't look at her as he said it.

She felt her toes tingle. She hated the rush of pleasure she felt. "Really?"

He looked up. His pale blue eyes made sparks as they met hers. "Really."

She hesitated.

"I never should have believed a man I just met, who sat in my office and told lies about you with perfect innocence. But, then, I was afraid you were too good to be true."

"Nobody's perfect."

"I realize that. You don't have to be perfect. I just don't want to get in over my head and get kicked in the teeth again."

"I'm not that sort of person," she told him.

His eyes narrowed on her face. "He really hurt you, didn't he?"

"I thought I loved him," she said quietly. "He seemed to be kind and considerate…but the first date we had, he kicked my cat. I should have known then. Kind people aren't cruel to animals, ever. I found out later that he'd been abusive to at least two other women he dated, but they were too afraid of him to press charges."

She smiled wanly. "Well, so was I. But Kell insisted. He said that Frank might end up killing someone if I didn't have him prosecuted. Then I'd have it on my conscience. I just didn't realize that it might be me that Frank killed." She put her face in her hands. "It won't ever end. Even if he goes back to trial, he could get off, or they could release him for good behavior, or he could break out…I'll never be free of him as long as I live."

"Don't talk like that," he said softly. "I won't let him hurt you."

She took her hands away. She looked older. "What if he hurt you? What if he killed you? Anybody around me will be a target. I almost put Brenda in danger without even realizing it."

"I'm not afraid of the little weasel," he told her. "And you're not going to be afraid of him, either. That's how he controls women. With fear. Don't give him a foothold in your mind."

She bit her lip. "I'm just scared, Bentley."

"Yes, but you did the right thing. And you'll do it again, anytime you have to. You aren't the type of person who runs from trouble, any more than I am."

"You think so?"

"I know so."

She searched his eyes. "I was scared to death of you, at first. Then I was in a wreck and you drove me home." She smiled. "You aren't as horrible as you seem."

"Thanks. I think." He smiled back.

"Okay. I'll stick it out. If Frank escapes another jail

sentence, maybe I can get Rourke to hide him in a jungle overseas, so deep that he'd never find his way out."

"Ahem," her purse replied, "I do not kidnap American citizens and carry them out of the country for nefarious purposes. Not even for pretty women."

"Spoilsport," she told him.

"However, I know people who would," he added, with a smile in his voice.

"Good man," Bentley said.

"Why don't you marry him?" Rourke asked. "At least he'd make sure you were never in harm's way."

"If you'll give me your boss's telephone number," Bentley told the purse, "I'll call him and give you a glowing recommendation."

"What a pal!"

"I always…"

Bentley stopped talking because three people were standing at their table with open mouths, watching him speak into Cappie's purse. He cleared his throat. "There, the radio's turned off now," he said in a deep, deliberate tone. He handed her back the purse.

The three people looked sheepish, smiled and left the cafeteria in a bit of a rush.

Cappie burst out laughing. Bentley's cheeks were the color of bubble gum.

"Quick thinking, there, Dr. Rydel," Rourke called over the radio. "Want to come work for us?"

"Go away," Cappie told him. "I am not going to consider marrying anybody in your line of work."

"Spoilsport," Rourke said. "Shutting up now."

Cappie met Bentley's eyes, and they both laughed.

Kell was groggy and quiet. The pain must have been pretty bad, Cappie thought, once the anesthetic wore off. He was much less talkative than he'd been when he was just out of the recovery room. He was pale and he looked as if it was an effort to say anything at all. They only stayed a couple of minutes. Kell was asleep before they got out the door.

"Do you think it would be safe to step outside just for a minute and get a breath of air?" Cappie asked. "There are people everywhere."

"I don't know," Bentley said, his eyes roving.

"Rourke, what do you think?" she asked her purse.

But there was no reply. She looked around. She didn't see Rourke or Chet. That was odd. They'd been visible every minute since she came to San Antonio.

"Maybe it would be all right," she said. "I just want to stretch my legs for a minute."

"All right," Bentley said. "But you stay close to me." He slid his big hand into her small one and closed it warmly. "I'll take care of you."

She smiled wearily and laid her head against his shoulder for a minute. "Okay."

They walked out into the cold night air. The sidewalk was crowded. Traffic passed by. There was a policeman on the corner, leaning back against a storefront, talking into a cell phone. Nearby, two men in suits were talking, oblivious to passersby.

All around them, neon signs and holiday lights brightened the darkness. "It's almost Christmas," she exclaimed. "With all that's happened, I forgot." She grimaced. "We won't get to open presents under the tree this year. Kell will never be able to go home by Christmas Eve."

"Then we'll put up a small tree in his room and transfer the presents up here from Jacobsville," he promised her. "We'll have Christmas here."

She looked up at him with soft, quiet eyes. "We?"

His jaw tautened. "I'm not leaving you again. Not even for a day," he said huskily.

The words made tears brim in her eyes. The way he said it was so poignant, so passionate. He didn't even need to say what he was feeling. She read it in his face.

He pulled her into his arms and held her close, hugged her tight, buried his face in her long, soft hair. "Marry me."

She closed her eyes. "Yes. Yes!" she whispered.

His chest rose and fell heavily. "Of all the places to get engaged," he groaned. "With a thousand eyes watching."

"It doesn't matter," she whispered.

No, he thought. It didn't.

"Hold him! I'll get her!"

The voices came suddenly into what was the

sweetest dream of Cappie's life. She was so relaxed, so happy, that it took precious seconds for her to realize what was about to happen. She felt Bentley torn from her arms. Two men were pulling his arms behind him. A violent jerk brought her around as two bruising hands caught her shoulders and twisted them. Above her, Frank Bartlett's angry, contorted features came into view, his narrow dark eyes promising retribution.

"Got you at last, didn't I?" he growled. "Now, you're going to pay for what you did to me!"

She cried out and tried to pull away from him, but his hands were too strong. He drew one back and slapped her as hard as he could, so hard that she staggered and would have fallen if he hadn't jerked her back up brutally with the other hand.

Her face stung like fire. There would be a bruise. But it only made her mad. She drew back her high-heeled foot and kicked him in the calf muscle as hard as she could. He yelled in pain and slapped her again. But before he could draw back another time, he suddenly went down under a vicious tackle.

"That's the way, brother!" came a cheering cry from the sidelines.

"Go get him!" came another hearty voice.

Bentley was knocking the stuffing out of Frank Bartlett, his big fists making the other man, a match for him pound for pound, cry out in pain.

"Now isn't he talented?" Rourke murmured as he drew a shaky Cappie back from the crowd. He looked at her bruised face and winced. "Sorry we didn't rush right in, but we wanted to make sure we had plenty of witnesses and an excellent case for the prosecution." He jerked his head toward Chet and the two men in suits. They had the two men with Frank subdued and handcuffed. The uniformed officer who'd been on the corner was standing with them.

"We had you staked out," Rourke told her. "I wouldn't have done it this way, if there had been any other choice."

She reached up and patted his cheek. "You did good, Dead-Eye," she said with a smile, and winced when it hurt. "I'm going to look like an accident victim for a few days, I'm afraid."

"No doubt about that. Your poor face!"

She glanced back toward Frank. Bentley was still pounding him. "Shouldn't you save Bentley?"

"Bentley?" he exclaimed.

"From a homicide charge, I mean," she clarified.

"Oh. Right. Probably should."

He moved forward and pulled Bentley off the other man. It took some doing. The veterinarian was obviously reluctant to give up his pastime.

"Now, now," Rourke calmed him, "we have to have enough left to prosecute. Besides, Cappie needs some TLC. She's pretty bruised."

Bentley was catching his breath as he walked quickly back to Cappie. He winced at the sight of her face. "My poor baby," he exclaimed, bending to kiss her bruised cheek with exquisite tenderness. "Let me just go back over there and hit him one more time…!"

"No," she protested, grabbing his suit coat. "Rourke's right, we have to have enough of him left to prosecute. Bentley, you were magnificent!"

"So were you, kicking him in the leg," he chuckled.

"I guess we make a pretty good team," she mused.

"You can say that again."

She put a hand to her cheek. "Boy, that stings."

"It looks like hell. You'll have to see a doctor."

"Fortunately there are plenty of those right inside," Rourke came back in time to reply. "See the letters? They spell out *hospital*."

She drew back a fist.

Rourke held up both hands. "Now, now, I'm on your side." He nodded toward one of the men in suits who had a long black ponytail. "Recognize him?"

She frowned. "No…"

"That's Detective Sergeant Rick Marquez," he told her. "He was just on his way to the opera when we phoned and said an assault with intent was going down in front of the hospital. He broke speed records getting here."

"How kind of him," Cappie said.

"Not really. He always goes to the opera alone. He can't get women."

"But, why not?" she wondered. "He's a dish."

"He carries a gun," Rourke pointed out.

"You carry a gun."

"I can't get women, either."

"What a shame."

He moved closer. "I'm available."

She laughed as Bentley stepped in front of her, glowering.

"Wait, scratch that, I just remembered, I'm not available," Rourke said quickly.

"Even if you were, she's not," Bentley said.

"There you are, again, starting trouble," Rick Marquez chuckled, joining them. He looked at Cappie's face and grimaced. "Damn, I'm sorry we didn't get here sooner," he apologized. "I couldn't get a cab and I had to run all the way."

"Fortunately you're in great shape," Rourke said.

"Fortunately I am," Marquez agreed. "What are you and Billings doing here?"

"Trading favors with Eb Scott." Rourke grinned. "We're bodyguards. Well, not anymore. Not now that you have those three jackals in custody."

Marquez moved a step closer to him. "How about telling Chet that he's not allowed to smoke here?"

"Why don't you tell him?" Rourke asked, surprised.

"Too many windows overlook my apartment," came the amused reply. "He might not be able to resist the temptation to get even."

"Good point. I'll just pass that along. About the smoking!" Rourke added quickly. "Anyway, he wouldn't shoot you. He's not sanctioned."

"Yet," Marquez enunciated.

Rourke shrugged, grinned and went to find his partner.

"They really were great," Cappie told the detective. "I've never felt safer. Well, until tonight."

"We let you walk into the trap," Marquez replied quietly. "It was the only way we could guarantee a case against Bartlett that he couldn't escape. His sort doesn't give up."

"Yes, but he could get out again..."

"He won't," Marquez said curtly. "I promise you that. See that guy I was standing with? He's the assistant D.A. who put Frank away in the first place."

"I thought he looked familiar," Cappie returned.

"He cursed a blue streak because the judge gave him such an easy sentence. He's been working behind the scenes to get depositions in case Frank slipped." He grinned. "And did Frank ever slip! In front of all these witnesses, too." He indicated the uniformed officer, and two others who'd joined him, who were questioning bystanders. "Frank is going back in jail for a long time."

"What about his friends?" Cappie asked.

"I know what they helped him do to your brother. We couldn't have proved it, before, but I'm betting one of them will be happy to turn state's evidence in return for a reduced sentence."

"Meanwhile," Bentley said, sliding an affectionate arm around Cappie, "we're going to have a nice Christmas celebration with Kell in the hospital and then plan a wedding."

"A wedding?" Marquez sighed. "I used to think I'd

find a nice woman someday who liked cops and opera, who'd love to marry me. But, I'm really happy to be single. I mean, I have all sorts of free time, and I get to watch whatever television programs I like, and TV dinners are just wonderful. In fact, I think I might like to do commercials for them." He smiled.

"They have psychiatrists in there, don't they?" Bentley asked, nodding toward the hospital.

Marquez glared at him. "I'm happy, I said! I love living alone! I never want my private life messed up by some sweet, loving woman who can cook!"

"Anybody got a straitjacket?" Bentley asked.

Marquez threw up his hands and walked away.

Cappie felt her face begin to throb. Tears stung her eyes. "Could we go back inside and find the emergency room, you think?" she asked Bentley.

"Right this minute," he said with obvious concern.

Marquez followed them inside. "I've got my digital camera with me," he said, suddenly all business. "We want to get photos, to make sure a jury sees what Frank did to you."

"Be my guest," Cappie replied. "But then I want aspirin and an ice pack!"

"You can come down to my office in the morning to give me a statement. For now, we'll get the photos and have a doctor look at your face. After that, you can even have a beer if you like, and I'll buy," Marquez promised.

She made a face. "Sorry, but I'd rather have the ice pack."

Bentley's arm contracted. "Then we have to find some way to keep Kell from seeing your poor face, until he's through the worst of his own ordeal."

"Yes, we do," she said. "That isn't going to be easy."

Marquez, seeing the bruising increase by the second, had to agree. And she didn't know yet how it was going to look a day later. But he did.

They did take X-rays of Cappie's face. Marquez got his photos and left. The doctor treating her came back into the cubicle where she and Bentley were waiting in the busy emergency room.

"There are two small broken bones," he said. "I want you to take these X-rays to your primary physician and let him refer you to a good plastic surgeon. Meanwhile, I'm going to write you something for pain. Keep ice on the swelling. Nothing is going to disguise the bruises, I'm afraid." He glanced curiously at Bentley.

"I didn't do it," Bentley said easily. "The man who did was taken away in a squad car, with his accomplices, and he's going to be prosecuted to the full extent of the law. Those X-rays we asked for a copy of are going to help put him away."

The young resident nodded somberly. "I see far too many injuries like this. A boyfriend?" he queried.

"No," Cappie said heavily. "An ex-boyfriend who spent six months in jail for breaking my arm," she added. "He got out and came looking for me. This time, I hope he'll stay as a guest of the state for much longer."

"I'll be happy to testify," the resident said. He pulled a card out of his wallet and handed it to her. "That happens too often, you know, a brutal man seeking revenge. We had a young woman killed a few weeks ago for the same thing."

Cappie felt sick to her stomach.

Bentley put his arm around her. "Nobody's killing you," he said.

She leaned her head against him. "Thanks."

They took the extra X-ray in its envelope, paid the bill and left the emergency room, hand-in-hand.

"Do you want to go and see Kell tonight?" Bentley asked.

She shook her head, wincing, because it hurt. "I'm too sick. I just want to lie down." She looked up. "Will you go with me to Marquez's office in the morning?"

"You'd better believe I will."

"Thanks."

His arm contracted around her. "Not necessary. Let's get you back to your room. It's been a long day."

"Tell me about it," she mused. At least, she thought, her ordeal was over for the moment. Tomorrow she could worry about the details, including telling poor Kell what had happened.

CHAPTER TEN

CAPPIE GROANED at her own reflection in the hotel mirror when she climbed out of bed the next morning. One whole side of her face was a brilliant purple, and swollen to boot.

"You okay in there?"

She smiled. Bentley had insisted on sleeping on the sofa in the suite, just in case. Rourke and Chet were already up and packing their things for the trip back to Jacobsville. Cappie and Bentley were staying for another day or two, while she gave statements to the police and looked after Kell.

"I think so," she said. "I just can't bear to look at myself."

"I'll bet Chet knows exactly how that feels!" Rourke called from the doorway of the room he and Chet had shared.

"Will you shut up?" Chet muttered.

"Now, that's a good example of how much work your diplomatic skills need," Rourke admonished.

"I'm through trying to be diplomatic," Chet said curtly. "I'm going back to the company and let them send me off on lone assignments, all by myself. Anywhere I don't have to try to be nice to people!"

"Yes, and you can take those smokes with you," Rourke added. "Having to share a room with you is punishment enough for any lawbreaker! Man, you reek!"

"Cigarette smoke is beneficial," Chet told him.

"It is not!"

"If your quarry smokes, you can smell him from five hundred meters," Chet returned, and he actually smiled.

Rourke's jaw dropped. He'd never seen the other man smile.

Chet gave him a haughty, arrogant stare, picked up his bag and walked out. "Hope things go well for you, Miss Drake," he said as she came out of her room wrapped in a thick robe. He winced. "It will look much better in a week or so," he assured her.

She tried to smile, but it hurt too much. "Thanks for helping keep me alive, Chet."

"My pleasure. See you back at Scott's place, Rourke."

"You wait for me—I'm not paying cab fare back to Jacobsville all alone," Rourke said. He picked up his own bag, shook hands with Bentley and bent to kiss Cappie's undamaged cheek. "If he ever walks out on you, just get word to me, and I'll bring him back to you in a net," he said in a stage whisper.

"Thanks, Rourke. But I don't think that will ever happen."

Bentley smiled. "I can guarantee it won't."

"Cheers, then. See you."

They waved the two men off. Bentley studied her poor, damaged face warily. "I wish there had been some way to prevent that."

"Me, too. But it's insurance. Let's get breakfast. Then we can go down to Detective Marquez's office and start giving statements. Later," she added reluctantly, "we can go see Kell and try not to upset him too much when we tell him what happened."

"Suits me."

Detective Marquez had a small office in a big department. It was noisy and people seemed to come and go constantly. The phones rang off the hook.

"This looks like those crime shows on television," Cappie remarked.

Marquez chuckled. "It's much worse. You can't get five minutes' peace to type up a report." He got up to retrieve the report he'd typed at the computer as he questioned her. He took it out of the printer tray and handed it to her. "Check over that, if you will, and see if I've got it right." He pulled out another one. "This one's for you, Dr. Rydel." He handed the vet another sheet of paper.

They went over their statements, made a couple of corrections. Marquez inserted the corrections and printed the statements out again. They signed them.

"I'll bet Frank's foaming at the mouth," Cappie mused.

"He really is, but this time he's not going to fool any jury into thinking he's the injured party," Marquez assured her.

"I'll bet that judge is feeling bad about now," Bentley muttered.

"The judge did feel bad," Marquez agreed. "So did the district attorney, especially after Frank and his cohorts beat up your brother. The whole justice system here in San Antonio went into overdrive to catch the perp."

"Really?" Cappie asked, surprised.

"Really. The assistant district attorney who prosecuted your case was in the vanguard."

"Somebody needs to take him out for a big steak dinner," Cappie commented.

"I'm taking him out for one, at my mother's café in Jacobsville," he chuckled. "Of course, he's eligible and so is my mother."

"I see wheels turning in your head," Cappie said.

He grinned. "Always," Marquez said easily. "He and I have worked several cases together. I like him."

"Me, too," Cappie said. She hesitated. "Frank won't get out until the trial, will he?"

Marquez shook his head. "The assistant D.A. is having the bond set in the six-figure range. I don't think Frank knows a bail bondsman who'll take a chance on him for that amount of money."

"Let's hope not," Bentley said.

Marquez gave him a keen glance. "He'll probably stay in jail voluntarily, to keep from having you come at him again. That was some tackle."

Bentley shrugged. "I used to play football in college."

"I played soccer. Don't get to do much tackling, but I can knock a ball half a block with my head."

"Is that why it looks that way?" a familiar voice drawled from the cubicle doorway.

"Kilraven," Marquez grumbled, "will you stop stalking me?"

"I'm not stalking you," the tall man said easily. "I'm just waiting for you to answer my ten phone calls, six voice mails and twenty e-mails." He glowered at the younger man.

Marquez held up his hands. "Okay. Just let me finish up with Miss Drake and Dr. Rydel and I'll be right with you. Honest."

"No hurry," Kilraven said, smiling. "I'll be standing right out here, intimidating lawbreakers."

"Thanks for looking out for Kell," Cappie told him.

"What are friends for?" he asked.

"How would you know, Kilraven, you don't have any friends," a passing detective drawled.

"I have lots of friends!"

"Oh, yeah? Name one."

"Marquez!"

"He's your friend?" the detective asked Marquez, sticking his head into the cubicle.

"He is not," Marquez said without looking up as he glanced over the statements one last time.

"I am so," Kilraven said in a surly tone.

Marquez gave him a speaking glance.

Kilraven moved back out of the cubicle, muttering to himself in some foreign language.

"I know what that means in Arabic," Marquez called after him. "Your brother speaks Farsi fluently and he taught me what those words mean!"

A rolling barrage in yet another language came lilting into the cubicle.

"What's that?" Marquez asked.

Kilraven poked his head in and grinned. "Lakota. And Jon can't teach you that—he doesn't speak it. Ha!"

He left.

Marquez grimaced.

"He's really very nice," Cappie said.

Marquez leaned toward her. "He is, but I'm not saying it out loud." His expression became somber. "I'm working on a cold case with him and another detective," he said quietly. "It involves him. He's impatient, because we got a new lead."

Bentley nodded quietly. "I know about that one. One of my vet techs is married to the best friend of our local sheriff. I hear most of what's going on."

"Tragic case," Marquez agreed. "But hopefully we're going to crack it."

Bentley got to his feet, tugging Cappie up with him. He winced as she turned toward him.

"I appreciate the copies of those X-rays," Marquez added, walking out with them. "Everything we can throw against Bartlett will help put him away."

"He'd better hope he never gets out," Cappie said. "My brother will be waiting for him if he does."

Marquez chuckled. "If it hadn't been three to one against, and your brother hadn't been in a wheelchair, I'd probably be helping defend him on homicide charges."

"No doubt," Bentley replied somberly.

Cappie frowned. "Is there a conversation going on that I don't know anything about?" she asked.

Bentley and Marquez exchanged covert glances. "Just commenting on your brother's justifiable anger," Bentley told her easily. He caught her fingers in his. "Let's go see your brother and tell him he's about to have a new brother-in-law."

Kell was a little better, until he saw Cappie's face. He swore brilliantly.

"I know how you feel," Bentley said. "But for what it's worth, Bartlett probably looks much worse. It took two detectives to pull me off him."

Kell brightened. "Good man." He winced at his sister's face, though. "I'm so sorry."

"I'll heal." She didn't mention the potential surgery she might have to undergo. There was no need to worry him even more. "Detective Marquez said that Frank won't get out for a long time. He expects one of Frank's accomplices to turn state's evidence. If they charge him with battery on both of us, he'll do some serious time."

"I expected Hayes Carson to show up here and ask me for a statement for what Frank did to me in Comanche Wells," he murmured.

"I imagine he's giving you time to get over the surgery," Cappie said.

"Probably so."

"Have you spoken to the surgeon yet?" Cappie asked.

He smiled. "Yes. He's optimistic, especially since I have feeling in my legs now."

"At least something good may come out of all this misery," she said gently.

Kell was looking at Bentley. "Just before we came up here to the hospital, she said she didn't want to live in a town that also contained you. You told me part of the story, but not any more than you had to. She was going to explain, then they knocked me out with a shot. Care to comment?"

"I made a stupid decision," Bentley said with a sigh. "I expect to be apologizing for it for the rest of my life. But she's going to marry me anyway." He gave her a tender smile, which she returned. "I can eat crow at every meal, for however long it takes."

"I stopped being mad at you while you were beating the stuffing out of Frank Bartlett," she pointed out.

He glanced at his bruised, swollen knuckles. "I'll have permanent mementoes of the occasion, I expect."

"You're getting married?" Kell asked.

"Yes," Cappie said. She touched her face gingerly. "Not until the swelling goes down, though."

"And not until I'm able to walk down the aisle and give you away," Kell interjected.

Bentley pursed his lips. "I could get Chet and Rourke to carry you down the aisle to give her away," he offered.

"The last wedding Chet went to, he spent the night in jail for inciting a riot," Kell pointed out.

Cappie frowned. "Exactly how well do you know Chet and Rourke?" she asked pointedly.

He groaned. "Oh. The pain. I need to rest. I really can't talk anymore right now."

Cappie's eyes narrowed on the drip catheter. "Doesn't that thing automatically inject painkiller into the drip while you're post-surgical?" she asked.

Kell kept his eyes closed. "I don't know. I feel terrible. You have to leave now." He opened one eye. "You can come back later, when I'll be much better as long as you don't ask potentially embarrassing questions. If you do, I may have a relapse."

"All right," Cappie sighed.

He brightened. "Be good and I'll tell you how to get past the Hunters in ODST."

"Cash told you?" she asked.

He chuckled and winced, because moving hurt. "Not without a bribe."

"What sort of bribe?"

"Remember that old Bette Davis movie, where she murders her lover and then has to blackmail the man's widow over a letter that could convict her?" he asked.

"Yes. It's called *The Letter*...it's one of my favorite..." She stopped. "You didn't!"

"Hey, it's not as if you watch it that much," Kell protested.

"Kell!"

"Do you want to get past the Hunters, or don't you?" he asked.

She sighed. "I guess I can always find another copy of it somewhere."

"That's a nice sister," Kell said.

"If I buy you another one," Bentley interrupted, "will you tell *me* how to get past the Hunters?" he asked her.

They all laughed.

Two weeks later, Kell was walking down the hall, wobbling a little, in his pajamas and robe while Cappie held him up. The swelling in her cheek had gone down, but it still had a yellowish tinge to it. Kell was much better. He was learning how to walk all over again, courtesy of the rehab department in the Jacobsville hospital.

"This is slow," he muttered.

"It is not," Bentley retorted, and the sound of gunfire came from the television in the living room. "Ha! That's one Hunter down!"

"Rub it in," she called. "It wasn't even your favorite movie you had to sacrifice to learn how to do that!"

"I bought you a new one. It's in the DVD player," he called back.

"Fat lot of good it's doing me, since that game console hasn't been off for five minutes all day," she muttered.

"Stop picking on my future brother-in-law," Kell chided. "It isn't every man who can make tortillas from scratch."

"He only did it to butter you up," she told him.

"It worked. When's the wedding, again?"

"Three weeks from now. Micah Steele says you'll be able to manage the church aisle with just a cane by then. And we can hope there won't be a large animal emergency anywhere in the county during the ceremony!" she raised her voice.

"I'm borrowing a vet from San Antonio to cover the practice for me until we're back from our honeymoon in Cancún," he said. They'd picked the exotic spot because it had been the dream of Cappie's life to see Chichen Itza, the Mayan ruin.

"I hope the vet knows he's covering for you," she said.

He chuckled. "He does."

"The guest list just keeps growing," Cappie sighed. "I've already sent out fifty invitations."

"Did you put Marquez and the assistant D.A. on the list?"

"Yes," she said. "And Rourke and Chet, too."

Kell groaned.

"Chet won't start any riots. I'll have a talk with him,"

she promised. "They took good care of me in San Antonio," she added.

"Yes, but I was the one who took down Frank," Bentley called. "Can you believe that little weasel tried to sue me for assault?" he added huffily.

"He didn't get as far as first base," Kell assured him. "Blake Kemp had a long talk with his attorney."

"Why would our D.A. be talking to a defense attorney in San Antonio?" Cappie wanted to know.

"Because the defense attorney wasn't aware of the familial connections of the defendant's assailant," Bentley murmured. "Ha! There went another Hunter!" he exclaimed.

Cappie blinked. "Familial connections…?"

Kell leaned down to her ear. "Don't ask. The upshot is that the lawsuit is going nowhere. Fast."

Cappie was still staring at Bentley. "What familial connections?" she persisted.

"The governor is my first cousin. Ha! Another one!"

"Our governor?" she exclaimed.

"We only have one. This game is great!"

Cappie sighed. She looked up at her handsome big brother. "The game is not going with us on our honeymoon," she said firmly.

Bentley gave her a roguish glance. "Not even if I tell you how to get past the Hunters?"

"Well, in that case, maybe I could reconsider," she chuckled.

* * *

Kell did make it down the aisle with a cane. The little country church in Comanche Wells was filled to capacity. Only people they knew got an invitation, but there was still standing room only. A good many of the guests were in uniform, either military or law enforcement, on one side of the church, while a number of Eb Scott's guys were seated across the aisle from them. Covert glares were exchanged. Down the center aisle marched Cappie in her lovely white gown with what seemed acres of lace and a pretty fingertip veil. She was carrying a bouquet of yellow roses and wearing a smile that went from ear to ear.

She held on to Kell's arm tightly, so proud of his progress that she beamed with happiness. He was already talking about a new job working for Eb Scott at his anti-terrorism school. She was really curious about how well her brother seemed to know any number of Eb's employees, but she hadn't made any comments. She was still indebted to Eb for lending her Chet and Rourke, who were seated together in the front of the church. Around them were her former and present co-workers, including Keely and Boone Sinclair. Boone's sister, Winnie, was being watched with real intensity by Kilraven, dressed in an expensive suit in the row behind her.

She and Kell stopped at the altar, where he gave her hand to Bentley. He was beaming, too, so handsome that Cappie just sighed, looking up at him with gray eyes that adored him.

The wedding service was brief, but poignant. Bentley lifted the veil and bent to kiss her with such tenderness that she had to fight tears.

Then he led her down the aisle to the back of the church. The people who hadn't been able to squeeze into the church were waiting outside with what seemed like buckets of rice and confetti. They were totally drenched in both as they ran to the white limousine that was to take them to the town civic center, for the reception.

They fed each other cake, posed for wedding pictures and generally had a wonderful time. There was a live band and they danced together to a slow, romantic tune, which lasted for all of two minutes before Cash Grier, with his beautiful wife, Tippy, signaled to the band leader.

There were grins, a fanfare and then a furious and delicious rendition of the classic tune "Brazil." But Cash didn't start dancing, as everyone expected him to. He glanced toward Bentley with a chuckle and a flourish.

Bentley gave Cappie a wicked look. "Shall we?"

"But, Bentley, you can't dance…can you?" she exclaimed.

"I couldn't," he confessed, taking her onto the dance floor. "But Cash gave me lessons. Okay. One, two… three!"

He twirled her around in the most professional sort of way, in a mixture of samba, cha-cha and mambo that she followed with consummate ease while people on the sidelines began to clap.

"You're terrific!" Cappie panted.

"So are you, gorgeous," he chuckled. "Are we good, or what?"

About a day and a half later, they repeated the same exact dialog to each other, but for a totally different reason.

Lying exhausted and bathed in sweat in a huge double bed in a beachfront hotel in Cancún, they could barely move.

"And I thought you danced well!" she laughed. "You're just amazing!"

"Why, thank you," he drawled, grinning. "May I return the compliment?"

"Yes, well, I think I'm a quick study," she sighed.

"Not so nervous anymore, I notice," he murmured.

She laughed. She was almost a basket case of nerves when they checked into the hotel that afternoon. She loved Bentley, but she had no real idea of what it was going to be like when they were alone together. But he was understanding, patient and gentle as he cradled her in his arms in a big easy chair and fed her shrimp from a big platter of seafood that room service had brought up. Of course, he'd also fed her champagne in increasing amounts, until she was so relaxed that nothing he suggested seemed to disturb her.

Slow, tender kisses grew slower and more insistent. He coaxed her out of her clothing with such ease that she barely noticed until she felt the cool air on her skin. Even then, the way he was touching her was so electrifying that her only conscious thought was to see how much closer to him she could get. There was one little flash of pain, easily forgotten as he kissed her with delicate sensuality and lifted her back into the fiery hunger the hesitation had briefly interrupted. Her mind had gone into eclipse while her body demanded and pleaded for an end to the tension which he built in her so effortlessly. Finally, finally, she fell over the edge of it into a blazing heat of fulfillment that exceeded her wildest expectations.

"And I used to think you were reserved!" she laughed.

"Only when I'm wearing a white lab coat," he murmured drowsily. He opened his eyes, rolled over and studied her pretty pink nudity with lazy appreciation. "Would you like me to get up and put on a lab coat, and be reserved?"

"I would not," she retorted, pulling him back down. She kissed him intensely. "I'd like you to be unreserved all over again, starting right now."

He slid over her, his hair-roughened chest grazing the hard tips of her pretty breasts. "I can't think of anything I'd enjoy more, Mrs. Rydel."

She would have answered him back, but she was much too involved for speech.

They wandered through the ruins at Chichen Itza hand in hand, fascinated as they strolled around the wide plain that contained the pyramidal Castillo and the other buildings that made up the Mayan complex.

"It must have looked much different when it was occupied, all those hundreds of years ago," Cappie mused, her eyes everywhere.

"There were probably even more people," he chuckled, glancing at the crowds of tourists that abounded, even this time of year. He handed her his huge water bottle and waited for her to take a sip before he followed suit. The bus trip here was hours long, and it would be after dark before they got back to their hotel. It was something they'd both wanted to see.

"It's a lot different, being here, than seeing it on television," she remarked.

"Most things are," he replied. "Until they can discover a way to let you touch and smell distant ruins, it won't be as much fun to watch it on a small screen."

She stopped and looked up at him with her heart in her gray eyes. "I never thought being married would be so much fun."

He hugged her close. "And we're only at the beginning of our marriage," he agreed, his blue eyes soft as they scanned her face. "I hope we have a hundred years ahead of us."

"Me, too." She pressed into his arms and closed her eyes. "Me, too, Bentley."

She went back to work for him in the practice. She'd argued that if Keely, who was happily married and well-off, could keep working, she could, too. He hadn't protested too much. It delighted him to be able to see her all day long.

"Don't you want a cat?" Keely coaxed the week after they came back from their honeymoon. "I've got six little white kittens that Grace Grier asked me to find homes for, and I've only placed four of them."

Cappie laughed. "I'd love one."

"Me, too," Bentley agreed, poking his head around the corner. "Did Cy Parks call back about that new bull of his that got cut on the barbed wire?"

"He did. He said if you'd drop by on your way home, he and Lisa would feed you both," Keely chuckled. "They're having homemade chili and corn bread."

"My favorite," Bentley said.

"Mine, too," Cappie replied almost at the same time as Bentley.

"He said you could bring Kell along," the other girl added.

"Kell's gone off somewhere with Rourke and Chet," Cappie sighed. "No telling where. They vanish for days at a time, and nobody knows where. He's my own brother. You'd think he could trust me."

"And me," Bentley added.

"I'm sure he has his reasons," Cappie said. "Whatever they are."

"It's bound to be something covert and dangerous and exciting," Keely said out loud.

"More than likely, they're helping Detective Marquez

stake out a nightclub or something," Bentley chuckled. "He did mention that he needed a couple of willing volunteers for a special project he and that assistant district attorney are working on."

"We owe that district attorney," Cappie agreed. "He talked Frank's accomplices into testifying against him for reduced sentences. He says Frank won't get out until his hair turns gray. Made my day," she added.

"Mine, too," Bentley assured her. "Okay, people, back to work."

"Yes, sir, Dr. Rydel, sir," Cappie said, saluting him.

He made a face at her. Then he grinned.

She grinned back, turning back to her coworker behind the counter. "Who's next, Keely?"

"Mrs. Anderson and her Chihuahua. Got the chart right here."

Cappie took it from her and went out into the waiting room, which was full. Her eyes were bright with happiness as she exchanged a glance with her handsome husband, just before he went into the back to examine a surgical patient. She felt as if she could walk on air.

"Okay, Mrs. Anderson," she told an elderly little woman with a smile. "If you'll bring Tweedle on back, we'll get Dr. Rydel to take a look at his bruised paw."

"He's a very nice doctor," the little woman told Cappie. "You're a lucky young woman!"

"Yes, you are!" Bentley called from the back. "Not every woman gets a husband who's as accomplished and modest as I am! You should be proud of yourself!"

"I am, dear, and how do you like your potatoes… burned or charbroiled?"

There was a pause. "Not every husband gets a wife as accomplished and modest as you are, dear!" he called back.

She chuckled. "Now that will get you a nice scalloped potato dish and a beautifully cooked pot roast!"

An amused Mrs. Anderson wiggled her eyebrows at Cappie as she followed her to a treatment room. Cappie just grinned.

* * * * *

PASSION FLOWER

To Victoria, Texas, with love

CHAPTER ONE

JENNIFER KING eyed the closed hotel room door nervously. She hadn't wanted this assignment, but she hadn't had much choice, either. Her recent illness had left her savings account bare, and this job was all she had to hold on to. It was a long way from the brilliant career in interior decorating she'd left behind in New York. But it was a living.

She pushed back a loose strand of blond hair and hoped she looked sedate enough for the cattleman behind the door. The kind of clothes she'd favored in New York were too expensive for her budget in Atlanta.

She knocked at the door and waited. It seemed to take forever for the man inside to get there. Finally, without warning, the door swung open.

"Miss King?" he asked, smiling pleasantly.

She smiled back. He was much younger than she'd expected him to be. Tall and fair and pleasant. "Yes," she said. "You rang for a temporary secretary?"

"Just need a few letters done, actually," he said,

taking the heavy portable typewriter from her hand. "I'm buying some cattle for my brother."

"Yes, Miss James at the agency told me it had to do with cattle." She sat down quickly. She was pale and wan, still feeling the after-effects of a terrible bout with pneumonia.

"Say, are you all right?" he asked, frowning.

"Fine, thank you, Mr. Culhane," she said, remembering his name from Miss James's description of the job. "I'm just getting over pneumonia, and I'm a little weak."

He sat down across from her on the sofa, lean and rangy, and smiled. "I guess it does take the whip out of you. I've never had it myself, but Everett nearly died on us one year. He smokes too much," he confided.

"Your brother?" she asked with polite interest as she got her steno pad and pen from her large purse.

"My brother. The senior partner. Everett runs the show." He sounded just a little jealous. She glanced up. Jennifer was twenty-three, and he couldn't have been much older. She felt a kinship with him. Until their deaths three years back, her parents had pretty much nudged her into the job they thought she wanted. By the sound of it, Everett Culhane had done the same with this young man.

She dug out her pad and pen and crossed her thin legs. All of her was thin. Back in New York, before the frantic pace threatened her health, she'd been slender and poised and pretty enough to draw any man's eye.

But now she was only a pale wraith, a ghost of the woman she'd been. Her blond hair was brittle and lusterless, her pale green eyes were dull, without their old sparkle. She looked bad, and that fact registered in the young man's eyes.

"Are you sure you feel up to this?" he asked gently. "You don't look well."

"I'm a little frail, that's all," she replied proudly. "I'm only just out of the hospital, you see."

"I guess that's why," he muttered. He got up, pacing the room, and found some notes scribbled on lined white paper. "Well, this first letter goes to Everett Culhane, Circle C Ranch, Big Spur, Texas."

"Texas?" Her pale eyes lit up. "Really?"

His eyebrows lifted, and he grinned. "Really. The town is named after a king-size ranch nearby—the Big Spur. It's owned by Cole Everett and his wife Heather, and their three sons. Our ranch isn't a patch on that one, but big brother has high hopes."

"I've always wanted to see a real cattle ranch," she confided. "My grandfather went cowboying out to Texas as a boy. He used to talk about it all the time, about the places he'd seen, and the history..." She sat up straight, poising her pen over the pad. "Sorry. I didn't mean to get off the track."

"That's all right. Funny, you don't look like a girl who'd care for the outdoors," he commented as he sat back down with the sheaf of papers in his hand.

"I love it," she said quietly. "I lived in a small town

until I was ten and my parents moved to Atlanta. I missed it terribly. I still do."

"Can't you go back?" he asked.

She shook her head sadly. "It's too late. I have no family left. My parents are dead. There are a few scattered relatives, but none close enough to visit."

"That's rough. Kind of like me and Everett," he added. "We got raised by our aunt and uncle. At least, I did. Everett wasn't so lucky. Our dad was still alive while he was a boy." His face clouded, as if with an unpleasant memory. He cleared his throat. "Well, anyway, back to the letter…"

He began to dictate, and she kept up with him easily. He thought out the sentences before he gave them to her, so there were few mistakes or changes. She wondered why he didn't just call his brother, but she didn't ask the question. She took down several pages of description about bulls and pedigrees and bloodlines. There was a second letter, to a bank executive in Big Spur, detailing the method the Culhane brothers had devised to pay back a sizeable loan. The third letter was to a breeder in Carrollton, outlining transport for a bull the man had evidently purchased from the Culhanes.

"Confused?" he murmured dryly when he stopped.

"It's not my business…" she began gently.

"We're selling off one of our best bulls," he said, "to give us enough down payment on another top breeding bull. Everett is trying for a purebred Hereford herd. But we don't have the cash, so I've come down here to do some fancy trading. I sold the bull we had. Now I'm trying to get a potential seller to come down on his price."

"Wouldn't a phone call to your brother be quicker?" she asked.

"Sure. And Everett would skin my head. I came out here on a bus, for God's sake, instead of a plane. We're just about mortgaged to the hilt, you see. Everett says we can't afford not to pinch pennies." His eyes twinkled. "We've got Highland Scots in our ancestry, you see."

She smiled. "Yes, I suppose so. I can see his point. Phone calls are expensive."

"Especially the kind it would take to relay this much information," he agreed, nodding toward what he'd dictated. "If I get it off today, he'll have it in a day or two. Then, if he thinks it's worth giving what the man wants, he can call me and just say a word or two. In the meantime, I've got other business to attend to."

"Shrewd idea," she murmured.

"Just a couple more," he continued. He leaned back and studied a magazine. "Okay, this one goes to…" He gave her a name and address in north Georgia, and dictated a letter asking if the breeder could give him a call at the hotel on Friday at 1:00 p.m. Then he dictated a second letter to a breeder in south Georgia, making the same request for 2:00 p.m. He grinned at her faint smile.

"Saving money," he assured her. "Although why Everett wants to do it the hard way is beyond me.

There's a geologist who swears we've got one hell of a lot of oil on our western boundary, but Everett dug in his heels and refused to sell off the drilling rights. Even for a percentage. Can you beat that? We could be millionaires, and here I sit writing letters asking people to call me, just to save money."

"Why won't he sell?" she asked, curious.

"Because he's a purist," he grumbled. "He doesn't want to spoil the land. He'd rather struggle to make the cattle pay. Fat chance. The way things have been going, we're going to wind up eating those damned purebreds, paper and all."

She laughed helplessly at his phrasing and hid her face in her hand. "Sorry," she mumbled. "I didn't mean to laugh."

"It is kind of funny," he confessed. "But not when you're cutting corners like we are."

She got up and started to lift the typewriter onto the desk by the window, struggling with it.

"Here, let me do that," he said, and put it onto the flat surface for her. "You're pretty weak, little lady."

"I'm getting back on my feet," she assured him. "Just a little wobbly, that's all."

"Well, I'll leave you to it. I'm going down to get a sandwich. Can I bring you something?"

She'd have loved a sandwich, but she wasn't going to put any further drain on his resources. "No, thank you," she said, politely and with a smile. "I just had lunch before I came over here."

"Okay, then. See you in a half hour or so."

He jammed a straw cowboy hat on his head and went out the door, closing it softly behind him.

Jennifer typed the letters quickly and efficiently, even down to the cattle's pedigrees. It was a good thing she'd taken that typing course when she was going through the school of interior design in New York, she thought. It had come in handy when the pressure of competition laid her out. She wasn't ready to handle that competitive rat race again yet. She needed to rest, and by comparison typing letters for out-of-town businessmen was a piece of cake.

She felt oddly sorry for this businessman, and faintly sympathetic with his brother, who'd rather go spare than sell out on his principles. She wondered if he looked like his younger brother.

Her eyes fell on the name she was typing at the bottom of the letter. Robert G. Culhane. That must be the man who'd dictated them. He seemed to know cattle, from his meticulous description of them. Her eyes wandered over what looked like a production record for a herd sire, and she sighed. Texas and cattle. She wondered what the Circle C Ranch was like and while she finished up the letters, lost herself in dreams of riding horseback over flat plains. Pipe dreams, she thought, smiling as she stacked the neat letters with their accompanying envelopes. She'd never see Texas.

Just as she rose from the typewriter, the door opened, and Robert Culhane was back. He smiled at her.

"Taking a break?" he asked as he swept off his hat and whirled it onto a table.

"No, I'm finished," she said, astounding him.

"Already?" He grabbed up the letters and bent over the desk, proofreading them one by one and shaking his head. "Damn, you're fast."

"I do around a hundred words a minute," she replied. "It's one of my few talents."

"You'd be a godsend at the ranch," he sighed. "It takes Everett an hour to type one letter. He cusses a blue streak when he has to write anything on that infernal old machine. And there are all the production records we have to keep, and the tax records, and the payroll…" His head lifted and he frowned. "I don't suppose you'd like a job?"

She caught her breath. "In Texas?"

"You make it sound like a religious experience," he murmured on a laugh.

"You can't imagine how much I hate the city," she replied, brushing back a strand of dull hair. "I still cough all the time because of the pollution, and the apartment where I live has no space at all. I'd almost work for free just to be out in the country."

He cocked his head at her and pursed his boyish lips. "It wouldn't be easy, working for Everett," he said. "And you'd have to manage your own fare to Big Spur. You see, I'll need a little time to convince him. You'd barely get minimum wage. And knowing Everett, you'd wind up doing a lot of things besides typing. We don't have a housekeeper…"

Her face lit up. "I can make curtains and cook."

"Do you have a telephone?"

She sighed. "No."

"Kind of in the same boat we are in, aren't you?" he said with a sympathetic smile. "I'm Robert Culhane, by the way."

"Jennifer King," she said for the second time that day, and extended her hand.

"Nice to meet you, Jenny. How can I reach you?"

"The agency will take a message for me," she said.

"Fine. I'll be in town for several more days. I'll be in touch with you before I go back to Texas. Okay?"

She beamed. "You're really serious?"

"I'm really serious. And this is great work," he added, gesturing toward the letters. "Jenny, it won't be an easy life on the Circle C. It's nothing like those fancy ranches you see on the television."

"I'm not expecting it to be," she said honestly, and was picturing a ramshackle house that needed paint and curtains and overhauling, and two lonely men living in it. She smiled. "I'm just expecting to be needed."

"You'll be that," he sighed, staring at her critically. "But are you up to hard work?"

"I'll manage," she promised. "Being out in the open, in fresh air, will make me strong. Besides, it'll be dry air out there, and it's summer."

"You'll burn up in the heat," he promised.

"I burn up in the heat here," she said. "Atlanta is a

southern city. We get hundred-degree temperatures here."

"Just like home," he murmured with a smile.

"I'd like to come," she said as she got her purse and closed up the typewriter. "But I don't want to get you into any trouble with your brother."

"Everett and I hardly ever have anything except trouble," he said easily. "Don't worry about me. You'd be doing us a big favor. I'll talk Everett into it."

"Should I write you another letter?" She hesitated.

He shook his head. "I'll have it out with him when I get home," he said. "No sweat. Thanks for doing my letters. I'll send the agency a check, you tell them."

"I will. And thank you!"

She hardly felt the weight of the typewriter on her way back to the agency. She was floating on a cloud.

Miss James gave her a hard look when she came back in. "You're late," she said. "We had to refuse a call."

"I'm sorry. There were several letters..." she began.

"You've another assignment. Here's the address. A politician. Wants several copies of a speech he's giving, to hand out to the press. You're to type the speech and get it photostatted for him."

She took the outstretched address and sighed. "The typewriter...?"

"He has his own, an electric one. Leave that one here, if you please." Miss James buried her silver head in paperwork. "You may go home when you finish. I'll see you in the morning. Good night."

"Good night," Jennifer said quietly, sighing as she went out onto the street. It would be well after quitting time when she finished, and Miss James knew it. But perhaps the politician would be generous enough to tip her. If only the Texas job worked out! Jennifer was a scrapper when she was at her peak, but she was weary and sick and dragged out. It wasn't a good time to get into an argument with the only employer she'd been able to find. All the other agencies were overstaffed with out-of-work people begging for any kind of job.

The politician was a city councilman, in a good mood and very generous. Jennifer treated herself to three hamburgers and two cups of coffee on the way back to her small apartment. It was in a private home, and dirt cheap. The landlady wasn't overly friendly, but it was a roof over her head and the price was right.

She slept fitfully, dreaming about the life she'd left behind in New York. It all seemed like something out of a fantasy. The competition for the plum jobs, the cocktail parties to make contacts, the deadlines, the endless fighting to land the best accounts, the agonizing perfecting of color schemes and coordinating pieces to fit fussy tastes… Her nerves had given out, and then her body.

It hadn't been her choice to go to New York. She'd have been happy in Atlanta. But the best schools were up north, and her parents had insisted. They wanted her to have the finest training available, so she let herself be gently pushed. Two years after she graduated, they were dead. She'd never truly gotten over their deaths in the plane crash. They'd been on their way to a party on Christmas Eve. The plane went down in the dark, in a lake, and it had been hours before they were missed.

In the two years since her graduation, Jennifer had landed a job at one of the top interior-decoration businesses in the city. She'd pushed herself over the limit to get clients, going to impossible lengths to please them. The outcome had been inevitable. Pneumonia landed her in the hospital for several days in March, and she was too drained to go back to work immediately after. An up-and-coming young designer had stepped neatly into her place, and she had found herself suddenly without work.

Everything had to go, of course. The luxury apartment, the furs, the designer clothes. She'd sold them all and headed south. Only to find that the job market was overloaded and she couldn't find a job that wouldn't finish killing her. Except at a temporary agency, where she could put her typing skills to work. She started working for Miss James, and trying to recover. But so far she'd failed miserably. And now the only bright spot in her future was Texas.

She prayed as she never had before, struggling from one assignment to the next and hoping beyond hope that the phone call would come. Late one Friday afternoon, it did. And she happened to be in the office when it came.

"Miss King?" Robert Culhane asked on a laugh. "Still want to go to Texas?"

"Oh, yes!" she said fervently, holding tightly to the telephone cord.

"Then pack a bag and be at the ranch bright and early a week from Monday morning. Got a pencil? Okay, here's how to get there."

She was so excited she could barely scribble. She got down the directions. "I can't believe it, it's like a dream!" she said enthusiastically. "I'll do a good job, really I will. I won't be any trouble, and the pay doesn't matter!"

"I'll tell Everett," he chuckled. "Don't forget. You needn't call. Just come on out to the ranch. I'll be there to smooth things over with old Everett, okay?"

"Okay. Thank you!"

"Thank *you,* Miss King," he said. "See you a week from Monday."

"Yes, sir!" She hung up, her face bright with hope. She was actually going to Texas!

"Miss King?" Miss James asked suspiciously.

"Oh! I won't be back in after today, Miss James," she said politely. "Thank you for letting me work with you. I've enjoyed it very much."

Miss James looked angry. "You can't just walk out like this," she said.

"But I can," Jennifer said, with some of her old spirit. She picked up her purse. "I didn't sign a contract, Miss James. And if you were to push the point, I'd tell you that I worked a great deal of overtime for which I wasn't paid," she added with a pointed stare. "How would you explain that to the people down at the state labor department?"

Miss James stiffened. "You're ungrateful."

"No, I'm not. I'm very grateful. But I'm leaving, all the same. Good day." She nodded politely just before she went out, and closed the door firmly behind her.

CHAPTER TWO

IT WAS blazing hot for a spring day in Texas. Jennifer stopped in the middle of the ranch road to rest for a minute and set her burdens down on the dusty, graveled ground. She wished for the tenth time in as many minutes that she'd let the cab driver take her all the way to the Culhanes' front door. But she'd wanted to walk. It hadn't seemed a long way from the main road. And it was so beautiful, with the wildflowers strewn across the endless meadows toward the flat horizon. Bluebonnets, which she'd only read about until then, and Mexican hat and Indian paintbrush. Even the names of the flowers were poetic. But her enthusiasm had outweighed her common sense. And her strength.

She'd tried to call the ranch from town—apparently Everett and Robert Culhane did have the luxury of a telephone. But it rang and rang with no answer. Well, it was Monday, and she'd been promised a job. She hefted her portable typewriter and her suitcase and started out again.

Her pale eyes lifted to the house in the distance. It was a two-story white frame building, with badly peeling paint and a long front porch. Towering live oaks protected it from the sun, trees bigger than anything Jennifer had seen in Georgia. And the feathery green trees with the crooked trunks had to be mesquite. She'd never seen it, but she'd done her share of reading about it.

On either side of the long, graveled driveway were fences, gray with weathering and strung with rusting barbed wire. Red-coated cattle grazed behind the fences, and her eyes lingered on the wide horizon. She'd always thought Georgia was big—until now. Texas was just unreal. In a separate pasture, a mare and her colt frolicked in the hot sun.

Jennifer pushed back a strand of dull blond hair that had escaped from her bun. In a white shirtwaist dress and high heels, she was a strange sight to be walking up the driveway of a cattle ranch. But she'd wanted to make a good impression.

Her eyes glanced down ruefully at the red dust on the hem of her dress, and the scuff marks on her last good pair of white sling pumps. She could have cried. One of her stockings had run, and she was sweating. She could hardly have looked worse if she'd planned it.

She couldn't help being a little nervous about the older brother. She had Everett Culhane pictured as a staid old rancher with a mean temper. She'd met businessmen like that before, and dealt with them. She wasn't afraid of him. But she hoped that he'd be glad of her help. It would make things easier all around.

Her footsteps echoed along the porch as she walked up the worn steps. She would have looked around more carefully weeks ago, but now she was tired and run-down and just too exhausted to care what her new surroundings looked like.

She paused at the screen door, and her slender fingers brushed the dust from her dress. She put the suitcase and the typewriter down, took a steadying breath, and knocked.

There was no sound from inside the house. The wooden door was standing open, and she thought she heard the whir of a fan. She knocked again. Maybe it would be the nice young man she'd met in Atlanta who would answer the door. She only hoped she was welcome.

The sound of quick, hard footsteps made her heart quicken. Someone was home, at least. Maybe she could sit down. She was feeling a little faint.

"Who the hell are you?" came a harsh masculine voice from behind the screen door, and Jennifer looked up into the hardest face and the coldest dark eyes she'd ever seen.

She couldn't even find her voice. Her immediate reaction was to turn around and run for it. But she'd come too far, and she was too tired.

"I'm Jennifer King," she said as professionally as she could. "Is Robert Culhane home, please?"

She was aware of the sudden tautening of his big body, a harsh intake of breath, before she looked up and saw the fury in his dark eyes.

"What the hell kind of game are you playing, lady?" he demanded.

She stared at him. It had been a long walk, and now it looked as if she might have made a mistake and come to the wrong ranch. Her usual confidence faltered. "Is this the Circle C Ranch?" she asked.

"Yes, it is."

He wasn't forthcoming, and she wondered if he might be one of the hired hands. "Is this where Robert Culhane lives?" she persisted, trying to peek past him—there was a lot of him, all hard muscle and blue denim.

"Bobby was killed in a bus wreck a week ago," he said harshly.

Jennifer was aware of a numb feeling in her legs. The long trip on the bus, the heavy suitcase, the effects of her recent illness—all of it added up to exhaustion. And those cold words were the final blow. With a pitiful little sound, she sank down onto the porch, her head whirling, nausea running up into her throat like warm water.

The screen door flew open and a pair of hard, impatient arms reached down to lift her. She felt herself effortlessly carried, like a sack of flour, into the cool house. She was unceremoniously dumped down onto a worn brocade sofa and left there while booted feet stomped off into another room. There were muttered words that she was glad she couldn't understand, and clinking sounds. Then, a minute later, a glass of dark amber liquid was held to her numb lips and a hard hand raised her head.

She sipped at the cold, sweet iced tea like a runner on the desert when confronted with wet salvation. She struggled to catch her breath and sat up, gently nudging the dark, lean hand holding the glass to one side. She breathed in deeply, trying to get her whirling mind to slow down. She was still trying to take it all in. She'd been promised a job, she'd come hundreds of miles at her own expense to work for minimum wage, and now the man who'd offered it to her was dead. That was the worst part, imagining such a nice young man dead.

"You look like a bleached handkerchief," the deep, harsh voice observed.

She sighed. "You ought to write for television. You sure do have a gift for prose."

His dark eyes narrowed. "Walking in this heat without a hat. My God, how many stupid city women are there in the world? And what landed you on my doorstep?"

She lifted her eyes then, to look at him properly. He was darkly tanned, and there were deep lines in his face, from the hatchet nose down to the wide, chiseled mouth. His eyes were deep-set, unblinking under heavy dark brows and a wide forehead. His hair was jet-black, straight and thick and a little shaggy. He was wearing what had to be work clothes: faded denim jeans that emphasized long, powerfully muscled legs, and a matching shirt whose open neck revealed a brown chest thick with short, curling hair. He had the look of a man who was all business, all the time. All at once she realized that this man wasn't the hired hand she'd mistaken him for.

"You're Everett Culhane," she said hesitantly.

His face didn't move. Not a muscle in it changed position, but she had the distinct feeling that the sound of his name on her lips had shocked him.

She took another long sip of the tea and sighed at the pleasure of the icy liquid going down her parched throat.

"How far did you walk?" he asked.

"Just from the end of your driveway," she admitted, looking down at her ruined shoes. "Distance is deceptive out here."

"Haven't you ever heard of sunstroke?"

She nodded. "It just didn't occur to me."

She put the glass down on the napkin he'd brought with it. Well, this was Texas. How sad that she wouldn't see anything more of it.

"I'm very sorry about your brother, Mr. Culhane," she said with dignity. "I didn't know him very well, but he seemed like a nice man." She got up with an odd kind of grace despite the unsteadiness of her legs. "I won't take up any more of your time."

"Why did you come, Miss King?"

She shook her head. "It doesn't matter now in the least." She turned and went out the screen door, lifting her suitcase and typewriter from where they'd fallen when she fainted. It was going to be a long walk back to town, but she'd just have to manage it. She had bus fare back home and a little more. A cab was a luxury now, with no job at the end of her long ride.

"Where do you think you're going?" Everett Culhane asked from behind her, his tone like a whiplash.

"Back to town," she said without turning. "Goodbye, Mr. Culhane."

"Walking?" he mused. "In this heat, without a hat?"

"Got here, didn't I?" she drawled as she walked down the steps.

"You'll never make it back. Wait a minute. I'll drive you."

"No, thanks," she said proudly. "I get around all right by myself, Mr. Culhane. I don't need any handouts."

"You'll need a doctor if you try that walk," he said, and turned back into the house.

She thought the matter was settled, until a battered red pickup truck roared up beside her and stopped. The passenger door flew open.

"Get in," he said curtly, in a tone that made it clear he expected instant obedience.

"I said…" she began irritatedly.

His dark eyes narrowed. "I don't mind lifting you in and holding you down until we get to town," he said quietly.

With a grimace, she climbed in, putting the typewriter and suitcase on the floorboard.

There was a marked lack of conversation. Everett

smoked his cigarette with sharp glances in her direction when she began coughing. Her lungs were still sensitive, and he seemed to be smoking shucks or something equally potent. Eventually he crushed out the cigarette and cracked a window.

"You don't sound well," he said suddenly.

"I'm getting over pneumonia," she said, staring lovingly at the horizon. "Texas sure is big."

"It sure is." He glanced at her. "Which part of it do you call home?"

"I don't."

The truck lurched as he slammed on the brakes. "What did you say?"

"I'm not a Texan," she confessed. "I'm from Atlanta."

"Georgia?"

"Is there another one?"

He let out a heavy breath. "What the hell did you mean, coming this distance just to see a man you hardly knew?" he burst out. "Surely to God, it wasn't love at first sight?"

"Love?" She blinked. "Heavens, no. I only did some typing for your brother."

He cut off the engine. "Start over. Start at the beginning. You're giving me one hell of a headache. How did you wind up out here?"

"Your brother offered me a job," she said quietly. "Typing. Of course, he said there'd be other duties as well. Cooking, cleaning, things like that. And a very small salary," she added with a tiny smile.

"He was honest with you, at least," he growled. "But then why did you come? Didn't you believe him?"

"Yes, of course," she said hesitantly. "Why wouldn't I want to come?"

He started to light another cigarette, stared hard at her, and put the pack back in his shirt pocket. "Keep talking."

He was an odd man, she thought. "Well, I'd lost my old job, because once I got over the pneumonia I was too weak to keep up the pace. I got a job in Atlanta with one of the temporary talent agencies doing typing. My speed is quite good, and it was something that didn't wring me out, you see. Mr. Culhane wanted some letters typed. We started talking," she smiled, remembering how kind he'd been, "and when I found out he was from Texas, from a real ranch, I guess I just went crazy. I've spent my whole life listening to my grandfather relive his youth in Texas, Mr. Culhane. I've read everything Zane Grey and Louis L'Amour ever wrote, and it was the dream of my life to come out here. The end of the rainbow. I figured that a low salary on open land would be worth a lot more than a big salary in the city, where I was choking to death on smog and civilization. He offered me the job and I said yes on the spot." She glanced at him ruefully. "I'm not usually so slow. But I was feeling so bad, and it sounded so wonderful...I didn't even think about checking with you first. Mr. Culhane said he'd have it all worked out, and that I was just to get on a bus and come on out today." Her eyes clouded. "I'm so sorry about him. Losing the job isn't nearly as bad as hearing that he...was killed. I liked him."

Everett's fingers were tapping an angry pattern on the steering wheel. "A job." He laughed mirthlessly, then sighed. "Well, maybe he had a point. I'm so behind on my production records and tax records, it isn't funny. I'm choking to death on my own cooking, the house hasn't been swept in a month..." He glanced at her narrowly. "You aren't pregnant?"

Her pale eyes flashed at him. "That, sir, would make medical history."

One dark eyebrow lifted and he glanced at her studiously before he smiled. "Little Southern lady, are you really that innocent?"

"Call me Scarlett and, unemployment or no unemployment, I'll paste you one, cowboy," she returned with a glimmer of her old spirit. It was too bad that the outburst triggered a coughing spree.

"Damn," he muttered, passing her his handkerchief. "All right, I'll stop baiting you. Do you want the job, or don't you? Robert was right about the wages. You'll get bed and board free, but it's going to be a frugal existence. Interested?"

"If it means getting to stay in Texas, yes, I am."

He smiled. "How old are you, schoolgirl?"

"I haven't been a schoolgirl for years, Mr. Culhane," she told him. "I'm twenty-three, in fact." She glared at him. "How old are you?"

"Make a guess," he invited.

Her eyes went from his thick hair down the hawklike features to his massive chest, which tapered to narrow hips, long powerful legs, and large, booted feet. "Thirty," she said.

He chuckled softly. It was the first time she'd heard the deep, pleasant sound, and it surprised her to find that he was capable of laughter. He didn't seem like the kind of man who laughed very often.

His eyes wandered over her thin body with amused indifference, and she regretted for a minute that she was such a shadow of her former self. "Try again, honey," he said.

She noticed then the deep lines in his darkly tanned face, the sprinkling of gray hair at his temples. In the open neck of his shirt, she could see threads of silver among the curling dark hair. No, he wasn't as young as she'd first thought.

"Thirty-four," she guessed.

"Add a year and you've got it."

She smiled. "Poor old man," she said with gentle humor.

He chuckled again. "That's no way to talk to your new boss," he cautioned.

"I won't forget again, honestly." She stared at him. "Do you have other people working for you?"

"Just Eddie and Bib," he said. "They're married." He nodded as he watched her eyes become wide and apprehensive. "That's right. We'll be alone. I'm a bachelor and there's no staff in the house."

"Well…"

"There'll be a lock on your door," he said after a

minute. "When you know me better, you'll see that I'm pretty conventional in my outlook. It's a big house. We'll rattle around like two peas in a pod. It's only on rare occasions that I'm in before bedtime." His dark eyes held hers. "And for the record, my taste doesn't run to city girls."

That sounded as if there was a good reason for his taste in women, but she didn't pry. "I'll work hard, Mr. Culhane."

"My name is Everett," he said, watching her. "Or Rett, if you prefer. You can cook meals and do the laundry and housekeeping. And when you have time, you can work in what passes for my office. Wages won't be much. I can pay the bills, and that's about it."

"I don't care about getting rich." Meanwhile she was thinking fast, sorely tempted to accept the offer, but afraid of the big, angry man at her side. There were worse things than being alone and without money, and she didn't really know him at all.

He saw the thoughts in her mind. "Jenny Wren," he said softly, "do I look like a mad rapist?"

Hearing her name that way on his lips sent a surge of warmth through her. No one had called her by a pet name since the death of her parents.

"No," she said quietly. "Of course you don't. I'll work for you, Mr. Culhane."

He didn't answer her. He only scanned her face and nodded. Then he started the truck, turned it around, and headed back to the Circle C Ranch.

CHAPTER THREE

TWO HOURS later, Jennifer was well and truly in residence, to the evident amusement of Everett's two ranch hands. They apparently knew better than to make any snide comments about her presence, but they did seem to find something fascinating about having a young woman around the place.

Jennifer had her own room, with peeling wallpaper, worn blue gingham curtains at the windows, and a faded quilt on the bed. Most of the house was like that. Even the rugs on the floor were faded and worn from use. She'd have given anything to be robust and healthy and have a free hand to redecorate the place. It had such wonderful potential with its long history and simple, uncluttered architecture.

The next morning she slept late, rising to bright sunlight and a strange sense that she belonged there. She hadn't felt that way since her childhood, and couldn't help wondering why. Everett had been polite, but not much more. He wasn't really a welcoming kind of man. But, then, he'd just lost his brother. That must account for his taciturn aloofness.

He was long gone when she went downstairs. She fixed herself a cup of coffee and two pieces of toast and then went to the small room that doubled as his office. As he'd promised the day before, he'd laid out a stack of production records and budget information that needed typing. He'd even put her electric typewriter on a table and plugged it in. There was a stack of white paper beside it, and a note.

"Don't feel obliged to work yourself into a coma the first day," it read. And his bold signature was slashed under the terse sentence. She smiled at the flowing handwriting and the perfect spelling. He was a literate man, at least.

She sat down in her cool blue shirtwaist dress and got to work. Two hours later, she'd made great inroads into the paperwork and was starting a new sheet when Everett's heavy footsteps resounded throughout the house. The door swung open and his dark eyebrows shot straight up.

"Aren't you going to eat lunch?" he asked.

More to the point, wasn't she going to feed him, she thought, and grinned.

"Something funny, Miss King?" he asked.

"Oh, no, boss," she said, leaving the typewriter behind. He was expecting that she'd forgotten his noon meal, but she had a surprise in store for him.

She led him into the kitchen, where two places were

set. He stood there staring at the table, scowling, while she put out bread, mayonnaise, some thick ham she'd found in the refrigerator, and a small salad she'd made with a bottled dressing.

"Coffee?" she asked, poised with the pot in her hand.

He nodded, sliding into the place at the head of the table.

She poured it into his thick white mug and then filled her own.

"How did you know I wanted coffee instead of tea?" he asked with a narrow gaze as she seated herself beside him.

"Because the coffee cannister was half empty and the tea had hardly been touched," she replied with a smile.

He chuckled softly as he sipped the black liquid. "Not bad," he murmured, glancing at her.

"I'm sorry about breakfast," she said. "I usually wake up around six, but this morning I was kind of tired."

"No problem," he told her, reaching for bread. "I'm used to getting my own breakfast."

"What do you have?"

"Coffee."

She gaped at him. "Coffee?"

He shrugged. "Eggs bounce, bacon's half raw, and the toast hides under some black stuff. Coffee's better."

Her eyes danced as he put some salad on her plate. "I guess so. I'll try to wake up on time tomorrow."

"Don't rush it," he said, glancing at her with a slight frown. "You look puny to me."

"Most people would look puny compared to you," she replied.

"Have you always been that thin?" he persisted.

"No. Not until I got pneumonia," she said. "I just went straight downhill. I suppose I just kept pushing too hard. It caught up with me."

"How's the paperwork coming along?"

"Oh, I'm doing fine," she said. "Your handwriting is very clear. I've had some correspondence to type for doctors that required translation."

"Who did you get to translate?"

She grinned. "The nearest pharmacist. They have experience, you see."

He smiled at her briefly before he bit into his sandwich. He made a second one, but she noticed that he ignored the salad.

"Don't you want some of this?" she asked, indicating the salad bowl.

"I'm not a rabbit," he informed her.

"It's very good for you."

"So is liver, I'm told, but I won't eat that either." He finished his sandwich and got up to pour himself another cup of coffee."

"Then why do you keep lettuce and tomatoes?"

He glanced at her. "I like it on sandwiches."

This was a great time to tell her, after she'd used it all up in the salad. Just like a man…

"You could have dug it out of here," she said weakly.

He cocked an eyebrow. "With salad dressing all over it?"

"You could scrape it off…"

"I don't like broccoli or cauliflower, and never fix creamed beef," he added. "I'm more or less a meat and potatoes man."

"I'll sure remember that from now on, Mr. Culhane," she promised. "I'll be careful to use potatoes instead of apples in the pie I'm fixing for supper."

He glared at her. "Funny girl. Why don't you go on the stage?"

"Because you'd starve to death and weigh heavily on my conscience," she promised. "Some man named Brickmayer called and asked did you have a farrier's hammer he could borrow." She glanced up. "What's a farrier?"

He burst out laughing. "A farrier is a man who shoes horses."

"I'd like a horse," she sighed. "I'd put him in saddle oxfords."

"Go back to work. But slowly," he added from the doorway. "I don't want you knocking yourself into a sickbed on my account."

"You can count on me, sir," she promised, with a wry glance. "I'm much too afraid of your cooking to ever be at the mercy of it."

He started to say something, turned, and went out the door.

Jennifer spent the rest of the day finishing up the typing. Then she swept and dusted and made supper—a ham-and-egg casserole, biscuits, and cabbage. Supper sat on the table, however, and began to congeal. Eventually, she warmed up a little of it for herself, ate it, put the rest in the refrigerator, and went to bed. She had a feeling it was an omen for the future. He'd mentioned something that first day about rarely being home before bedtime. But couldn't he have warned her at lunch?

She woke up on time her second morning at the ranch. By 6:15 she was moving gracefully around the spacious kitchen in jeans and a green T-shirt. Apparently, Everett didn't mind what she wore, so she might as well be comfortable. She cooked a huge breakfast of fresh sausage, eggs, and biscuits, and made a pot of coffee.

Everything was piping hot and on the table when Everett came into the kitchen in nothing but his undershorts. Barefooted and bare-chested, he was enough to hold any woman's eyes. Jennifer, who'd seen her share of almost-bare men on the beaches, stood against the counter and stared like a starstruck girl. There wasn't an ounce of fat anywhere on that big body and he was covered with thick black hair—all over his chest, his flat stomach, his broad thighs. He was as sensuously male as any leading man on television, and she couldn't drag her fascinated eyes away.

He cocked an eyebrow at her, his eyes faintly amused

at what he recognized as shocked fascination. “I thought I heard something moving around down here. It’s just as well I took time to climb into my shorts.” And he turned away to leave her standing there, gaping after him.

A minute later he was back, whipping a belt around the faded blue denims he’d stepped into. He was still barefooted and bare-chested as he sat down at the table across from her.

“I thought I told you to stay in bed,” he said as he reached for a biscuit.

“I was afraid you’d keel over out on the plains and your horse wouldn’t be able to toss you onto his back and bring you home.” She grinned at his puzzled expression. “Well, that’s what Texas horses do in western movies.”

He chuckled. “Not my horse. He’s barely smart enough to find the barn when he’s hungry.” He buttered the biscuit. “My aunt used to cook like this,” he remarked. “Biscuits as light as air.”

“Sometimes they bounce,” she warned him. “I got lucky.”

He gave her a wary glance. “If these biscuits are any indication, so did I,” he murmured.

“I saw a henhouse out back. Do I gather the eggs every day?”

“Yes, but watch where you put your hand,” he cautioned. “Snakes have been known to get in there.”

She shuddered delicately, nodding.

They ate in silence for several minutes before he spoke again. "You're a good cook, Jenny."

She grinned. "My mother taught me. She was terrific."

"Are your parents still alive?"

She shook her head, feeling a twinge of nostalgia. "No. They died several months ago, in a plane crash."

"I'm sorry. Were you close?"

"Very." She glanced at him. "Are your parents dead?"

His face closed up. "Yes," he said curtly, and in a tone that didn't encourage further questions.

She looked up again, her eyes involuntarily lingering on his bare chest. She felt his gaze, and abruptly averted her own eyes back to her empty plate.

He got up after a minute and went back to his bedroom. When he came out, he was tucking in a buttoned khaki shirt, and wearing boots as well. "Thanks for breakfast," he said. "Now, how about taking it easy for the rest of the day? I want to be sure you're up to housework before you pitch in with both hands."

"I won't do anything I'm not able to do," she promised.

"I've got some rope in the barn," he said with soft menace, while his eyes measured her for it.

She stared at him thoughtfully. "I'll be sure to carry a pair of scissors on me."

He was trying not to grin. "My God, you're stubborn."

"Look who's talking."

"I've had lots of practice working cattle," he replied. He picked up his coffee cup and drained it. "From now on, I'll come to the table dressed. Even at six o'clock in the morning."

She looked up, smiling. "You're a nice man, Mr. Culhane," she said. "I'm not a prude, honestly I'm not. It's just that I'm not accustomed to sitting down to breakfast with men. Dressed or undressed."

His dark eyes studied her. "Not liberated, Miss King?" he asked.

She sensed a deeper intent behind that question, but she took it at face value. "I was never unliberated. I'm just old-fashioned."

"So am I, honey. You stick to your guns." He reached for his hat and walked off, whistling.

She was never sure quite how to take what he said. As the days went by, he puzzled her more and more. She noticed him watching her occasionally, when he was in the house and not working with his cattle. But it wasn't a leering kind of look. It was faintly curious and a little protective. She had the odd feeling that he didn't think of her as a woman at all. Not that she found the thought surprising. Her mirror gave her inescapable proof that she had little to attract a man's eyes these days. She was still frail and washed out.

Eddie was the elder of the ranchhands, and Jenny liked him on sight. He was a lot like the boss. He hardly ever smiled, he worked like two men, and he almost never sat down. But Jenny coaxed him into the kitchen with a cold glass of tea at the end of the week, when he brought her the eggs before she could go looking for them.

"Thank you, ma'am. I can sure use this." He sighed, and drained almost the whole glass in a few swallows. "Boss had me fixing fences. Nothing I hate worse than fixing fences," he added with a hard stare.

She tried not to grin. With his jutting chin and short graying whiskers and half-bald head, he did look fierce.

"I appreciate your bringing in the eggs for me," she replied. "I got busy mending curtains and forgot about them."

He shrugged. "It wasn't much," he murmured. He narrowed one eye as he studied her. "You ain't the kind I'd expect the boss to hire."

Her eyebrows arched and she did grin this time. "What would you expect?"

He cleared his throat. "Well, the boss being the way he is…an older lady with a mean temper." He moved restlessly in the chair he was straddling. "Well, it takes a mean temper to deal with him. I know, I been doin' it for nigh on twenty years."

"Has he owned the Circle C for that long?" she asked.

"He ain't old enough," he reminded her. "I mean, I knowed him that long. He used to hang around here with his Uncle Ben when he was just a tadpole. His parents never had much use for him. His mama run off with some man when he was ten and his daddy drank hisself to death."

It was like having the pins knocked out from under her. She could imagine Everett at ten, with no mother and an alcoholic father. Her eyes mirrored the horror she felt. "His brother must have been just a baby," she burst out.

"He was. Old Ben and Miss Emma took him in. But Everett weren't so lucky. He had to stay with his daddy."

She studied him quietly, and filled the tea glass again. "Why doesn't he like city women?"

"He got mixed up with some social-climbing lady from Houston," he said curtly. "Anybody could have seen she wouldn't fit in here, except Everett. He'd just inherited the place and had these big dreams of making a fortune in cattle. The fool woman listened to the dreams and came harking out here with him one summer." He laughed bitterly. "Took her all of five minutes to give Everett back his ring and tell him what she thought of his plans. Everett got drunk that night, first time I ever knew him to take a drink of anything stronger than beer. And that was the last time he brought a woman here. Until you come along, at least."

She sat back down, all too aware of the faded yellow shirt and casual jeans she was wearing. The shirt was Everett's. She'd borrowed it while she washed her own in the ancient chugging washing machine. "Don't look at me like a contender," she laughed, tossing back her long dark-blond hair. "I'm just a hanger-on myself, not a chic city woman."

"For a hanger-on," he observed, indicating the scrubbed floors and clean, pressed curtains at the windows and the food cooking on the stove, "you do get through a power of work."

"I like housework," she told him. She sipped her own tea. "I used to fix up houses for a living, until it got too much for me. I got frail during the winter and I haven't quite picked back up yet."

"That accent of yours throws me," he muttered. "Sounds like a lot of Southern mixed up with Yankee."

She laughed again. "I'm from Georgia. Smart man, aren't you?"

"Not so smart, lady, or I'd be rich, too," he said with a rare grin. He got up. "Well, I better get back to work. The boss don't hold with us lollygagging on his time, and Bib's waiting for me to help him move cattle."

"Thanks again for bringing my eggs," she said.

He nodded. "No trouble."

She watched him go, sipping her own tea. There were a lot of things about Everett Culhane that were beginning to make sense. She felt that she understood him a lot better now, right down to the black moods that made him walk around brooding sometimes in the evening.

It was just after dark when Everett came in, and Jenny put the cornbread in the oven to warm the minute she heard the old pickup coming up the driveway. She'd learned that Everett Culhane didn't work banker's hours. He went out at dawn and might not come home until bedtime. But he had yet to find himself without a meal. Jenny prided herself in keeping not only his office, but his home, in order.

He tugged off his hat as he came in the back door. He looked even more weary than usual, covered in dust, his eyes dark-shadowed, his face needing a shave.

She glanced up from the pot of chili she was just taking off the stove and smiled. "Hi, boss. How about some chili and Mexican cornbread?"

"I'm hungry enough to even eat one of those damned salads," he said, glancing toward the stove. He was still wearing his chaps and the leather had a fine layer of dust over it. So did his arms and his dark face.

"If you'll sit down, I'll feed you."

"I need a bath first, honey," he remarked.

"You could rinse off your face and hands in the sink," she suggested, gesturing toward it. "There's a hand towel there, and some soap. You look like you might go to sleep in the shower."

He lifted an eyebrow. "I can just see you pulling me out."

She turned away. "I'd call Eddie or Bib."

"And if you couldn't find them?" he persisted, shedding the chaps on the floor.

"In that case," she said dryly, "I reckon you'd drown, tall man."

"Sassy lady," he accused. He moved behind her and

suddenly caught her by the waist with his lean, dark hands. He held her in front of him while he bent over her shoulder to smell the chili. She tried to breathe normally and failed. He was warm and strong at her back, and he smelled of the whole outdoors. She wanted to reach up and kiss that hard, masculine face, and her heart leaped at the uncharacteristic longing.

"What did you put in there?" he asked.

"One armadillo, two rattlers, a quart of beans, some tomatoes, and a hatful of jalapeño peppers."

His hands contracted, making her jump. "A hatful of jalapeño peppers would take the rust off my truck."

"Probably the tires, too," she commented, trying to keep her voice steady. "But Bib told me you Texans like your chili hot."

He turned her around to face him. He searched her eyes for a long, taut moment, and she felt her feet melting into the floor as she looked back. Something seemed to link them for that tiny space of time, joining them soul to soul for one explosive second. She heard him catch his breath and then she was free, all too soon.

"Would...would you like a glass of milk with this?" she asked after she'd served the chili into bowls and put it on the table, along with the sliced cornbread and some canned fruit.

"Didn't you make coffee?" he asked, glancing up.

"Sure. I just thought..."

"I don't need anything to put out the fire," he told her with a wicked smile. "I'm not a tenderfoot from *Jawja.*"

She moved to the coffeepot and poured two cups. She set his in front of him and sat down. "For your information, suh," she drawled, "we Georgians have been known to eat rattlesnakes while they were still wiggling. And an aunt of mine makes a barbecued sparerib dish that makes Texas chili taste like oatmeal by comparison."

"Is that so? Let's see." He dipped into his chili, savored it, put the spoon down, and glared at her. "You call this hot?" he asked.

She tasted hers and went into coughing spasms. While she was fanning her mouth wildly, he got up with a weary sigh, went to the cupboard, got a glass, and filled it with cold milk.

He handed it to her and sat back down, with a bottle of Tabasco sauce in his free hand. While she gulped milk, he poured half the contents of the bottle into his chili and then tasted it again.

"Just right." He grinned. "But next time, honey, it wouldn't hurt to add another handful of those peppers."

She made a sound between a moan and a gasp and drained the milk glass.

"Now, what were you saying about barbecued spareribs making chili taste like oatmeal?" he asked politely. "I especially liked the part about the rattlers…"

"Would you pass the cornbread, please?" she asked proudly.

"Don't you want the rest of your chili?" he returned.

"I'll eat it later," she said. "I made an apple pie for dessert."

He stifled a smile as he dug into his own chili. It got bigger when she shifted her chair so that she didn't have to watch him eat it.

CHAPTER FOUR

IT HAD BEEN a long time since Jennifer had been on a horse, but once Everett decided that she was going riding with him one morning, it was useless to argue.

"I'll fall off," she grumbled as she stared up at the palomino gelding he'd chosen for her. "Besides, I've got work to do."

"You've ironed every curtain in the house, washed everything that isn't tied down, scrubbed all the floors, and finished my paperwork. What's left?" he asked, hands low on his hips, his eyes mocking.

"I haven't started supper," she said victoriously.

"So we'll eat late," he replied. "Now, get on."

With a hard glare, she let him put her into the saddle. She was still weak, but her hair had begun to regain its earlier luster and her spirit was returning with a vengeance.

"Were you always so domineering, or did you take lessons?" she asked.

"It sort of comes naturally out here, honey," he told

her with a hard laugh. “You either get tough or you go broke.”

His eyes ran over her, from her short-sleeved button-up blue print blouse down to the legs of her worn jeans, and he frowned. “You could use some more clothes,” he observed.

“I used to have a closetful,” she sighed. “But in recent months my clothing budget has been pretty small. Anyway, I don’t need to dress up around here, do I?”

“You could use a pair of new jeans, at least,” he said. His lean hand slid along her thigh gently, where the material was almost see-through, and the touch quickened her pulse.

“Yours aren’t much better,” she protested, glancing down from his denim shirt to the jeans that outlined his powerful legs.

“I wear mine out fast,” he reminded her. “Ranching is tough on clothes.”

She knew that, having had to get four layers of mud off his several times. “Well, I don’t put mine to the same use. I don’t fix fences and pull calves and vet cattle.”

He lifted an eyebrow. His hand was still resting absently on her thin leg. “You work hard enough. If I didn’t already know it, I’d be told twice a day by Eddie or Bib.”

“I like your men,” she said.

“They like you. So do I,” he added on a smile. “You brighten up the place.”

But not as a woman, she thought, watching him. He was completely unaware of her sexually. Even when his eyes did wander over her, it was in an indifferent way. It disturbed her, oddly enough, that he didn't see her as a woman. Because she sure did see him as a man. That sensuous physique was playing on her nerves even now as she glanced down at it with a helpless appreciation.

"All we need is a violin," she murmured, grinning.

He stared up at her, but he didn't smile. "Your hair seems lighter," he remarked.

The oddest kind of pleasure swept through her. He'd noticed. She'd just washed it, and the dullness was leaving it. It shimmered with silvery lights where it peeked out from under her hat.

"I just washed it," she remarked.

He shook his head. "It never looked that way before."

"I wasn't healthy before," she returned. "I feel so much better out here," she remarked, sighing as she looked around, with happiness shining out of her like a beacon. "Oh, what a marvelous view! Poor city people."

He turned away and mounted his buckskin gelding. "Come on. I'll show you the bottoms. That's where I've got my new stock."

"Does it flood when it rains?" she asked. It was hard getting into the rhythm of the horse, but somehow she managed it.

"Yes, ma'am, it does," he assured her in a grim tone.

"Uncle Ben lost thirty head in a flood when I was a boy. I watched them wash away. Incredible, the force of the water when it's unleashed."

"It used to flood back home sometimes," she observed.

"Yes, but not like it does out here," he commented. "Wait until you've seen a Texas rainstorm, and you'll know what I mean."

"I grew up reading Zane Grey," she informed him. "I know all about dry washes and flash floods and stampeding."

"Zane Grey?" he asked, staring at her. "Well, I'll be."

"I told you I loved Texas," she said with a quick smile. She closed her eyes, letting the horse pick its own way beside his. "Just breathe that air," she said lazily. "Rett, I'll bet if you bottled it, you could get rich overnight!"

"I could get rich overnight by selling off oil leases if I wanted to," he said curtly. He lit a cigarette, without looking at her.

She felt as if she'd offended him. "Sorry," she murmured. "Did I hit a nerve?"

"A raw one," he agreed, glancing at her. "Bobby was forever after me about those leases."

"He never won," she said, grinning. "Did he?"

His broad shoulders shifted. "I thought about it once or twice, when times got hard. But it's like a cop-out. I want to make this place pay with cattle, not oil. I don't want my land tied up in oil rigs and pumps cluttering up my landscape." He gestured toward the horizon. "Not too far out there, Apaches used to camp. Santa Ana's troops cut through part of this property on their way to the Alamo. After that, the local cattlemen pooled their cattle here to start them up the Chisolm Trail. During the Civil War, Confederates passed through on their way to Mexico. There's one hell of a lot of history here, and I don't want to spoil it."

She was watching him when he spoke, and her eyes involuntarily lingered on his strong jaw, his sensuous mouth. "Yes," she said softly, "I can understand that."

He glanced at her over his cigarette and smiled. "Where did you grow up?" he asked curiously.

"In a small town in south Georgia," she recalled. "Edison, by name. It wasn't a big place, but it had a big heart. Open fields and lots of pines and a flat horizon like this out beyond it. It's mostly agricultural land there, with huge farms. My grandfather's was very small. Back in his day, it was cotton. Now it's peanuts and soybeans."

"How long did you live there?"

"Until I was around ten," she recalled. "Dad got a job in Atlanta, and we moved there. We lived better, but I never liked it as much as home."

"What did your father do?"

"He was an architect," she said, smiling. "A very good one, too. He added a lot to the city's skyline in his day." She glanced at him. "Your father…"

"I don't discuss him," he said matter-of-factly, with a level stare.

"Why?"

He drew in an impatient breath and reined in his horse to light another cigarette. He was chain smoking, something he rarely did. "I said, I don't discuss him."

"Sorry, boss," she replied, pulling her hat down over her eyes in an excellent imitation of tall, lean Bib as she mimicked his drawl. "I shore didn't mean to rile you."

His lips tugged up. He blew out a cloud of smoke and flexed his broad shoulders, rippling the fabric that covered them. "My father was an alcoholic, Jenny."

She knew that already, but she wasn't about to give Eddie away. Everett wouldn't like being gossiped about by his employees. "It must have been a rough childhood for you and Robert," she said innocently.

"Bobby was raised by Uncle Ben and Aunt Emma," he said. "Bobby and I inherited this place from them. They were fine people. Ben spent his life fighting to hold this property. It was a struggle for him to pay taxes. I helped him get into breeding Herefords when I moved in with them. I was just a green kid," he recalled, "all big ears and feet and gigantic ideas. Fifteen, and I had all the answers." He sighed, blowing out another cloud of smoke. "Now I'm almost thirty-five, and every day I come up short of new answers."

"Don't we all?" Jennifer said with a smile. "I was lucky, I suppose. My parents loved each other, and me, and we were well-off. I didn't appreciate it at the time. When I lost them it was a staggering blow." She leaned forward in the saddle to gaze at the horizon. "How about your mother?"

"A desperate woman, completely undomesticated," he said quietly. "She ran off with the first man who offered her an alternative to starvation. An insurance salesman," he scoffed. "Bobby was just a baby. She walked out the door and never looked back."

"I can't imagine a woman that callous," she said, glancing at him. "Do you ever hear from her now? Is she still alive?"

"I don't know. I don't care." He lifted the cigarette to his chiseled lips. His eyes cut around to meet hers, and they were cold with memory and pain. "I don't much like women."

She felt the impact of the statement to her toes. She knew why he didn't like women, that was the problem, but she was too intelligent to think that she could pry that far, to mention the city woman who'd dumped him because he was poor.

"It would have left scars, I imagine," she agreed.

"Let's ride." He stuck the cigarette between his lips and urged his mount into a gallop.

Riding beside him without difficulty now, Jennifer felt alive and vital. He was such a devastating man, she thought, glancing at him, so sensuous even in faded jeans and shirt. He was powerfully built, like an athlete, and she didn't imagine many men could compete with him.

"Have you ever ridden in rodeo competition?" she asked suddenly without meaning to.

He glanced at her and slowed his mount. "Have I what?"

"Ridden in rodeos?"

He chuckled. "What brought that on?"

"You're so big..."

He stopped his horse and stared at her, his wrists crossed over the pommel of his saddle. "Too big," he returned. "The best riders are lean and wiry."

"Oh."

"But in my younger days, I did some bareback riding and bulldogging. It was fun until I broke my arm in two places."

"I'll bet that slowed you down," she murmured dryly.

"It's about the only thing that ever did." He glanced at her rapt face. Live oaks and feathery mesquite trees and prickly pear cactus and wildflowers filled the long space to the horizon and Jennifer was staring at the landscape as if she'd landed in heaven. There were fences everywhere, enclosing pastures where Everett's white-faced Herefords grazed. The fences were old, graying and knotty and more like posts than neatly cut wood, with barbed wire stretched between them.

"Like what you see?" Everett mused.

"Oh, yes," she sighed. "I can almost see it the way it would have been a hundred and more years ago, when settlers and drovers and cattlemen and gunfighters came through here." She glanced at him. "Did you know that Dr. John Henry Holliday, better known as Doc, hailed from Valdosta, Georgia?" she added. "Or that he went west because the doctors said he'd die of tuberculosis if he didn't find a drier climate quick? Or that he and his cousin were supposed to be married, and when they found out about the TB, he went west and she joined a nunnery in Atlanta? And that he once backed down a gang of cowboys in Dodge City and saved Wyatt Earp's life?"

He burst out laughing. "My God, you do know your history, don't you?"

"There was this fantastic biography of Holliday by John Myers Myers," she told him. "It was the most exciting book I ever read. I wish I had a copy. I tried to get one once, but it was out of print."

"Isn't Holliday buried out West somewhere?" he asked.

"In Glenwood Springs, Colorado," she volunteered. "He had a standing bet that a bullet would get him before the TB did, but he lost. He died in a sanitarium out there. He always said he had the edge in gunfights, because he didn't care if he died—and most men did." She smiled. "He was a frail little man, not at all the way he's portrayed in films most of the time. He was blond and blue-eyed and most likely had a slow Southern drawl. Gunfighter, gambler, and heavy drinker he might have been, but he had some fine qualities, too, like loyalty and courage."

"We had a few brave men in Texas, too," he said, smoking his cigarette with a grin. "Some of them fought a little battle with a few thousand Mexicans in a Spanish mission in San Antonio."

"Yes, in the Alamo," she said, grinning. "In 1836, and some of those men were from Georgia."

He burst out laughing. "I can't catch you out on anything, can I?"

"I'm proud of my state," she told him. "Even though Texas does feel like home, too. If my grandfather hadn't come back, I might have been born here."

"Why did he go back?" he asked, curious.

"I never knew," she said. "But I expect he got into trouble. He was something of a hell-raiser even when I knew him." She recalled the little old man sitting astride a chair in her mother's kitchen, relating hair-raising escapes from the Germans during World War I while he smoked his pipe. He'd died when she was fourteen, and she still remembered going to Edison for the funeral, to a cemetery near Fort Gaines where Spanish moss fell from the trees. It had been a quiet place, a fitting place for the old gentleman to be laid to rest. In his home country. Under spreading oak trees.

"You miss him," Everett said quietly.

"Yes."

"My Uncle Ben was something like that," he murmured, lifting his eyes to the horizon. "He had a big heart and a black temper. Sometimes it was hard to see the one for the other," he added with a short laugh. "I idolized him. He had nothing, but he bowed to no man. He'd have approved of what I'm doing with this place. He'd have fought the quick money, too. He liked a challenge."

And so, she would have bet, did his nephew. She couldn't picture Everett Culhane liking anything that came too easily. He would have loved living in the nineteenth century, when a man could build an empire.

"You'd have been right at home here in the middle eighteen hundreds," she remarked, putting the thought into words. "Like John Chisum, you'd have built an empire of your own."

"Think so?" he mused. He glanced at her. "What do you think I'm trying to do now?"

"The same thing," she murmured. "And I'd bet you'll succeed."

He looked her over. "Would you?" His eyes caught hers and held them for a long moment before he tossed his cigarette onto the ground and stepped down out of the saddle to grind it under his boot.

A sudden sizzling sound nearby shocked Jennifer, but it did something far worse to the horse she was riding. The gelding suddenly reared up, and when it came back down again it was running wild.

She pulled back feverishly on the reins, but the horse wouldn't break its speed at all. "Whoa!" she yelled into its ear. "Whoa, you stupid animal!"

Finally, she leaned forward and hung on to the reins and the horse's mane at the same time, holding on with her knees as well. It was a wild ride, and she didn't have time to worry about whether or not she was going to survive it. In the back of her mind she recalled Everett's sudden shout, but nothing registered after that.

The wind bit into her face, her hair came loose from its neat bun. She closed her eyes and began to pray. The jolting pressure was hurting, actually jarring her bones. If only she could keep from falling off!

She heard a second horse gaining on them, then, and she knew that everything would be all right. All she had to do was hold on until Everett could get to her.

But at that moment, the runaway gelding came to a fence and suddenly began to slow down. He balked at the fence, but Jennifer didn't. She sailed right over the animal's head to land roughly on her back in the pasture on the other side of the barbed wire.

The breath was completely knocked out of her. She lay there staring up at leaves and blue sky, feeling as if she'd never get a lungful of air again.

Nearby, Everett was cursing steadily, using words she'd never heard before, even from angry clients back in New York City. She saw his face come slowly into focus above her and was fascinated by its paleness. His eyes were colorful enough, though, like brown flames glittering at her.

"Not…my…fault," she managed to protest in a thin voice.

"I know that," he growled. "It was mine. Damned rattler, and me without my gun…"

"It didn't…bite you?" she asked apprehensively, her eyes widening with fear.

He blew out a short breath and chuckled. "No, it

didn't. Sweet Jenny. Half dead in a fall, and you're worried about me. You're one in a million, honey."

He bent down beside her. "Hurt anywhere?" he asked gently.

"All over," she said. "Can't get…my breath."

"I'm not surprised. Damned horse. We'll put him in your next batch of chili, I promise," he said on a faint smile. "Let's see how much damage you did."

His lean, hard hands ran up and down her legs and arms, feeling for breaks. "How about your back?" he asked, busy with his task.

"Can't…feel it yet."

"You will," he promised ruefully.

She was still just trying to breathe. She'd heard of people having the breath knocked out of them, but never knew what it was until now. Her eyes searched Everett's quietly.

"Am I dead?" she asked politely.

"Not quite." He brushed the hair away from her cheeks. "Feel like sitting up?"

"If you'll give me a hand, I'll try," she said huskily.

He raised her up and that was when she noticed that her blouse had lost several buttons, leaving her chest quite exposed. And today of all days she hadn't worn a bra.

Her hands went protectively to the white curves of her breasts, which were barely covered.

"None of that," he chided. "We don't have that kind of relationship. I'm not going to embarrass you by staring. Now get up."

That was almost the final blow. Even half dressed, he still couldn't accept her as a woman. She wanted to sit down on the grass and bawl. It wouldn't have done any good, but it might have eased the sudden ache in her heart.

She let him help her to her feet and staggered unsteadily on them. Her pale eyes glanced toward the gelding, now happily grazing in the pasture across the fence.

"First," she sputtered, "I'm going to dig a deep pit. Then I'm going to fill it with six-foot rattlesnakes. Then I'm going to get a backhoe and shove that stupid horse in there!"

"Wouldn't you rather eat him?" he offered.

"On second thought, I'll gain weight," she muttered. "Lots of it. And I'll ride him two hours every morning."

"You could use a few pounds," he observed, studying her thinness. "You're almost frail."

"I'm not," she argued. "I'm just puny, remember? I'll get better."

"I guess you already have," he murmured dryly. "You sure do get through the housework."

"Slowly but surely," she agreed. She tugged her blouse together and tied the bottom edges together.

When she looked back up, his eyes were watching her hands with a strange, intent stare. He looked up and met her puzzled gaze.

"Are you okay now?" he asked.

"Just a little shaky," she murmured with a slight grin.

"Come here." He bent and lifted her easily into his

arms, shifting her weight as he turned, and walked toward the nearby gate in the fence.

She was shocked by her reaction to being carried by him. She felt ripples of pleasure washing over her body like fire, burning where his chest touched her soft breasts. Even through two layers of fabric, the contact was wildly arousing, exciting. She clamped her teeth together hard to keep from giving in to the urge to grind her body against his. He was a man, after all, and not invulnerable. She could start something that she couldn't stop.

"I'm too heavy," she protested once.

"No," he said gently, glancing down into her eyes unsmilingly. "You're like feathers. Much too light."

"Most women would seem light to you," she murmured, lowering her eyes to his shirt. Where the top buttons were undone, she saw the white of his T-shirt and the curl of dark, thick hair. He smelled of leather and wind and tobacco and she wanted so desperately to curl up next to him and kiss that hard, chiseled mouth…

"Open the gate," he said, nodding toward the latch.

She reached out and unfastened it, and pushed until it came free of the post. He went through and let her fasten it again. When she finished, she noticed that his gaze had fallen to her body. She followed it, embarrassed to find that the edges of her blouse gapped so much, that one creamy pink breast was completely bare to his eyes.

Her hand went slowly to the fabric, tugging it into place. "Sorry," she whispered self-consciously.

"So am I. I didn't mean to stare," he said quietly, shifting her closer to his chest. "Don't be embarrassed, Jenny."

She drew in a slow breath, burying her red face in his throat. He stiffened before he drew her even closer, his arms tautening until she was crushed to his broad, warm chest.

He didn't say a word as he walked, and neither did she. But she could feel the hard beat of his heart, the ragged sigh of his breath, the stiffening of his body against her taut breasts. In ways she'd never expected, her body sang to her, exquisite songs of unknown pleasure, of soft touches and wild contact. Her hands clung to Everett's neck, her eyes closed. She wanted this to last forever.

All too soon, they reached the horses. Everett let her slide down his body in a much too arousing way, so that she could feel the impact of every single inch of him on the way to the ground. And then, his arms contracted, holding her, bringing her into the length of him, while his cheek rested on her hair and the wind blew softly around them.

She clung, feeling the muscles of his back tense under her hands, loving the strength and warmth and scent of him. She'd never wanted anything so much as she wanted this closeness. It was sweet and heady and satisfying in a wild new way.

Seconds later, he let her go, just as she imagined she felt a fine tremor in his arms.

"Are you all right?" he asked softly.

"Yes," she said, trying to smile, but she couldn't look up at him. It had been intimate, that embrace. As intimate as a kiss in some ways, and it had caused an unexpected shift in their relationship.

"We'd better get back," he said. "I've got work to do."

"So have I," she said quickly, mounting the gelding with more apprehension than courage. "All right, you ugly horse," she told it. "You do that to me again, and I'll back the pickup truck over you!"

The horse's ears perked up and it moved its head slightly to one side. She burst into laughter. "See, Rett, he heard me!"

But Everett wasn't looking her way. He'd already turned his mount and was smoking another cigarette. And all the way back to the house, he didn't say a word.

As they reached the yard she felt uncomfortably tense. To break the silence, she broached a subject she'd had on her mind all day.

"Rett, could I have a bucket of paint?"

He stared at her. "What?"

"Can I have a bucket of paint?" she asked. "Just one. I want to paint the kitchen."

"Now, look, lady," he said, "I hired you to cook and do housework and type." His eyes narrowed and she fought not to let her fallen spirits show. "I like my house the way it is, with no changes."

"Just one little bucket of paint," she murmured.

"No."

She glared at him, but he glared back just as hard. "If you want to spend money," he said curtly, "I'll buy you a new pair of jeans. But we aren't throwing money away on decorating." He made the word sound insulting.

"Decorating is an art," she returned, defending her professional integrity. She was about to tell him what she'd done for a living, but as she opened her mouth, he was speaking again.

"It's a high-class con game," he returned hotly. "And even if I had the money, I wouldn't turn one of those fools loose on my house. Imagine paying out good money to let some tasteless idiot wreck your home and charge you a fortune to do it!" He leaned forward in the saddle with a belligerent stare. "No paint. Do we understand each other, Miss King?"

Do we ever, she thought furiously. Her head lifted. "You'd be lucky to get a real decorator in here, anyway," she flung back. "One who wouldn't faint at the way you combine beautiful old oriental rugs with ashtrays made of old dead rattlesnakes!"

His dark eyes glittered dangerously. "It's my house," he said coldly.

"Thank God!" she threw back.

"If you don't like it, close your eyes!" he said. "Or pack your damned bag and go back to Atlanta and turn your nose up…"

"I'm not turning my nose up!" she shouted. "I just wanted a bucket of paint!"

"You know when you'll get it, too, don't you?" he taunted. He tipped his hat and rode off, leaving her fuming on the steps.

Yes, she knew. His eyes had told her, graphically. When hell froze over. She remembered in the back of her mind that there was a place called Hell, and once it did freeze over and made national headlines. She only wished she'd saved the newspaper clipping. She'd shove it under his arrogant nose, and maybe then she'd get her paint!

She turned to go into the house, stunned to find Eddie coming out the front door.

He looked red-faced, but he doffed his hat. "Mornin', ma'am," he murmured. "I was just putting the mail on the table."

"Thanks, Eddie," she said with a wan smile.

He stared at her. "Boss lost his temper, I see."

"Yep," she agreed.

"Been a number of days before when he's done that."

"Yep."

"You going to keep it all to yourself, too, ain't you?"

"Yep."

He chuckled, tipped his hat, and went on down the steps. She walked into the house and burst out laughing. She was getting the hang of speaking Texan at last.

CHAPTER FIVE

JENNIFER SPENT the rest of the day feverishly washing down the kitchen walls. So decorators were con artists, were they? And he wouldn't turn one loose in his home, huh? She was so enraged that the mammoth job took hardly any time at all. Fortunately, the walls had been done with oil-based paint, so the dirt and grease came off without taking the paint along with them. When she was through, she stood back, worn out and damp with sweat, to survey her handiwork. She had the fan going full blast, but it was still hot and sticky, and she felt the same way herself. The pale yellow walls looked new, making the effort worthwhile.

Now, she thought wistfully, if she only had a few dollars' worth of fabric and some thread, and the use of the aging sewing machine upstairs, she could make curtains for the windows. She could even buy that out of her own pocket, and the interior-decorator-hating Mr. Everett Donald Culhane could just keep his nasty opinions to himself. She laughed, wondering what he'd have said if she'd used his full name while they were riding. Bib had told her his middle name. She wondered if anyone ever called him Donald.

She fixed a light supper of creamed beef and broccoli, remembering that he'd told her he hated both of those dishes. She deliberately made weak coffee. Then she sat down in the kitchen and pared apples while she waited for him to come home. Con artist, huh?

It was getting dark when he walked in the door. He was muddy and tired-looking, and in his lean, dark hand was a small bouquet of slightly wilted wildflowers.

"Here," he said gruffly, tossing them onto the kitchen table beside her coffee cup. The mad profusion of bluebonnets and Indian paintbrush and Mexican hat made blue and orange and red swirls of color on the white tablecloth. "And you can have your damned bucket of paint."

He strode past her toward the staircase, his face hard and unyielding, without looking back. She burst into tears, her fingers trembling as they touched the unexpected gift.

Never in her life had she moved so fast. She dried her tears and ran to pour out the pot of weak coffee. She put on a pot of strong, black coffee and dragged out bacon and eggs and flour, then put the broccoli and chipped beef, covered, into the refrigerator.

By the time Everett came back down, showered and

in clean denims, she had bacon and eggs and biscuits on the table.

"I thought you might like something fresh and hot for supper," she said quickly.

He glanced at her as he sat down. "I'm surprised. I was expecting liver and onions or broccoli tonight."

She flushed and turned her back. "Were you? How strange." She got the coffeepot and calmly filled his cup and her own. "Thank you for my flowers," she said without looking at him.

"Don't start getting ideas, Miss King," he said curtly, reaching for a biscuit. "Just because I backed down on the paint, don't expect it to become a habit around here."

She lowered her eyes demurely to the platter of eggs she was dishing up. "Oh, no, sir," she said.

He glanced around the room and his eyes darkened, glittered. They came back to her. He laid down his knife. "Did you go ahead and buy paint?" he asked in a softly menacing tone.

"No, I did not," she replied curtly. "I washed down the walls."

He blinked. "Washed down the walls?" He looked around again, scowling. "In this heat?"

"Look good, don't they?" she asked fiercely, smiling. "I don't need the paint, but thank you anyway."

He picked up his fork, lifting a mouthful of eggs slowly to his mouth. He finished his supper before he spoke again. "Why did it matter so much about the walls?" he asked. "The house is old. It needs thousands of dollars' worth of things I can't afford to have done. Painting one room is only going to make the others look worse."

She shrugged. "Old habits," she murmured with a faint smile. "I've been fixing up houses for a long time."

That went right past him. He looked preoccupied. Dark and brooding.

"Is something wrong?" she asked suddenly.

He sighed and pulled an envelope from his pocket and tossed it onto the table. "I found that on the hall table on my way upstairs."

She frowned. "What is it?"

"A notice that the first payment is due on the note I signed at the bank for my new bull." He laughed shortly. "I can't meet it. My tractor broke down and I had to use the money for the payment to fix it. Can't plant without the tractor. Can't feed livestock without growing feed. Ironically, I may have to sell the bull to pay back the money."

Her heart went out to him. Here she sat giving him the devil over a bucket of paint, and he was in serious trouble. She felt terrible.

"I ought to be shot," she murmured quietly. "I'm sorry I made such a fuss about the paint, Rett."

He laughed without humor. "You didn't know. I told you times were hard."

"Yes. But I didn't realize how hard until now." She sipped her coffee. "How much do you need…can I ask?" she asked softly.

He sighed. "Six hundred dollars." He shook his head. "I thought I could swing it, I really did. I wanted to pay it off fast."

"I've got last week's salary," she said. "I haven't spent any of it. That would help a little. And you could hold back this week's..."

He stared into her wide, soft eyes and smiled. "You're quite a girl, Jenny."

"I want to help."

"I know. I appreciate it. But spend your money on yourself. At any rate, honey, it would hardly be a drop in the bucket. I've got a few days to work it out. I'll turn up something."

He got up and left the table and Jennifer stared after him, frowning. Well, she could help. There had to be an interior-design firm in Houston, which was closer than San Antonio or Austin. She'd go into town and offer her services. With any luck at all, they'd be glad of her expert help. She could make enough on one job to buy Everett's blessed bull outright. She was strong enough now to take on the challenge of a single job. And she would!

As luck would have it, the next morning Eddie mentioned that his wife, Libby, was going to drive into the city to buy a party dress for his daughter. Jennifer hitched a ride with her after Everett went to work.

Libby was a talker, a blond bearcat of a woman with a fine sense of humor. She was good company, and Jennifer took to her immediately.

"I'm so glad Everett's got you to help around the

house," she said as they drove up the long highway to Houston. "I offered, but he wouldn't hear of it. Said I had enough to do, what with raising four kids. He even looks better since you've been around. And he doesn't cuss as much." She grinned.

"I was so delighted to have the job," Jennifer sighed, smiling. She brushed back a stray wisp of blond hair. She was wearing her best blue camisole with a simple navy blue skirt and her polished white sling pumps with a white purse. She looked elegant, and Libby remarked on it.

"Where are you going, all dressed up?" she asked.

"To get a second job," Jennifer confessed. "But you mustn't tell Everett. I want to surprise him."

Libby looked worried. "You're not leaving?"

"Oh, no! Not until he makes me! This is only a temporary thing," she promised.

"Doing what?"

"Decorating."

"That takes a lot of schooling, doesn't it?" Libby asked, frowning.

"Quite a lot. I graduated from interior-design school in New York," Jennifer explained. "And I worked in the field for two years. My health gave out and I had to give it up for a while." She sighed. "There was so much pressure, you see. So much competition. My nerves got raw and my resistance got low, and I wound up flat on my back in a hospital with pneumonia. I went home to Atlanta to recuperate, got a job with a temporary talent agency, and met Robert Culhane on an assignment. He offered me a job, and I grabbed it. Getting to work in Texas was pretty close to heaven, for me."

Libby shook her head. "Imagine that."

"I was sorry about Robert," Jennifer said quietly. "I only knew him slightly, but I did like him. Everett still broods about it. He doesn't say much, but I know he misses his brother."

"He was forever looking out for Bobby," Libby confirmed. "Protecting him and such. A lot of the time, Bobby didn't appreciate that. And Bobby didn't like living low. He wanted Everett to sell off those oil rights and get rich. Everett wouldn't."

"I don't blame him," Jennifer said. "If it was my land, I'd feel the same way."

Libby looked surprised. "My goodness, another one."

"I don't like strip-mining, either," Jennifer offered. "Or killing baby seals for their fur or polluting the rivers."

Libby burst out laughing. "You and Everett were made for each other. He's just that way himself." She glanced at Jennifer as the Houston skyline came into view. "Did Bobby tell you what Everett did the day the oil man came out here to make him that offer, after the geologists found what they believed was oil-bearing land?"

"No."

"The little oil man wanted to argue about it, and

Everett had just been thrown by a horse he was trying to saddle-break and was in a mean temper. He told the man to cut it off, and he wouldn't. So Everett picked him up," she said, grinning, "carried him out to his car, put him in, and walked away. We haven't seen any oil men at the ranch since."

Jennifer laughed. It sounded like Everett, all right. She sat back, sighing, and wondered how she was going to make him take the money she hoped to earn. Well, that worry could wait in line. First, she had to find a job.

While Libby went into the store, Jennifer found a telephone directory and looked up the addresses of two design shops. The first one was nearby, so she stopped to arrange a time and place to rendezvous with Libby that afternoon, and walked the two blocks.

She waited for fifteen minutes to see the man who owned the shop. He listened politely, but impatiently, while she gave her background. She mentioned the name of the firm she'd worked with in New York, and saw his assistant's eyebrows jump up. But the manager was obviously not impressed. He told her he was sorry but he was overstaffed already.

Crestfallen, she walked out and called a taxi to take her to the next company. This time, she had better luck. The owner was a woman, a veritable Amazon, thin and dark and personable. She gave Jennifer a cup of coffee, listened to her credentials, and grinned.

"Lucky me." She laughed. "To find you just when I was desperate for one more designer!"

"You mean, you can give me work?" Jennifer burst out, delighted.

"Just this one job, right now, but it could work into a full-time position," she promised.

"Part-time would be great. You see, I already have a job I'd rather not leave," Jennifer replied.

"Perfect. You can do this one in days. It's only one room. I'll give you the address, and you can go and see the lady yourself. Where are you staying?"

"Just north of Victoria," Jennifer said. "In Big Spur."

"How lovely!" the lady said. "The job's in Victoria! No transportation problem?"

She thought of asking Libby, and smiled. "I have a conspirator," she murmured. "I think I can manage." She glanced up. "Can you estimate my commission?"

Her new employer did, and Jennifer grinned. It would be more than enough for Everett to pay off his note. "Okay!"

"The client, Mrs. Whitehall, doesn't mind paying for quality work," came the lilting reply. "And she'll be tickled when she hears the background of her designer. I'll give her a ring now, if you like."

"Would I! Miss...Mrs...Ms...?"

"Ms. Sally Ward," the owner volunteered. "I'm glad to meet you, Jennifer King. Now, let's get busy."

Libby was overjoyed when she heard what Jennifer was plotting, and volunteered to drive her back and forth to the home she'd be working on. She even agreed to pinch-hit in the house, so that Everett wouldn't know what was going on. It would be risky, but Jennifer felt it would be very much worth the risk.

As it turned out, Mrs. Whitehall was an elderly lady with an unlimited budget and a garage full of cars. She was more than happy to lend one to Jennifer so that she could drive back and forth to Victoria to get fabric and wallcoverings and to make appointments with painters and carpet-layers.

Jennifer made preliminary drawings after an interview with Mrs. Whitehall, who lived on an enormous estate called Casa Verde.

"My son Jason and his wife, Amanda, used to live with me," Mrs. Whitehall volunteered. "But since their marriage, they've built a house of their own farther down the road. They're expecting their first child. Jason wants a boy and Amanda a girl." She grinned. "From the size of her, I'm expecting twins!"

"When is she due?" Jennifer asked.

"Any day," came the answer. "Jason spends part of the time pacing the floor and the other part daring Amanda to lift, move, walk, or breathe hard." She laughed delightedly. "You'd have to know my son, Miss King, to realize how out of character that is for him. Jason was always such a calm person until Amanda got pregnant. I think it's been harder on him than it has on her."

"Have they been married long?"

"Six years," Mrs. Whitehall said. "So happily. They wanted a child very much, but it took a long time for Amanda to become pregnant. It's been all the world to them, this baby." She stared around the room at the fading wallpaper and the worn carpet. "I've just put this room off for so long. Now I don't feel I can wait any longer to have it done. Once the baby comes, I'll have so many other things to think of. What do you suggest, my dear?"

"I have some sketches," Jennifer said, drawing out her portfolio.

Mrs. Whitehall looked over them, sighing. "Just what I wanted. Just exactly what I wanted." She nodded. "Begin whenever you like, Jennifer. I'll find somewhere else to sit while the workmen are busy."

And so it began. Jennifer spent her mornings at Casa Verde, supervising the work. Afternoons she worked at Everett's ranch. And amazingly, she never got caught.

It only took a few days to complete the work. Luckily, she found workmen who were between jobs and could take on a small project. By the end of the week, it was finished.

"I can't tell you how impressed I am." Mrs. Whitehall sighed as she studied the delightful new decor, done in soft green and white and dark green.

"It will be even lovelier when the furniture is delivered tomorrow." Jennifer grinned. "I'm so proud of it. I hope you like it half as much as I do."

"I do, indeed," Mrs. Whitehall said. "I…"

The ringing of the phone halted her. She picked up the extension at her side. "Hello?" She sat up straight. "Yes, Jason! When?" She laughed, covering the receiver. "It's a boy!" She moved her hand. "What are you going to name him? Oh, yes, I like that very much. Joshua Brand Whitehall. Yes, I do. How is Amanda? Yes, she's tough, all right. Dear, I'll be there in thirty minutes. Now you calm down, dear. Yes, I know it isn't every day a man has a son. I'll seen you soon. Yes, dear."

She hung up. "Jason's beside himself," she said, smiling. "He wanted a boy so much. And they can have others. Amanda will get her girl yet. I must rush."

Jennifer stood up. "Congratulations on that new grandbaby," she said. "And I've enjoyed working with you very much."

"I'll drop you off at the ranch on my way," Mrs. Whitehall offered.

"It's a good little way," Jennifer began, wondering how she'd explain it to Everett. Mrs. Whitehall drove a Mercedes-Benz.

"Nonsense." Mrs. Whitehall laughed. "It's no trouble at all. Anyway, I want to talk to you about doing some more rooms. This is delightful. Very creative. I never enjoyed redecorating before, but you make it exciting."

After that, how could Jennifer refuse? She got in the car.

Luckily enough, Everett wasn't in sight when she reached the ranch. Mrs. Whitehall let her out at the steps and Jennifer rushed inside, nervous and wild-eyed. But the house was empty. She almost collapsed with relief. And best of all, on the hall table was an envelope addressed to her from Houston, from the interior-design agency. She tore it open and found a check and a nice letter offering more work. The check was for the amount Everett needed, plus a little. Jennifer endorsed it, grinning, and went in to fix supper.

CHAPTER SIX

EVERETT CAME home just before dark, but he didn't come into the house. Jennifer had a light supper ready, just cold cuts and bread so there wouldn't be anything to reheat. When he didn't appear after she heard the truck stop, she went out to look for him.

He was standing by the fence, staring at the big Hereford bull he'd wanted so badly. Jennifer stood on the porch and watched him, her heart aching for him. She'd decided already to cash her check first thing in the morning and give it to him at breakfast. But she wondered if she should mention it now. He looked so alone…

She moved out into the yard, the skirt of her blue shirtwaist dress blowing in the soft, warm breeze.

"Rett?" she called.

He glanced at her briefly. "Waiting supper on me again?" he asked quietly.

"No. I've only made cold cuts." She moved to the fence beside him and stared at the big, burly bull. "He sure is big."

"Yep." He took out a cigarette and lit it, blowing out a cloud of smoke. He looked very western in his worn jeans, batwing chaps, and close-fitting denim shirt, which was open halfway down his chest. He was a sensuous man, and she loved looking at him. Her eyes went up to his hard mouth and she wondered for what seemed the twentieth time how it would feel on her own. That made her burn with embarrassment, and she turned away.

"Suppose I offered you what I've saved?" she asked.

"We've been through all that. No. Thank you," he added. "I can't go deeper in debt, not even to save my bull. I'll just pay off the note and start over. The price of beef is expected to start going up in a few months. I'll stand pat until it does."

"Did anyone ever tell you that you have a double dose of pride?" she asked, exasperated.

He looked down at her, his eyes shadowed in the dusk by the brim of his hat. "Look who's talking about pride, for God's sake," he returned. "Don't I remember that you tried to walk back to town carrying a suitcase and a typewriter in the blazing sun with no hat? I had to threaten to tie you in the truck to get you inside it."

"I knew you didn't want me here," she said simply. "I didn't want to become a nuisance."

"I don't think I can imagine that. You being a nuisance, I mean." He took another draw from the cigarette and crushed it out. "I've had a good offer for the bull from one of my neighbors. He's coming over tomorrow to talk to me about it."

Well, that gave her time to cash the check and make one last effort to convince him, she thought.

"Why are you wearing a dress?" he asked, staring down at her. "Trying to catch my eye, by any chance?"

"Who, me?" she laughed. "As you told me the other day, we don't have that kind of relationship."

"You were holding me pretty hard that day the rattlesnake spooked your horse," he said unexpectedly, and he didn't smile. "And you didn't seem to mind too much that I saw you without your shirt."

She felt the color work its way into her hairline. "I'd better put supper on the…oh!"

He caught her before she could move away and brought her gently against the length of his body. His hand snaked around her waist, holding her there, and the other one spread against her throat, arching it.

"Just stand still," he said gently. "And don't start anything. I know damned good and well you're a virgin. I'm not going to try to seduce you."

Her breath was trapped somewhere below her windpipe. She felt her knees go wobbly as she saw the narrowness of his eyes, the hard lines of his face. She'd wanted it so much, but now that it was happening, she was afraid.

She stilled and let her fingers rest over his shirt, but breathing had become difficult. He felt strong and warm and she wanted to touch his hair-roughened skin. It looked so tantalizing to her innocent eyes.

He was breathing slowly, steadily. His thumb nudged

her chin up so that he could look into her eyes. "You let me look at you," he said under his breath. "I've gone half mad remembering that, wondering how many other men have seen you that way."

"No one has," she replied quietly. She couldn't drag her eyes from his. She could feel his breath, taste the smokiness of it, smell the leather and tobacco smells of his big, hard body so close to hers. "Only you."

His chest rose heavily. "Only me?"

"I was career-minded," she said hesitantly. "I didn't want commitment, so I didn't get involved. Everett…"

"No. I don't want to fight." He took her hands and slid them up and down over the hard muscles of his chest. His breathing changed suddenly.

He bent and drew her lower lip down with the soft pressure of his thumb. He fit his own mouth to it with exquisite patience, opening it slowly, tempting it, until she stood very still and closed her eyes.

His free hand brought her body close against his. The other one slowly undid the top two buttons of her dress and moved inside to her throat, her shoulder, her collarbone. His mouth increased its ardent pressure as his fingers spread, and his breathing became suddenly ragged as he arched her body and found the soft rise of her breast with his whole hand.

She gasped and instinctively caught his wrist. But he lifted his mouth and looked into her eyes and slowly shook his head. "You're old enough to be taught this," he said quietly. "I know how delicate you are here," he breathed, brushing his fingers over the thin lace. "I'm going to be very gentle, and you're going to enjoy what I do to you. I promise. Close your eyes, honey."

His mouth found hers again, even as he stopped speaking. It moved tenderly on her trembling lips, nibbling, demanding, in a silence bursting with new sensations and promise.

She clung to his shirtfront, shocked to find that her legs were trembling against his, that her breath was coming quick enough to be audible. She tried to pull away, but his fingers slid quietly under the bra and found bare, vulnerable skin, and she moaned aloud.

Her nails bit into his chest. "Rett!" she gasped, on fire with hunger and frightened and embarrassed that he could see and feel her reaction to him.

"Shh," he whispered at her mouth, gentling her. "It's all right. It's all right to let me see. You're so sweet, Jenny Wren. Like a bright new penny without a single fingerprint except mine." His mouth touched her closed eyelids, her forehead. His fingers contracted gently, his palm feeling the exquisite tautening of her body as she clung to him and shuddered. "Yes, you like that, don't you?" he breathed. His mouth brushed her eyelids again, her nose, her mouth. "Jenny, put your hand inside my shirt."

His voice was deep and low and tender. She obeyed him blindly, on fire with reckless hunger, needing to touch and taste and feel him. Her hands slid under his shirt and flattened on hair and warm muscle, and he tautened.

"Does that…make you feel the way…I feel?" she whispered shakily, looking up at him.

"Exactly," he whispered back. He moved his hand from her breast to her neck and pressed her face slowly against his bare chest.

She seemed to sense what he wanted. Her mouth touched him there tentatively, shyly, and he moaned. He smelled of faint cologne and tobacco, and she liked the way his hard muscles contracted where she touched them with her hands and her lips. He was all man. All man. And her world was suddenly narrowed to her senses, and Everett.

He took her face in his hands and tilted it, bending to kiss her with a hungry ferocity that would have frightened her minutes before. But she went on tiptoe and linked her arms around his neck and gave him back the kiss, opening her mouth under his to incite him to further intimacy, shivering wildly when he accepted the invitation and his tongue went into the sweet darkness in a slow, hungry tasting.

When he finally released her, he was shaking too. His eyes burned with frustrated desire, his hands framed her face, hot and hard.

"We have to stop. Now."

She took a slow, steadying breath. "Yes."

He took his hands away and moved toward the house, lighting a cigarette eventually after two fumbles.

She followed him, drunk on sensual pleasure, awed by what she'd felt with him, by what she'd let him do.

She felt shy when they got into the house, into the light, and she couldn't quite meet his eyes.

"I'll get supper on the table," she said.

He didn't even reply. He followed her into the kitchen, and with brooding dark eyes watched her move around.

She poured coffee and he sat down, still watching her.

Her hands trembled as she put the cream pitcher beside his cup. He caught her fingers, looking up at her with a dark, unsmiling stare.

"Don't start getting self-conscious with me," he said quietly. "I know you've never let another man touch you like that. I'm proud that you let me."

She stared at him, eyes widening. Of all the things she'd expected he might say, that wasn't one of them.

His nostrils flared and his hand contracted. "After supper," he said slowly, holding her eyes, "I'm going to carry you into the living room and lay you down on the sofa. And I'm going to make love to you, in every way I know. And when I get through, you'll shudder at the thought of another man's hands on you."

His eyes were blazing, and her own kindled. Her lips parted. "Rett, I can't…you know."

He nodded. "We won't go that far." His fingers caressed her wrist and his face hardened. "How hungry are you?" he asked under his breath.

Her heart was beating wildly. She looked at him and it was suicide. She felt shaky to her toes.

"Make love to me," she whispered blindly as she reached for him.

He twisted her down across his lap and found her mouth in a single motion. He groaned as he kissed her, his breath sighing out raggedly.

"Oh, God, I need you," he ground out, standing with her in his arms. "I need you so much!"

He turned, still kissing her, and carried her through into the living room, putting her gently down on the worn couch. After giving her a hot stare, he turned and methodically drew all the curtains and closed and locked the door. Then he came back, sitting down so that he was facing her.

"Now," he whispered, bending with trembling hands to the bodice of her dress. "Now, let's see how much damage we can do to each other's self-control, Jenny Wren. I want to look at you until I ache to my toes!"

He unbuttoned it and she sank back against the pillows, watching unprotestingly. He half lifted her and slipped the dress down her arms. Her bra followed it. And then he leaned over her, just looking at the soft mounds he'd uncovered.

His fingers stroked one perfect breast, lingering on the tip until she cried out.

"Does that hurt?" he whispered, looking into her eyes.

She was trembling, and it was hard to talk. "No," she breathed.

He smiled slowly, in a tender, purely masculine way, and repeated the brushing caress. She arched up, and his eyes blazed like dark fires.

"Jenny!" he growled. His fingers held her breasts up

to his hard mouth. He took her by surprise, and she moaned wildly as she felt the warm moistness envelop her. Her hands dug into his hair and she dragged his head closer, whimpering as if she were being tortured.

"Not so hard, baby," he whispered raggedly, lifting his head. "You're too delicate for that, Jenny."

"Rett," she moaned, her eyes wild.

"Like this, then," he whispered, bending to grind his mouth into hers. His hand swallowed her, stroking, molding, and she trembled all over as if with a fever, clinging to him, needing something more than this, something closer, something far, far more intimate….

Her hands moved against his chest, trembling as they explored the hard muscles.

"Be still now," he whispered, easing her back into the cushions. "Don't move under me. Just lie still, Jenny Wren, and let me show you…how bodies kiss."

She held her breath as his body moved completely onto hers. She felt the blatant maleness of it, the warmth, the tickle of hair against her soft breasts, the exquisite weight, and her hungry eyes looked straight into his as they joined.

"Oh," she whispered jerkily.

"Sweet, sweet Jenny," he breathed, cupping her face in his hands. "It's like moving on velvet. Do you feel me…all of me?"

"Yes." Her own hands went to his back, found their way under his shirt. "Rett, you're very heavy," she said with a shaky smile.

"Too heavy?" he whispered.

"Oh, no," she said softly. "I…like the way it feels."

"So do I." He bent and kissed her, tenderly, in a new and delicious way. "Not afraid?"

"No."

"You will be," he whispered softly. His hands moved down, sliding under her hips. He lifted his head and looked down at her just as his fingers contracted and ground her hips up into his in an intimacy that made her gasp and cry out.

He shuddered, and she buried her face in his hot throat, dizzy and drowning in deep water, burning with exquisite sensation and blinding pleasure.

"Jenny," he groaned. His hands hurt. "Jenny, Jenny, if you weren't a virgin, I'd take you. I'd take you, here, now, in every way there is…!"

She barely heard him, she was shaking so badly. All at once, he eased himself down beside her and folded her into his arms in a strangely protective way. His hands smoothed her back, his lips brushed over her face in tiny, warm kisses. All the passion was suddenly gone, and he was comforting her.

"I never believed…what my mother used to say about…passion," Jenny whispered at his ear, still trembling. "Rett, it's exquisite…isn't it? So explosive and sweet and dangerous!"

"You've never wanted a man before?" he breathed.

"No."

"I'll tell you something, Jenny. I've never wanted a

woman like this. Not ever." He kissed her ear softly. "I want you to know something. If it ever happened, even accidentally, you'd never want to forget it. I'd take you so tenderly, so slowly, that you'd never know anything about pain."

"Yes, I know that," she murmured, smiling. Her arms tightened. "You could have had me, then, lofty principles and all," she added ruefully. "I didn't realize how easy it was to throw reason to the wind."

"You're a very passionate woman." He lifted his head and searched her eyes. "I didn't expect that."

"You didn't seem much like a passionate man either," she confessed, letting her eyes wander slowly over his hard, dark face. "Oh, Rett, I did want you in the most frightening way!"

His chest expanded roughly. "Jenny, I think we'd better get up from here. My good intentions only seem to last until I get half your clothes off."

She watched him draw away, watched how his eyes clung to her bare breasts, and she smiled and arched gently.

"Oh, God, don't do that!" he whispered, shaken, as he turned away.

She laughed delightedly and sat up, getting back into her clothes as she stared at his broad back. He was smoking a cigarette, running a restless hand through his hair. And he was the handsomest man she'd ever seen in her life. And the most… loved.

I love you, she thought dreamily. I love every line and

curve and impatient gesture you make. I'd rather live here, in poverty, with you than to have the world in the bank.

"I'm decent now," she murmured, smiling when he turned hesitantly around. "My gosh, you make me feel good. I was always self-conscious about being so small."

His eyes narrowed. "You're not small, baby," he said in a gruff tone. "You're just delicate."

Her face glowed with pride. "Thank you, Rett."

"Let's see if the coffee's still warm," he said softly, holding out his hand.

She took it, and he pulled her up, pausing to bend and kiss her slowly, lingering over the soft, swollen contours of her warm mouth.

"I've bruised your lips," he whispered. "Are they sore?"

"They're delightfully sensitive," she whispered back, going on tiptoe. "You know a lot about kissing for a cattleman."

"You know a lot for a virgin," he murmured, chuckling.

"Pat yourself on the back, I'm a fast study." She slid her hand pertly inside his shirt and stroked him. "See?"

He took her hand away and buttoned his shirt to the throat. "I'm going to have to watch you, lady," he murmured, "or you'll wrestle me down on the couch and seduce me one dark night."

"It's all right," she whispered. "I won't get you pregnant. You can trust me, honey," she added with a wicked smile.

He burst out laughing and led her into the kitchen. "Feed me," he said, "before we get in over our heads."

"Spoilsport. Just when things were getting interesting."

"Another minute, and they'd have gone past interesting to educational," he murmured dryly, with a pointed glance. "Men get hot pretty fast that way, Jenny. Don't rely on my protective instincts too far. I damned near lost my head."

"Did you, really?" she asked, all eyes. "But I don't know anything."

"That's why," he sighed. "I…haven't touched a virgin since I was one myself. Funny, isn't it, that these days it's become a stigma. Back when I was a kid, decent boys wouldn't be seen with a girl who had a reputation for being easy. Now it's the virgins who take all the taunting." He stopped, turning her, and his face was solemn. "I'm glad you're still innocent. I'm glad that I can look at you and make you blush, and watch all those first reactions that you've never shown anybody else. To hell with modern morality, Jenny. I love the fact that you're as old-fashioned as I am."

"So do I. Now," she added, studying him warmly. "Rett…" Her fingers went up and touched his hard mouth. "Rett, I think I…" She was about to say "love you" when a piece of paper on the floor caught his eye.

"Hey, what's this?" he asked, bending to pick it up.

Her heart stopped. It was the check she'd gotten in the mail. She'd stuck it in her pocket, but it must have fallen out. She watched him open it and read the logo at the top with a feeling of impending disaster. She hadn't meant to tell him where it came from just yet…

His lean hand closed around the check, crumpling it. "Where did you get this kind of money, and what for?" he demanded.

"I…I worked part-time for a design house in Houston, decorating a lady's living room," she blurted out. "It's for you. To pay off your bull," she said, her face bright, her eyes shining. "I went to Houston and got a part-time job decorating a living room. That's my commission. Surprise! Now you won't have to sell that mangy old Hereford bull!"

He looked odd. As if he'd tried to swallow a watermelon and couldn't get it down. He stood up, still staring at the crumpled check, and turned away. He walked to the sink, staring out the darkened window.

"How did you get a job decorating anything?"

"I studied for several years at an excellent school of interior design in New York," she said. "I got a job with one of the leading agencies and spent two years developing my craft. That's why I got so angry when you made the remark about interior decorators being con artists," she added. "You see, I am one."

"New York?"

"Yes. It's the best place to learn, and to work."

"And you got pneumonia…"

"And had to give it up temporarily," she agreed. She frowned. He sounded strange. "Thanks to you, I'm back on my feet now and in fine form. The lady I did the design for was really pleased with my work, too. But the reason I did it was to get you enough money to pay off your note…"

"I can't take this," he said in a strained tone. He put it gently on the table and started out the door.

"But, Everett, your supper…!" she called.

"I'm not hungry." He kept walking. A moment later, the front door slammed behind him.

She sat there at the table, alone, staring at the check for a long time, until the numbers started to blur. Her eyes burned with unshed tears. She loved him. She loved Everett Culhane. And in the space of one night, her good intentions had lost her the pleasure of being near him. She knew almost certainly that he was going to fire her now. Too late, she remembered his opinion of city women. She hadn't had time to explain that it was her parents' idea for her to study and to work in New York, not her own. Nor that the pressure had been too much. He thought it was only pneumonia. Could she convince him in time that she wasn't what he was sure she was? That she wanted to stay here forever, not just as a temporary thing. She glanced toward the door with a quiet sigh. Well, she'd just sit here and wait until the shock wore off and he came back.

She did wait. But when three o'clock in the morning came, with no sign of Everett, she went reluctantly upstairs and lay down. It didn't help that she still smelled leather and faint cologne, and that her mind replayed the fierce ardor she'd learned from him until, exhausted, she slept.

When her eyes slowly opened the next morning, she felt as if she hadn't slept at all. And the first thing she remembered was Everett's shocked face when she'd told him what she used to do for a living. She couldn't understand why he'd reacted that way. After the way it had been between them, she hadn't expected him to walk off without at least discussing it. She wondered if it was going to be that way until he fired her. Because she was sure he was going to. And she knew for a certainty that she didn't want to go. She loved him with all her heart.

CHAPTER SEVEN

IF SHE'D hoped for a new start that morning, she was disappointed. She fixed breakfast, but Everett went out the front door without even sticking his head in the kitchen. Apparently, he'd rather have starved than eat what she'd cooked for him.

That morning set the pattern for the next two days. Jennifer cooked and wound up eating her efforts by herself. Everett came home in the early hours of the morning, arranging his schedule so that she never saw him at all.

He'd sold the bull. She found it out from Eddie, who was in a nasty temper of his own.

"I practically begged him to wait and see what happened," Eddie spat as he delivered the eggs to Jennifer the second morning. "When that neighbor didn't want the bull, Everett just loaded it up and took it to the sale without a word. He looks bad. He won't talk. Do you know what's eating him?"

She avoided that sharp look. "He's worried about

money, I think," she said. "I offered him what I had. He got mad and stomped off and he hasn't spoken to me since."

"That don't sound like Everett."

"Yes, I know." She sighed, smiling at him. "I think he wants me to go away, Eddie. He's done everything but leave the ranch forever to get his point across."

"Money troubles are doing it, not you." Eddie grinned. "Don't back off now. He needs us all more than ever."

"Maybe he does," Jennifer said. "I just wish he'd taken the money I offered to lend him."

"That would be something, all right, to watch Everett take money from a lady. No offense, Miss Jenny, but he's too much man. If you know what I mean."

She did, unfortunately. She'd experienced the male in him, in ways that would haunt her forever. And worst of all was the fact that she was still hungry for him. If anything, that wild little interlude on the sofa had whetted her appetite, not satisfied it.

For lunch, she put a platter of cold cuts in the refrigerator and left a loaf of bread on the table along with a plate and cup; there was coffee warming on the stove. She pulled on a sweater and went down to visit Libby. It was like baiting a trap, she thought. Perhaps he'd enjoy eating if he didn't have to look at a city woman.

Libby didn't ask any obvious questions. She simply enjoyed the visit, since the children were in school and she could talk about clothes and television programs with the younger woman.

At one o'clock, Jennifer left the house and walked slowly back to see if Everett had eaten. It was something of a shock to find him wandering wildly around the kitchen, smoking like a furnace.

"So there you are!" he burst out, glaring at her with menacing brown eyes. "Where in hell have you been? No note, no nothing! I didn't know if you'd left or been kidnapped, or stepped into a hole…"

"What would you care if I had?" she demanded. "You've made it obvious that you don't care for my company!"

"What did you expect?" he burst out, his eyes dangerous. "You lied to me."

"I didn't," she said in defense.

"I thought you were a poor little secretary in danger of starving if I didn't take you in," he said through his teeth. He let his eyes wander with slow insolence over the white blouse and green skirt she was wearing. "And what do I find out? That you lived and worked in New York at a job that would pay you more in one week than I can make here in two months!"

So that was it. His pride was crushed. He was poor and she wasn't, and that cut him up.

But knowing it wasn't much help. He was as unapproachable as a coiled rattler. In his dusty jeans and boots and denim shirt, he looked as wild as an outlaw.

"I had pneumonia," she began. "I had to come south…"

"Bobby didn't know?" he asked.

"No," she said. "I didn't see any reason to tell him. Everett…!"

"Why didn't you say something at the beginning?" he demanded, ramming his hand into his pocket to fish for another cigarette.

"What was there to say?" she asked impotently. She took the sweater from around her shoulders, and her green eyes pleaded with him. "Everett, I'm just the same as I always was."

"Not hardly," he said. His jaw clenched as he lit the cigarette. "You came here looking like a straggly little hen. And now…" He blew out a cloud of smoke, letting his eyes savor the difference. They lingered for a long time on her blouse, narrowing, burning. "I brought a city girl here once," he said absently. His eyes caught hers. "When she found out that I had more ideas than I had money, she turned around and ran. We were engaged," he said on a short laugh. "I do have the damndest blind spot about women."

She wrapped her arms around her chest. "Why does it make so much difference?" she asked. "I only took the designing job to help, Rett," she added. She moved closer. "I just wanted to pay you back, for giving me a job when I needed it. I knew you couldn't afford me, but I was in trouble, and you sacrificed for me." Her eyes searched his dark, hard face. "I wanted to do something for you. I wanted you to have your bull."

His face hardened and he turned away, as if he

couldn't bear the sight of her. He raised the cigarette to his lips and his back was ramrod straight.

"I want you to leave," he said.

"Yes, I know," she said on a soft little sigh. "When?"

"At the end of the week."

So soon? she thought miserably. Her eyes clouded as she stared at his back, seeing the determination in every hard line of it. "Do you hate me?" she asked in a hurting tone.

He turned around slowly, the cigarette held tautly in one hand, and his eyes slashed at her. He moved closer, with a look in his dark eyes that was disturbing.

With a smooth motion, he tossed the unfinished cigarette into an ashtray on the table and reached for her.

"I could hate you," he said harshly. "If I didn't want you so damned much." He bent his head and caught her mouth with his.

She stiffened for an instant, because there was no tenderness in this exchange. He was rough and hurting, deliberately. Even so, she loved him. If this was all he could give, then it would be enough. She inched her trapped hands up to his neck and slid them around it. Her soft mouth opened, giving him all he wanted of it. She couldn't respond, he left her no room. He was taking without any thought of giving back the pleasure.

His hard hands slid roughly over her breasts and down to her hips and ground her against him in a deep, insolent rhythm, letting her feel what she already knew—that he wanted her desperately.

"Was it all a lie?" he ground out against her mouth. "Are you really a virgin?"

Her lips felt bruised when she tried to speak. "Yes," she said shakily. He was still holding her intimately, and when she tried to pull back, he only crushed her hips closer.

"No, don't do that," he said with a cruel smile. "I like to feel you. Doesn't it give you a sense of triumph, city girl, knowing how you affect me?"

Her hands pushed futilely at his hard chest. "Everett, don't make me feel cheap," she pleaded.

"Could I?" He laughed coldly. "With your prospects?" His hands tightened, making her cry out. His mouth lowered. This time it was teasing, tantalizing. He brushed it against her own mouth in whispery motions that worked like a narcotic, hypnotizing her, weakening her. She began to follow those hard lips with her own, trying to capture them in an exchange that would satisfy the ache he was creating.

"Do you want to stay with me, Jenny?" he whispered.

"Yes," she whispered back, her whole heart in her response. She clutched at his shirtfront with trembling fingers. Her mouth begged for his. "Yes, Everett, I want to stay…!"

His breath came hard and fast at her lips. "Then come upstairs with me, now, and I'll let you," he breathed.

It took a minute for his words to register, and then she realized that his hands had moved to the very base of her spine, to touch her in ways that shocked and frightened her.

She pulled against his hands, her face red, her eyes wild. “What do you mean?” she whispered.

He laughed, his eyes as cold as winter snow. “Don’t you know? Sleep with me. Or would you like to hear it in a less formal way?” he added, and put it in words that made her hand come up like a whip.

He caught it, looking down at her with contempt and desire and anger all mixed up in his hard face. “Not interested?” he asked mockingly. “You were a minute ago. You were the other night, when you let me strip you.”

Her teeth clenched as she tried to hang on to her dignity and her pride. “Let me go,” she whispered shakily.

“I could please you, city girl,” he said with a bold, slow gaze down her taut body. “You’re going to give in to a man someday. Why not me? Or do I need to get rich first to appeal to you?”

Tears welled up in her eyes. His one hand was about to crack the delicate bone in her wrist, and the other was hurting her back. She closed her eyelids to shut off the sight of his cold face. She loved him so. How could he treat her this way? How could he be so cruel after that tenderness they’d shared!

“No comment?” he asked. He dropped his hands and retrieved his still-smoking cigarette from the ashtray. “Well, you can’t blame a man for trying. You seemed willing enough the other night. I thought you might like some memories to carry away with you.”

She'd had some beautiful ones, she thought miserably, until now. Her hands reached, trembling, for her sweater. She held it over her chest and wouldn't look up.

"I've got some correspondence on the desk you can type when you run out of things to do in the kitchen," he said, turning toward the door. He looked back with a grim smile on his lips. "That way you can make up some of the time you spent decorating that woman's house for her."

She still didn't speak, didn't move. The world had caved in on her. She loved him. And he could treat her like this, like some tramp he'd picked up on the street!

He drew in a sharp breath. "Don't talk, then," he said coldly. "I don't give a damn. I never did. I wanted you, that's all. But if I had the money, I could have you and a dozen like you, couldn't I?"

She managed to raise her ravaged face. He seemed almost to flinch at the sight of it, but he was only a blur through the tears in her eyes, and she might have been mistaken.

"Say something!" he ground out.

She lifted her chin. Her pale, swollen eyes just stared at him accusingly, and not one single word left her lips. Even if he threw her against the wall, she wouldn't give him the satisfaction of even one syllable!

He drew in a furious breath and whirled on his heel, slamming out the door.

She went upstairs like a zombie, hardly aware of her surroundings at all. She went into her room and took the uncashed checks that he'd signed for her salary and put them neatly on her dresser. She packed very quickly and searched in her purse. She had just enough pocket money left to pay a cab. She could cash the design firm's check in town when she got there. She called the cab company and then lifted her case and went downstairs to wait for it.

Everett was nowhere in sight, neither were Eddie and Bib, when the taxi came winding up the driveway. She walked down the steps, her eyes dry now, her face resolved, and got inside.

"Take me into town, please," she said quietly.

The cab pulled away from the steps, and she scanned the ranchhouse and the corrals one last time. Then she turned away and closed her eyes. She didn't look back, not once.

Fortunately, Jennifer had no trouble landing a job. Sally Wade had been so impressed with the work that she'd done for Mrs. Whitehall that she practically created a position for Jennifer in her small, and still struggling, design firm. Jennifer loved the work, but several weeks had passed before she was able to think about Everett without crying.

The cup of coffee at Jennifer's elbow was getting cold. She frowned at it as her hand stilled on the sketch she was doing for a new client.

"Want some fresh?" Sally Wade asked from the

doorway, holding her own cup aloft. "I'm just going to the pot."

"Bless you," Jennifer laughed.

"That's the first time you've really looked happy in the three months since you've been here," Sally remarked, cocking her head. "Getting over him?"

"Over whom?" came the shocked reply.

"That man, whoever he was, who had you in tears your first week here. I didn't pry, but I wondered," the older woman confessed. "I kept waiting for the phone to ring, or a letter to come. But nothing did. I kind of thought that he had to care, because you cared so much."

"He wanted a mistress," Jennifer said, putting it into words. "And I wanted a husband. We just got our signals crossed. Besides," she added with a wan smile, "I'm feeling worlds better. I've got a great job, a lovely boss, and even a part-time boyfriend. If you can call Drew a boy."

"He's delightful." Sally sighed. "Just what you need. A live wire."

"And not a bad architect, either. You must be pleased he's working with us." She grinned. "He did a great job on that office project last month."

"So did you," Sally said, smiling. She leaned against the doorjamb. "I thought it a marvelous idea, locating a group of offices in a renovated mansion. It only needed the right team, and you and Drew work wonderfully well together."

"In business, yes." Jennifer twirled her pencil around

in her slender fingers. "I just don't want him getting serious about me. If it's possible for him to get serious about anyone." She laughed.

"Don't try to bury yourself."

"Oh, I'm not. It's just..." She shrugged. "I'm only now getting over... I don't want any more risks. Not for a long time. Maybe not ever."

"Some men are kind-hearted," Sally ventured.

"So why are you single?" came the sharp reply.

"I'm picky," Sally informed her with a sly smile. "Very, very picky. I want Rhett Butler or nobody."

"Wrong century, wrong state."

"You're from Georgia. Help me out!"

"Sorry," Jennifer murmured. "If I could find one, do you think I'd tell anybody?"

"Point taken. Give me that cup and I'll fill it for you."

"Thanks, boss."

"Oh, boy, coffee!" a tall, redheaded man called from the doorway as he closed the door behind him. "I'll have mine black, with two doughnuts, a fried egg..."

"The breakfast bar is closed, Mr. Peterson," Jennifer told him.

"Sorry, Drew," Sally added. "You'll just have to catch your own chicken and do it the hard way."

"I could starve," he grumbled, ramming his hands in his pockets. He had blue eyes, and right now they were glaring at both women. "I don't have a wife or a mother. I live alone. My cook hates me..."

"You're breaking my heart," Sally offered.

"You can have the other half of my doughnut," Jennifer said, holding up a chunk of doughnut with chocolate clinging to it.

"Never mind." Drew sighed. "Thanks all the same, but I'll just wither away."

"That wouldn't be difficult," Jennifer told him. "You're nothing but skin and bones."

"I gained two pounds this week," he said, affronted.

"Where is it," Sally asked with a sweeping glance, "in your big toe?"

"Ha, ha," he laughed as she turned to go to the coffeepot.

"You *are* thin," Jennifer remarked.

He glared at her. "I'm still a growing boy." He stretched lazily. "Want to ride out to the new office building with me this morning?"

"No, thanks. I've got to finish these drawings. What do you think?"

She held one up, and he studied them with an architect's trained eye. "Nice. Just remember that this," he said, pointing to the vestibule, "is going to be a heavy-traffic area, and plan accordingly."

"There goes my white carpet," she teased.

"I'll white carpet you," he muttered. He pursed his lips as he studied her. "Wow, lady, what a change."

She blinked up at him. "What?"

"You. When you walked in here three months ago, you looked like a drowned kitten. And now…" He only sighed.

She was wearing a beige suit with a pink candy-striped blouse and a pink silk scarf. Her blond hair was almost platinum with its new body and sheen, and she'd had it trimmed so that it hung in wispy waves all around her shoulders. Her face was creamy and soft and she was wearing makeup again. She looked nice, and his eyes told her so.

"Thanks."

He pursed his lips. "What for?"

"The flattery," she told him. "My ego's been even with my ankles for quite a while."

"Stick with me, kid, I'll get it all the way up to your ears," he promised with an evil leer.

"Sally, he's trying to seduce me!" she called toward the front of the office.

She expected some kind of bantering reply, but none was forthcoming. She looked up at Drew contemplatively. "Reckon she's left?"

"No. She's answered the phone. You still aren't used to the musical tone, are you?"

No, she wasn't. There were quite a lot of things she wasn't used to, and the worst of them was being without Everett. She had a good job, a nice apartment, and some new clothes. But without him, none of that mattered. She was going through the motions, and little more. His contempt still stung her pride when she recalled that last horrible scene. But she couldn't get him out of her mind, no matter how she tried.

"Well!" Sally said, catching her breath as she rejoined

them. "If the rest of him looks like this voice, I may get back into the active part of the business. That was a potential client, and I think he may be the Rhett Butler I've always dreamed of. What a silky, sexy voice!"

"Dream on," Jennifer teased.

"He's coming by in the morning to talk to us. Wants his whole house done!" the older woman exclaimed.

"He must have a sizeable wallet, then," Drew remarked.

Sally nodded. "He didn't say where the house was, but I assume it's nearby. It didn't sound like a long-distance call." She glanced at Jennifer with a smile. "Apparently your reputation has gotten around, too," she laughed. "He asked if you'd be doing the project. I had the idea he wouldn't have agreed otherwise." She danced around with her coffee cup in her hand. "What a godsend. With the office building and this job, we'll be out of the red, kids! What a break!"

"And you were groaning about the bills just yesterday," Jennifer laughed. "I told you something would turn up, didn't I?"

"You're my lucky charm," Sally told her. "If I hadn't hired you, I shudder to think what would have happened."

"You know how much I appreciated getting this job," Jennifer murmured. "I was in pretty desperate circumstances."

"So I noticed. Well, we did each other a lot of good.

We still are," Sally said warmly. "Hey, let's celebrate. Come on. I'll treat you two to lunch."

"Lovely!" Jennifer got up and grabbed her purse. "Come on, Drew, let's hurry before she changes her mind!"

She rushed out the door, with Drew in full pursuit, just ahead of Sally. And not one of them noticed the man sitting quietly in the luxury car across the street, his fingers idly caressing a car phone in the backseat as he stared intently after them.

CHAPTER EIGHT

DREW HAD asked Jennifer to go out with him that night, but she begged off with a smile. She didn't care for the nightlife anymore. She went to company functions with Sally when it was necessary to attract clients or discuss new projects, but that was about the extent of her social consciousness. She spent most of her time alone, in her modest apartment, going over drawings and planning rooms.

She enjoyed working for Sally. Houston was a big city, but much smaller than New York. And while there was competition, it wasn't as fierce. The pressure was less. And best of all, Jennifer was allowed a lot of latitude in her projects. She had a free hand to incorporate her own ideas as long as they complemented the client's requirements. She loved what she did, and in loving it, she blossomed into the woman she'd once been. But this time she didn't allow herself to fall into the trap of overspending. She budgeted, right down to the pretty clothes she loved—she bought them on sale, a few at a time, and concentrated on mix-and-match outfits.

It was a good life. But part of her was still mourning Everett. Not a day went by when she couldn't see him, tall and unnerving, somewhere in her memory. They'd been so good for each other. She'd never experienced such tenderness in a man.

She got up from the sofa and looked out at the skyline of Houston. The city was bright and beautiful, but she remembered the ranch on starry nights. Dogs would howl far in the distance, crickets would sing at the steps. And all around would be open land and stars and the silhouettes of Everett's cattle.

She wrapped her arms around her body and sighed. Perhaps someday the pain would stop and she could really forget him. Perhaps someday she could remember his harsh accusations and not be wounded all over again. But right now, it hurt terribly. He'd been willing to let her stay as his mistress, as a possession to be used when he wanted her. But he wouldn't let her be part of his life. He couldn't have told her more graphically how little he thought of her. That had hurt the most. That even after all the caring, all the tenderness, she hadn't reached him at all. He hadn't seen past the shape of her body and his need of it. He hadn't loved her. And he'd made sure she knew it.

There were a lot of nights, like this one, when she paced and paced and wondered if he thought of her at all, if he regretted what had happened. Somehow, she doubted it. Everett had a wall like steel around him. He wouldn't let anyone inside it. Especially not a city woman with an income that could top his.

She laughed bitterly. It was unfortunate that she had fallen in love for the first time with such a cynical man. It had warped the way she looked at the world. She felt as if she, too, were impregnable now. Her emotions were carefully wrapped away, where they couldn't be touched. Nobody could reach her now. She felt safe in her warm cocoon. Of course, she was as incapable of caring now as he'd been. And in a way, that was a blessing. Because she couldn't be hurt anymore. She could laugh and carry on with Drew, and it didn't mean a thing. There was no risk in dating these days. Her heart was safely tucked away.

With a last uncaring look at the skyline, she turned off the lights and went to bed. Just as she drifted off, she wondered who the new client was going to be, and grinned at the memory of Sally's remark about his sexy voice.

She overslept the next morning for the first time in months. With a shriek as she saw the time, she dressed hastily in a silky beige dress and high heels. She moaned over her unruly hair that would curl and feather all around her shoulders instead of going into a neat bun. She touched up her face, stepped into her shoes, and rushed out into the chill autumn morning without a jacket or a sweater. Oh, well, maybe she wouldn't freeze, she told herself as she jumped into the cab she'd called and headed for the office.

"So there you are," Drew said with mock anger as

she rushed breathlessly in the door, her cheeks flushed, her eyes sparkling, her hair disheveled and sexy around her face. "I ought to fire you."

"Go ahead. I dare you." She laughed up at him. "And I'll tell Sally all about that last expense voucher you faked."

"Blackmailer!" he growled. He reached out and lifted her up in the air, laughing at her.

"Put me down, you male chauvinist." She laughed gaily. Her face was a study in beauty, her body lusciously displayed in the pose, her hands on his shoulders, her hair swirling gracefully as she looked down at him. "Come on, put me down," she coaxed. "Put me down, Drew, and I'll take you to lunch."

"In that case," he murmured dryly.

"Jennifer! Drew!" Sally exclaimed, entering the room with a nervous laugh. "Stop clowning. We've got business to discuss, and you're making a horrible first impression."

"Oops," Drew murmured. He turned his head just as Jennifer turned hers, and all the laughter and brightness drained out of her like air out of a balloon. She stared down at the newcomer with strained features and eyes that went from shock to extreme anger.

Drew set her down on her feet and turned, hand extended, grinning. "Sorry about that. Just chastising the staff for tardiness." He chuckled. "I'm Andrew Peterson, resident architect. This is my associate, Jennifer King."

"I know her name," Everett Culhane said quietly. His dark eyes held no offer of peace, no hint of truce. They were angry and cold, and he smiled mockingly as his eyes went from Jennifer to Drew. "We've met."

Sally looked poleaxed. It had just dawned on her who Everett was, when she got a look at Jennifer's white face.

"Uh, Mr. Culhane is our new client," Sally said hesitantly. Jennifer looked as if she might faint. "You remember, Jenny, I mentioned yesterday that he'd called."

"You didn't mention his name," Jennifer said in a cool voice that shook with rage. "Excuse me, I have a phone call to make."

"Not so fast," Everett said quietly. "First we talk."

Her eyes glittered at him, her body trembled with suppressed tension. "I have nothing to say to you, Mr. Culhane," she managed. "And you have nothing to say to me that I care to hear."

"Jennifer…" Sally began nervously.

"If my job depends on working for Mr. Culhane, you can have my resignation on the spot," Jennifer said unsteadily. "I will not speak to him, much less work with him. I'm sorry."

She turned and went on wobbly legs to her office, closing the door behind her. She couldn't even sit down. She was shaking like a leaf all over and tears were burning her eyes. She heard voices outside, but ignored them. She stared at an abstract painting on the wall until she thought she'd go blind.

The sound of the door opening barely registered. Then it closed with a firm snap, and she glanced over her shoulder to find Everett inside.

It was only then that she noticed he was wearing a suit. A very expensive gray one that made his darkness even more formidable; his powerful body was streamlined and elegant in its new garments. He was holding a silverbelly Stetson in one lean hand and staring at her quietly, calculatingly.

"Please go away," she said with as much conviction as she could muster.

"Why?" he asked carelessly, tossing his hat onto her desk. He dropped into an armchair and crossed one long leg over the other. He lit a cigarette and pulled the ashtray on her desk closer, but his eyes never left her ravaged face.

"If you want your house redone, there are other firms," she told him, turning bravely, although her legs were still trembling.

He saw that, and his eyes narrowed, his jaw tautened. "Are you afraid of me?" he asked quietly.

"I'm outraged," she replied in a voice that was little more than a whisper. Her hand brushed back a long, unruly strand of hair. "You might as well have taken a bullwhip to me, just before I left the ranch. What do you want now? To show me how prosperous you are? I've noticed the cut of your suit. And the fact that you can afford to hire this firm to redo the house does indicate a lot of money." She smiled unsteadily. "Congratulations. I hope your sudden wealth makes you happy."

He didn't speak for a long minute. His eyes wandered over her slowly, without any insult, as if he'd forgotten what she looked like and needed to stare at her, to fill his eyes. "Aren't you going to ask me how I came by it?" he demanded finally.

"No. Because I don't care," she said.

One corner of his mouth twitched a little. He took a draw from the cigarette and flicked an ash into the ashtray. "I sold off the oil rights."

So much for sticking to your principles, she wanted to say. But she didn't have the strength. She went behind her desk and sat down carefully.

"No comment?" he asked.

She blanched, remembering with staggering clarity the last time he'd said that. He seemed to remember it, too, because his jaw tautened and he drew in a harsh breath.

"I want my house done," he said curtly. "I want you to do it. Nobody else. And I want you to stay with me while you work on the place."

"Hell will freeze over first," she said quietly.

"I was under the impression that the firm wasn't operating in the black," he said with an insolent appraisal of her office. "The commission on this project will be pretty large."

"I told you once that you couldn't buy me," she said on a shuddering breath. "I'd jump off a cliff before I'd stay under the same roof with you!"

His eyes closed. When they opened again, he was staring down at his boot. "Is it that redheaded clown outside?" he asked suddenly, jerking his gaze up to catch hers.

Her lips trembled. "That's none of your business."

His eyes wandered slowly over her face. "You looked different with him," he said deeply. "Alive, vibrant, happy. And then, the minute you spotted me, every bit of life went out of you. It was like watching water drain from a glass."

"What did you expect, for God's sake!" she burst out, her eyes wild. "You cut me up!"

He drew in a slow breath. "Yes. I know."

"Then why are you here?" she asked wearily. "What do you want from me?"

He stared at the cigarette with eyes that barely saw it. "I told you. I want my house done." He looked up. "I can afford the best, and that's what I want. You."

There was an odd inflection in his voice, but she was too upset to hear it. She blinked her eyes, trying to get herself under control. "I won't do it. Sally will just have to fire me."

He got to his feet and loomed over the desk, crushing out the cigarette before he rammed his hands into his pockets and glared at her. "There are less pleasant ways to do this," he said. "I could make things very difficult for your new employer." His eyes challenged her. "Call my bluff. See if you can skip town with that on your conscience."

She couldn't, and he knew it. Her pride felt lacerated. "What do you think you'll accomplish by forcing me to come back?" she asked. "I'd put a knife in you if I could. I won't sleep with you, no matter what you do. So what will you get out of it?"

"My house decorated, of course," he said lazily. His eyes wandered over her. "I've got over the other. Out of sight, out of mind, don't they say?" He shrugged and turned away with a calculating look on his face. "And one body's pretty much like another in the dark," he added, reaching for his Stetson. His eyes caught the flutter of her lashes and he smiled to himself as he reached for the doorknob. "Well, Miss King, which is it? Do you come back to Big Spur with me or do I give Ms. Wade the sad news that you're leaving her in the lurch?"

Her eyes flashed green sparks at him. What choice was there? But he'd pay for this. Somehow, she'd make him. "I'll go," she bit off.

He didn't say another word. He left her office as though he were doing her a favor by letting her redecorate his house!

Sally came in the door minutes later, looking troubled and apologetic.

"I had no idea," she told Jennifer. "Honest to God, I had no idea who he was."

"Now you know," Jennifer said on a shaky laugh.

"You don't have to do it," the older woman said curtly.

"Yes, I'm afraid I do. Everett doesn't make idle

threats," she said, rising. "You've been too good to me, Sally. I can't let him cause trouble for you on my account. I'll go with him. After all, it's just another job."

"You look like death warmed over. I'll send Drew with you. We'll do something to justify him..."

"Everett would eat him alive," she told Sally with a level stare. "And don't pretend you don't know it. Drew's a nice man but he isn't up to Everett's weight or his temper. This is a private war."

"Unarmed combat?" Sally asked sadly.

"Exactly. He has this thing about city women, and I wasn't completely honest with him. He wants to get even."

"I thought revenge went out with the Borgias," Sally muttered.

"Not quite. Wish me luck. I'm going to need it."

"If it gets too rough, call for reinforcements," Sally said. "I'll pack a bag and move in with you, Everett or no Everett."

"You're a pal," Jennifer said warmly.

"I'm a rat," came the dry reply. "I wish I hadn't done this to you. If I'd known who he was, I'd never have told him you worked here."

Jennifer had hoped to go down to Big Spur alone, but Everett went back to her apartment with her, his eyes daring her to refuse his company.

He waited in the living room while she packed, and not one corner escaped his scrutiny.

"Looking for dust?" she asked politely, case in hand.

He turned, cigarette in hand, studying her. "This place must cost you an arm," he remarked.

"It does," she said with deliberate sarcasm. "But I can afford it. I make a lot of money, as you reminded me."

"I said a lot of cruel things, didn't I, Jenny Wren?" he asked quietly, searching her shocked eyes. "Did I leave deep scars?"

She lifted her chin. "Can we go? The sooner we get there, the sooner I can get the job done and come home."

"Didn't you ever think of the ranch as home?" he asked, watching her. "You seemed to love it at first."

"Things were different then," she said noncommittally, and started for the door.

He took her case, his fingers brushing hers in the process, and producing electric results.

"Eddie and Bib gave me hell when they found out you'd gone," he said as he opened the door for her.

"I imagine you were too busy celebrating to notice."

He laughed shortly. "Celebrating? You damned little fool, I...!" He closed his mouth with a rough sigh. "Never mind. You might have left a nasty note or something."

"Why, so you'd know where I went?" she demanded. "That was the last thing I wanted."

"So I noticed," he agreed. He locked the door, handed her the key, and started down the hall toward the elevator. "Libby told me the name of the firm you'd worked for. It wasn't hard to guess you'd get a job with them."

She tossed her hair. "So that was how you found me."

"We've got some unfinished business," he replied as they waited for the elevator. His dark eyes held hers and she had to clench her fists to keep from kicking him. He had a power over her that all her anger couldn't stop. Deep beneath the layer of ice was a blazing inferno of hunger and love, but she'd die before she'd show it to him.

"I hate you," she breathed.

"Yes, I know you do," he said with an odd satisfaction.

"Mr. Culhane..."

"You used to call me Rett," he recalled, studying her. "Especially," he added quietly, "when we made love."

Her face began to color and she aimed a kick at his shins. He jumped back just as the elevator door opened.

"Pig!" she ground out.

"Now, honey, think of the kids," he drawled, aiming a glance at the elevator full of fascinated spectators. "If you knock me down, how can I support the ten of you?"

Red-faced, she got in ahead of him and wished with all her heart that the elevator doors would close right dead center on him. They didn't.

He sighed loudly, glancing down at her. "I begged you not to run off with that salesman," he said in a sad drawl. "I told you he'd lead you into a life of sin!"

There were murmured exclamations all around and a buzz of conversation. She glared up at him. Two could play that game.

"Well, what did you expect me to do, sit at home and knit while you ran around with that black-eyed hussy?" she drawled back. "And me in my delicate condition…"

"Delicate condition…?" he murmured, shocked at her unexpected remark.

"And it's your baby, too, you animal," she said with a mock sob, glaring up at him.

"Darling!" he burst out. "You didn't tell me!"

And he grabbed her and kissed her hungrily right there in front of the whole crowd while she gasped and counted to ten and tried not to let him see that she was melting into the floor from the delicious contact with his mouth.

The elevator doors opened and he lifted his head as the other occupants filed out. He was breathing unsteadily and his eyes held hers. "No," he whispered when she tried to move away. His arm caught her and his head bent. "I need you," he whispered shakily. "Need you so…!"

That brought it all back. Need. He needed her. He just needed a body, that was all, and she knew it! She jerked herself out of his arms and stomped off the elevator.

"You try that again and I'll vanish!" she threatened, glaring up at him when they were outside the building. Her face was flushed, her breath shuddering. "I mean it! I'll disappear and you won't find me this time!"

He shrugged. "Suit yourself." He walked alongside her, all the brief humor gone out of his face. She wondered minutes later if it had been there at all.

CHAPTER NINE

HE HAD a Lincoln now. Not only the car, but a driver to go with it. He handed her bag to the uniformed driver and put Jennifer in the backseat beside him.

"Aren't we coming up in the world, though?" she asked with cool sarcasm.

"Don't you like it?" he replied mockingly. He leaned back against the seat facing her and lit a cigarette. "I didn't think a woman alive could resist flashy money."

She remembered reluctantly how he'd already been thrown over once for the lack of wealth. Part of her tender heart felt sorry for him. But not any part that was going to show, she told herself.

"You could buy your share now, I imagine," she said, glancing out the window at the traffic.

He blew out a thin cloud of smoke. The driver climbed in under the wheel and, starting the powerful car, pulled out into the street.

"I imagine so."

She stared at the purse in her lap. "They really did find oil out there?" she asked.

"Sure did. Barrels and barrels." He glanced at her over his cigarette. "The whole damned skyline's cluttered with rigs these days. Metal grasshoppers." He sighed. "The cattle don't even seem to mind them. They just graze right on."

Wouldn't it be something if a geyser blew out under one of his prize Herefords one day, she mused. She almost told him, and then remembered the animosity between them. It had been a good kind of relationship that they'd had. If only Everett hadn't ruined it.

"It's a little late to go into it now," he said quietly. "But I didn't mean to hurt you that much. Once I cooled down, I would have apologized."

"The apology wouldn't have meant much after what you said to me!" she said through her teeth, flushing at the memory of the crude phrase.

He looked away. For a long minute he just sat and smoked. "You're almost twenty-four years old, Jenny," he said finally. "If you haven't heard words like that before, you're overdue."

"I didn't expect to hear them from you," she shot back, glaring at him. "Much less have you treat me with less respect than a woman you might have picked up on the streets with a twenty-dollar bill!"

"One way or another, I'd have touched you like that eventually!" he growled, glaring at her. "And don't sit there like lily-white purity and pretend you don't know what I'm talking about. We were on the verge of becoming lovers that night on the sofa."

"You wouldn't have made me feel ashamed if it had happened that night," she said fiercely. "You wouldn't have made me feel cheap!"

He seemed about to explode. Then he caught himself and took a calming draw from the cigarette. His dark eyes studied the lean hand holding it. "You hurt me."

It was a shock to hear him admit it. "What?"

"You hurt me." His dark eyes lifted. "I thought we were being totally honest with each other. I trusted you. I let you closer than any other woman ever got. And then out of the blue, you hit me with everything at once. That you were a professional woman, a career woman. Worse," he added quietly, "a city woman, used to city men and city life and city ways. I couldn't take it. I'd been paying you scant wages, and you handed me that check..." He sighed wearily. "My God, I can't even tell you how I felt. My pride took one hell of a blow. I had nothing, and you were showing me graphically that you could outdo me on every front."

"I only wanted to help," she said curtly. "I wanted to buy you the damned bull. Sorry. If I had it to do all over again, I wouldn't offer you a dime."

"Yes, it shows." He sighed. He finished the cigarette and crushed it out. "Who's the redhead?"

"Drew? Sally told you. He's our architect. He has his own firm, of course, but he collaborates with us on big projects."

"Not on mine," he said menacingly, and his eyes darkened. "Not in my house."

She glared back. "That will depend on how much renovation the project calls for, I imagine."

"I won't have him on my place," he said softly.

"Why?"

"I don't like the way he looks at you," he said coldly. "Much less the way he makes free with his hands."

"I'm twenty-three years old," she reminded him. "And I like Drew, and the way he looks at me! He's a nice man."

"And I'm not," he agreed. "Nice is the last thing I am. If he ever touches you that way again when I'm in the same room, I'll break his fingers for him."

"Everett Donald Culhane!" she burst out.

His eyebrows arched. "Who told you my whole name?"

She looked away. "Never mind," she said, embarrassed.

His hand brushed against her hair, caressing it. "God, your hair is glorious," he said quietly. "It was nothing like this at the ranch."

She tried not to feel his touch. "I'd been ill," she managed.

"And now you aren't. Now you're…fuller and softer-looking. Even your breasts…"

"Stop it!" she cried, red-faced.

He let go of her hair reluctantly, but his eyes didn't leave her. "I'll have you, Jenny," he said quietly, his tone as soft as it had been that night when he was loving her.

"Only if you shoot me in the leg first!" she told him.

"Not a chance," he murmured, studying her. "I'll want you healthy and strong, so that you can keep up with me."

Her face did a slow burn again. She could have kicked him, but they were sitting down. "I don't want you!"

"You did. You will. I've got a whole campaign mapped out, Miss Jenny," he told her with amazing arrogance. "You're under siege. You just haven't realized it yet."

She looked him straight in the eye. "My grandfather held off a whole German company during World War I rather than surrender."

His eyebrows went up. "Is that supposed to impress me?"

"I won't be your mistress," she told him levelly. "No matter how many campaigns you map out or what kind of bribes or threats you try to use. I came with you to save Sally's business. But all this is to me is a job. I am not going to sleep with you."

His dark, quiet eyes searched over her face. "Why?"

Her lips opened and closed, opened again. "Because I can't do it without love," she said finally.

"Love isn't always possible," he said softly. "Sometimes, other things have to come first. Mutual respect, caring, companionship..."

"Can we talk about something else?" she asked tautly. Her fingers twisted the purse out of shape.

He chuckled softly. "Talking about sex won't get you pregnant."

"You've got money now. You can buy women," she ground out. "You said so."

"Honey, would you want a man you had to buy?" he asked quietly, studying her face.

Her lips parted. "Would I..." She searched his eyes. "Well, no."

"I wouldn't want a woman I had to buy," he said simply. "I'm too proud, Jenny. I said and did some harsh things to you," he remarked. "I can understand why you're angry and hurt about it. Someday I'll try to explain why I behaved that way. Right now, I'll settle for regaining even a shadow of the friendship we had. Nothing more. Despite all this wild talk, I'd never deliberately try to seduce you."

"Wouldn't you?" she asked bitterly. "Isn't that the whole point of getting me down here?"

"No." He lit another cigarette.

"You said you were going to..." she faltered.

"I want to," he admitted quietly. "God, I want to! But I can't quite take a virgin in my stride. Once, I thought I might," he confessed, his eyes searching her face. "That night... You were so eager, and I damned near lost my head when I realized that I could have you." He stared at the tip of his cigarette with blank eyes. "Would you have hated me if I hadn't been able to stop?"

Her eyes drilled into her purse. "There's just no point in going over it," she said in a studiously polite tone. "The past is gone."

"Like hell it's gone," he ground out. "I look at you and start aching," he said harshly.

Her lower lip trembled as she glared at him. "Then stop looking. Or take cold showers! Just don't expect me to do anything about it. I'm here to work, period!"

His eyebrows arched, and he was watching her with a faintly amused expression. "Where did you learn about cold showers?"

"From watching movies!"

"Is that how you learned about sex, from the movies?" he taunted.

"No, I learned in school! Sex education," she bit off.

"In my day, we had to learn it the hard way," he murmured. "It wasn't part of the core curriculum."

She glanced at him. "I can see you, doing extracurricular work in somebody's backseat."

He reached out and caught her hair again, tugging on it experimentally. "In a haystall, actually," he said, his voice low and soft and dark. Her head turned and he held her eyes. "She was two years older than I was, and she taught me the difference between sex and making love."

Her face flushed. He affected her in ways nobody else could. She was trembling from the bare touch of his fingers on her hair; her heart was beating wildly. How was she going to survive being in the same house with him?

"Everett..." she began.

"I'm sorry about what I said to you that last day, Jenny," he said quietly. "I'm sorry I made it into something cheap and sordid between us. Because that's the last thing it would have been if you'd given yourself to me."

She pulled away from him with a dry little laugh. "Oh, really?" she said shakenly, turning her eyes to the window. They were out of Houston now, heading south. "The minute you'd finished with me, you'd have kicked me out the door, and you know it, Everett Culhane. I'd have been no different from all the other women you've held in contempt for giving in to you."

"It isn't like that with you."

"And how many times have you told that story?" she asked sadly.

"Once. Just now."

He sounded irritated, probably because she wasn't falling for his practiced line. She closed her eyes and leaned her head against the cool window pane.

"I'd rather stay in a motel," she said, "if you don't mind."

"No way, lady," he said curtly. "The same lock's still on your door, if you can't trust me that far. But staying at Big Spur was part of the deal you and I negotiated."

She turned her head to glance at his hard, set profile. He looked formidable again, all dark, flashing eyes and coldness. He was like the man she'd met that first day at the screen door.

"What would you have done, if I'd given in?" she asked suddenly, watching him closely. "What if I'd gotten pregnant?"

His head turned and his eyes glittered strangely. "I'd have gotten down on my knees and thanked God for it," he said harshly. "What did you think I'd do?"

Her lips parted. "I hadn't really thought about it."

"I want children. A yardful."

That was surprising. Her eyes dropped to his broad chest, to the muscles that his gray suit barely contained, and remembered how it was to be held against him in passion.

"Libby said you loved the ranch," he remarked.

"I did. When I was welcome."

"You still are."

"Do tell?" She cocked her head. "I'm a career woman, remember? And I'm a city girl."

His mouth tugged up. "I think city girls are sexy." His dark eyes traveled down to her slender legs encased in pink hose. "I didn't know you had legs, Jenny Wren. You always kept them in jeans."

"I didn't want you leering at me."

"Ha!" he shot back. "You knew that damned blouse was torn, the day you fell off your horse." His eyes dared her to dispute him. "You wanted my eyes on you. I'll never forget the way you looked when you saw me staring at you."

Her chest rose and fell quickly. "I was shocked."

"Shocked, hell. Delighted." He lifted the cigarette to his mouth. "I didn't realize you were a woman until then. I'd seen you as a kid. A little helpless thing I needed to protect." His eyes cut sideways and he smiled mockingly. "And then that blouse came open and I saw a body I'd have killed for. After that, the whole situation started getting impossible."

"So did you."

"I know," he admitted. "My brain was telling me to keep away, but my body wouldn't listen. You didn't help a hell of a lot, lying there on that couch with your mouth begging for mine."

"Well, I'm human!" she burst out furiously. "And I never asked you to start kissing me."

"You didn't fight me."

She turned away. "Can't we get off this subject?"

"Just when it's getting interesting?" he mused. "Why? Don't you like remembering it?"

"No, I don't!"

"Does he kiss you the way I did?" he asked shortly, jerking her around by the arm, his lean hand hurting. "That redhead, have you let him touch you like I did?"

"No!" she whispered, shocking herself with the disgust she put into that one, telling syllable.

His nostrils flared and his dark eyes traveled to the bodice of her dress, to her slender legs, her rounded hips, and all the way back up again to her eyes. "Why not?" he breathed unsteadily.

"Maybe I'm terrified of men now," she muttered.

"Maybe you're just terrified of other men," he whispered. "It was so good, when we touched each other. So good, so sweet… I rocked you under me and felt you respond, here..." His fingers brushed lightly against the bodice of her dress.

Coming to her senses all at once, she caught his fingers and pushed them away.

"No!" she burst out.

His fingers curled around her hand. He brought her fingers to his mouth and nibbled at them softly, staring into her eyes. "I can't even get in the mood with other women," he said quietly. "Three long months and I still can't sleep for thinking how you felt in my arms."

"Don't," she ground out, bending her head. "You won't make me feel guilty."

"That isn't what I want from you. Not guilt."

Her eyes came up. "You just want sex, don't you? You want me because I haven't been with anyone else!"

He caught her face in his warm hands and searched it while the forgotten cigarette between his fingers sent up curls of smoke beside her head.

"Someday, I'll tell you what I really want," he said, his voice quiet and soft and dark. "When you've forgotten, and forgiven what happened. Until then, I'll just go on as I have before." His mouth twisted. "Taking cold showers and working myself into exhaustion."

She wouldn't weaken; she wouldn't! But his hands were warm and rough, and his breath was smoky against her parted lips. And her mouth wanted his.

He bent closer, just close enough to torment her. His eyes closed. His nose touched hers.

She felt reckless and hungry, and all her willpower wasn't proof against him.

"Jenny," he groaned against her lips.

"Isn't...fair," she whispered shakily.

"I know." His hands were trembling. They touched her face as if it were some priceless treasure. His mouth trembled, too, while it brushed softly over hers. "Oh, God, I'll die if I don't kiss you...!" he whispered achingly.

"No..." But it was only a breath, and he took it from her with the cool, moist pressure of his hard lips.

She hadn't dreamed of kisses this tender, this soft. He nudged her mouth with his until it opened. She shuddered with quickly drawn breaths. Her eyes slid open and looked into his slitted ones.

"Oh," she moaned in a sharp whisper.

"Oh," he whispered back. His thumbs brushed her cheeks. "I want you. I want to live with you and touch you and let you touch me. I want to make love with you and to you."

"Everett...you mustn't," she managed in a husky whisper as his mouth tortured hers. "Please, don't do this...to me. The driver..."

"I closed the curtain, didn't you notice?" he whispered.

She looked past him, her breath jerky and quick, her face flushed, her eyes wild.

"You see?" he asked quietly.

She swallowed, struggling for control. Her eyes closed and she pulled carefully away from his warm hands.

"No," she said then.

"All right." He moved back and finished his cigarette in silence.

She glanced at him warily, tucking back a loose strand of hair.

"There's nothing to be afraid of," he said, as if he sensed all her hidden fears. "I want nothing from you that you don't want to give freely."

She clasped her hands together. Her tongue touched her dry lips, and she could still taste him on them. It was so intimate that she caught her breath.

"I can't go with you," she burst out, all at once.

"Your door has a lock," he reminded her. "And I'll even give you my word that I won't force you."

Her troubled eyes sought his and he smiled reassuringly.

"Let me rephrase that," he said after a minute. "I won't take advantage of any…lapses. Is that better?"

She clutched her purse hard enough to wrinkle the soft leather wallet inside. "I hate being vulnerable!"

"Do you think I don't?" he growled, his eyes flashing. He crushed out his cigarette. "I'm thirty-five, and it's never happened to me before." He glared at her. "And it had to be with a damned virgin!"

"Don't you curse at me!"

"I wasn't cursing," he said harshly. He reached for another cigarette.

"Will you please stop that?" she pleaded. "I'm choking on the smoke as it is."

He made a rough sound and repocketed the cigarette. "That's it! I quit. You'll be carrying a noose around with you next."

"I'm glad you're quitting smoking, but I won't be throwing a rope around your neck," she promised him with a sweet smile. "Confirmed bachelors aren't my cup of tea."

"Career women aren't mine."

She turned her eyes out the window. And for the rest of the drive to the ranch she didn't say another word.

The room he gave her was the one she'd had before. But she was surprised to see that the linen hadn't been changed. And the checks he'd written for her were just where she'd left them, on the dresser.

She stared at him as he set her bag down. "It's…you haven't torn them up," she faltered.

He straightened, taking off his hat to run a hand through his thick, dark hair. "So what?" he growled, challenge in his very posture. He towered over her.

"Well, I don't want them!" she burst out.

"Of course not," he replied. "You've got a good paying job, now, don't you?"

Her chin lifted. "Yes, I do."

He tossed his hat onto the dresser and moved toward her.

"You promised!" she burst out.

"Sure I did," he replied. He reached out and jerked her up into his arms, staring into her eyes. "What if I lied?" he whispered gruffly. "What if I meant to throw you on that bed, and strip you, and make love to you until dawn?"

He was testing her. So that was how it was going to be. She stared back at him fearlessly. "Try it," she invited.

His mouth curled up. "No hysterics?"

"I stopped having hysterics the day that horse threw me and you got an anatomy lesson," she tossed back. "Go ahead, rape me."

His face darkened. "It wouldn't be rape. Not between you and me."

"If I didn't want you, it would be."

"Honey," he said softly, "you'd want me. Desperately."

She already did. The feel of him, the clean smell of his body, the coiled strength in his powerful muscles were all working on her like drugs. But she was too afraid of the future to slide backwards now. He wanted her. But nothing more. And without love, she wanted nothing he had to offer.

"You promised," she said again.

He sighed. "So I did. Damned fool." He set her down on her feet and moved away with a long sigh to pick up his hat. His eyes studied her from the doorway. "Well, come on down when you're rested, and I'll have Consuelo fix something to eat."

"Consuelo?"

"My housekeeper." His eyes watched the expressions that washed over her face. "She's forty-eight, nicely plump, and happily married to one of my new hands. All right?"

"Did you hope I might be jealous?" she asked.

His broad chest rose and fell swiftly. "I've got a lot of high hopes about you. Care to hear a few of them?"

"Not particularly."

"That's what I was afraid of." He went out and closed the door behind him with an odd laugh.

Consuelo shrugged at the penetrating look she got from the younger woman. "Sometimes at night, the señor, he would go up there and just sit. For a long time. I wonder, you see, but the only time I mention this strange habit, he says to mind my own business. So I do not question it."

How illuminating that was. Jennifer pondered on it long and hard. It was almost as if he'd missed her. But then, if he'd missed her, he'd have to care. And he didn't. He just wanted her because she was something different, a virgin. And perhaps because she was the only woman who'd been close to him for a long time. Under the same circumstances, it could very well have been any young, reasonably attractive woman.

He came in from the corral looking dusty and tired and out of humor. Consuelo glanced at him and he glared at her as he removed his wide-brimmed hat and sat down at the table with his chaps still on.

"Any comments?" he growled.

"Not from me, señor," Consuelo assured him. "As far as I am concerned, you can sit there in your overcoat. Lunch is on the table. Call if you need me."

Jennifer put a hand over her mouth to keep from laughing. Everett glared at her.

"My, you're in a nasty mood," she observed as she poured him a cup of coffee from the carafe. She filled her own cup, too.

"Pat yourself on the back," he returned.

She raised her eyebrows. "Me?"

CHAPTER TEN

CONSUELO WAS a treasure. Small, dark, very quick around the kitchen, and Jennifer liked her on sight.

"It is good that you are here, señorita," the older woman said as she put food on the new and very elegant dining room table. "So nice to see the señor do something besides growl and pace."

Jennifer laughed as she put out the silverware. "Yes, now he's cursing at the top of his lungs," she mused, cocking her ear toward the window. "Hear him?"

It would have been impossible not to. He was giving somebody hell about an open gate, and Jennifer was glad it wasn't her.

"Such a strange man," Consuelo sighed, shaking her head. "The room he has given you, señorita, he would not let me touch it. Not to dust, not even to change the linen."

"Did he say why?" Jennifer asked with studied carelessness.

"No. But sometimes at night…" She hesitated.

"Yes?"

"You." He picked up a roll and buttered it.

"I can leave?" she suggested.

"Go ahead."

She sat back in her chair, watching him. "What's wrong?" she asked quietly. "Something is."

"Bull died."

She caught her breath. "The big Hereford?"

He nodded. "The one I sold and then bought back when I leased the oil rights." He stared at his roll blankly. "The vet's going to do an autopsy. I want to know why. He was healthy."

"I'm sorry," she said gently. "You were very proud of him."

His jaw tautened. "Well, maybe some of those heifers I bred to him will throw a good bull."

She dished up some mashed potatoes and steak and gravy. "I thought heifers were cows that hadn't grown up,' she murmured. "Isn't that what you told me?"

"Heifers are heifers until they're two years old and bred for the first time. Which these just were."

"Oh."

He glanced at her. "I'm surprised you'd remember that."

"I remember a lot about the ranch," she murmured as she ate. "Are you selling off stock before winter?"

"Not a lot of it," he said. "Now that I can afford to feed the herd."

"It's an art, isn't it?" she asked, lifting her eyes to his. "Cattle-raising, I mean. It's very methodical."

"Like decorating?" he muttered.

"That reminds me." She got up, fetched her sketch pad, and put it down beside his plate. "I did those before I came down. They're just the living room and kitchen, but I'd like to see what you think."

"You're the decorator," he said without opening it. "Do what you please."

She glared at him and put down her fork. "Everett, it's your house. I'd at least like you to approve the suggestions I'm making."

He sighed and opened the sketch pad. He frowned. His head came up suddenly. "I didn't know you could draw like this."

"It kind of goes with the job," she said, embarrassed.

"Well, you're good. Damned good. Is this what it will look like when you're finished?" he asked.

"Something like it. I'll do more detailed drawings if you like the basic plan."

"Yes, I like it," he said with a slow smile. He ran a finger over her depiction of the sofa and she remembered suddenly that instead of drawing in a new one, she'd sketched the old one. The one they'd lain on that night....

She cleared her throat. "The kitchen sketch is just under that one."

He looked up. "Was that a Freudian slip, drawing that particular sofa?" he asked.

Her face went hot. "I'm human!" she grumbled.

His eyes searched hers. "No need to overheat, Miss King. I was just asking a question. I enjoyed what we did, too. I'm not throwing stones." He turned the page and pursed his lips. "I don't like the breakfast bar."

Probably because it would require the services of an architect, she thought evilly.

"Why?" she asked anyway, trying to sound interested.

He smiled mockingly. "Because, as I told you already, I won't have that redhead in my house."

She sighed angrily. "As you wish." She studied his hard face. "Will you have a few minutes to go over some ideas with me tonight? Or are you still trying to work yourself into an early grave?"

"Would you mind if I did, Jenny?" he mused.

"Yes. I wouldn't get paid," she said venomously.

He chuckled softly. "Hardhearted little thing. Yes, I'll have some free time tonight." He finished his coffee. "But not now." He got up from the table.

"I'm sorry about your bull."

He stopped by her chair and tilted her chin up. "It will all work out," he said enigmatically. His thumb brushed over her soft mouth slowly, with electrifying results. She stared up with an expression that seemed to incite violence in him.

"Jenny," he breathed gruffly, and started to bend.

"Señor," Consuelo called, coming through the door in time to break the spell holding them, "do you want dessert now?"

"I'd have had it but for you, woman," he growled. And with that he stomped out the door, rattling the furniture as he went.

Consuelo stared after him, and Jennifer tried not to look guilty and frustrated all at once.

For the rest of the day, Jennifer went from room to room, making preliminary sketches. It was like a dream come true. For a long time, ever since she'd first seen the big house, she'd wondered what it would be like to redo it. Now she was getting the chance, and she was overjoyed. The only sad part was that Everett wouldn't let her get Drew in to do an appraisal of the place. It would be a shame to redo it if there were basic structural problems.

That evening after a quiet supper she went into the study with him and watched him build a fire in the fireplace. It was late autumn and getting cold at night. The fire crackled and burned in orange and yellow glory and smelled of oak and pine and the whole outdoors.

"How lovely," she sighed, leaning back in the armchair facing it with her eyes closed. She was wearing jeans again, with a button-down brown patterned shirt, and she felt at home.

"Yes," he said.

She opened her eyes lazily to find him standing in front of her, staring quietly at her face.

"Sorry, I drifted off," she said quickly, and started to rise.

"Don't get up. Here." He handed her the sketch pad and perched himself on the arm of the chair, just close enough to drive her crazy with the scent and warmth and threat of his big body. "Show me."

She went through the sketches with him, showing the changes she wanted to make. When they came to his big bedroom, her voice faltered as she suggested new Mediterranean furnishings and a king-size bed.

"You're very big," she said, trying not to look at him. "And the room is large enough to accommodate it."

"By all means," he murmured, watching her. "I like a lot of room."

It was the way he said it. She cleared her throat. "And I thought a narrow chocolate-and-vanilla-stripe wallpaper would be nice. With a thick cream carpet and chocolate-colored drapes."

"Am I going to live in the room, or eat it?"

"Hush. And you could have a small sitting area if you like. A desk and a chair, a lounge chair…"

"All I want in my bedroom is a bed," he grumbled. "I can work down here."

"All right." She flipped the page, glad to be on to the next room, which was a guest bedroom. "This…"

"No."

She glanced up. "What?"

"No. I don't want another guest room there." He looked down into her eyes. "Make it into a nursery."

She felt her body go cold. "A nursery?"

"Well, I've got to have someplace to put the kids," he said reasonably.

"Where are they going to come from?" she asked blankly.

He sighed with exaggerated patience. “First you have a man. Then you have a woman. They sleep together and—”

“I know that!”

“Then why did you ask me?”

“Forgive me if I sound dull, but didn’t you swear that you’d rather be dead than married?” she grumbled.

“Sure. But being rich has changed my ideas around. I’ve decided that I’ll need somebody to leave all this to.” He pulled out a cigarette and lit it.

She stared at her designs with unseeing eyes. “Do you have a candidate already?” she asked with a forced laugh.

“No, not yet. But there are plenty of women around.” His eyes narrowed as he studied her profile. “As a matter of fact, I had a phone call last week. From the woman I used to be engaged to. Seems her marriage didn’t work out. She’s divorced now.”

That hurt. She hadn’t expected that it would, but it went through her like a dagger. “Oh?” she said. Her pencil moved restlessly on the page as she darkened a line. “Were you surprised?”

“Not really,” he said with cynicism. “Women like that are pretty predictable. I told you how I felt about buying them.”

“Yes.” She drew in a slow breath. “Well, Houston is full of debutantes. You shouldn’t have much trouble picking out one.”

“I don’t want a child.”

She glanced up. “Picky, aren’t you?”

His mouth curled. "Yep."

She laughed despite herself, despite the cold that was numbing her heart. "Well, I wish you luck. Now, about the nursery, do you want it done in blue?"

"No. I like girls, too. Make it pink and blue. Or maybe yellow. Something unisex." He got up, stretching lazily, and yawned. "God, I'm tired. Honey, do you mind if we cut this short? I'd dearly love a few extra hours' sleep."

"Of course not. Do you mind if I go ahead with the rooms we've discussed?" she asked. "I could go ahead and order the materials tomorrow. I've already arranged to have the wallpaper in the living room stripped."

"Go right ahead." He glanced at her. "How long do you think it will take, doing the whole house?"

"A few weeks, that's all."

He nodded. "Sleep well, Jenny. Good night."

"Good night."

He went upstairs, and she sat by the fire until it went out, trying to reconcile herself to the fact that Everett was going to get married and have children. It would be to somebody like Libby, she thought. Some nice, sweet country girl who had no ambition to be anything but a wife and mother. Tears dripped down her cheeks and burned her cool flesh. What a pity it wouldn't be Jennifer.

She decided that perhaps Everett had had the right idea in the first place. Exhaustion was the best way in the world to keep one's mind off one's troubles. So she got up at dawn to oversee the workmen who were tearing down wallpaper and repairing plaster. Fortunately the plasterwork was in good condition and wouldn't have to be redone. By the time they were finished with the walls, the carpet people had a free day and invaded the house. She escaped to the corral and watched Eddie saddlebreak one of the new horses Everett had bought.

Perched on the corral fence in her jeans and blue sweatshirt, with her hair in a ponytail, she looked as outdoorsy as he did.

"How about if I yell 'ride 'em, cowboy,' and cheer you on, Eddie?" she drawled.

He lifted a hand. "Go ahead, Miss Jenny!"

"Ride 'em, cowboy!" she hollered.

He chuckled, bouncing around on the horse. She was so busy watching him that she didn't even hear Everett ride up behind her. He reached out a long arm and suddenly jerked her off the fence and into the saddle in front of him.

"Sorry to steal your audience, Eddie," he yelled toward the older man, "but she's needed!"

Eddie waved. Everett's hard arm tightened around her waist, tugging her stiff body into the curve of his, as he urged the horse into a canter.

"Where am I needed?" she asked, peeking over her shoulder at his hard face.

"I've got a new calf. Thought you might like to pet it."

She laughed. "I'm too busy to pet calves."

"Sure. Sitting around on fences like a rodeo girl." His arm tightened. "Eddie doesn't need an audience to break horses."

"Well, it was interesting."

"So are calves."

She sighed and let her body slump back against his. She felt him stiffen at the contact, felt his breath quicken. She could smell him, and feel him, and her body sang at the contact. It had been such a long time since those things had disturbed her.

"Where are we going?" she murmured contentedly.

"Down to the creek. Tired?"

"Mmm," she murmured. "My arms ache."

"I've got an ache of my own, but it isn't in my arms," he mused.

She cleared her throat and sat up straight. "Uh, what kind of calf is it?"

He laughed softly. "I've got an ache in my back from lifting equipment," he said, watching her face burn. "What did you think I meant?"

"Everett," she groaned, embarrassed.

"You babe in the woods," he murmured. His fingers spread on her waist, so long that they trespassed onto her flat stomach as well. "Hold on."

He put the horse into a gallop and she caught her breath, turning in the saddle to cling to his neck and hide her face in his shoulder.

He laughed softly, coiling his arm around her. "I won't let you fall," he chided.

"Do we have to go so fast?"

"I thought you were in a hurry to get there." He slowed the horse as they reached a stand of trees beside the creek. Beyond it was a barbed-wire fence. Inside it was a cow and a calf, both Herefords.

He dismounted and lifted Jenny down. "She's gentle," he said, taking her hand to pull her along toward the horned cow. "I raised this one myself, from a calf. Her mama died of snakebite and I nursed her with a bottle. She's been a good breeder. This is her sixth calf."

The furry little thing fascinated Jenny. It had pink eyes and a pink nose and pink ears, and the rest of it was reddish-brown and white.

She laughed softly and rubbed it between the eyes. "How pretty," she murmured. "She has pink eyes!"

"He," he corrected. "It will be a steer."

She frowned. "Not a bull?"

He glowered down at her. "Don't you ever listen to me? A steer is a bull that's been converted for beef. A bull has…" He searched for the words. "A bull is still able to father calves."

She grinned up at him. "Not embarrassed, are you?" she taunted.

He cocked an eyebrow. "You're the one who gets embarrassed every time I talk straight," he said curtly.

She remembered then, and her smile faded. She touched the calf gently, concentrating on it instead of him.

His lean hands caught her waist and she gasped, stiffening. His breath came hard and fast at her back.

"There's a party in Victoria tomorrow night. One of the oil men's giving it. He asked me to come." His fingers bit into her soft flesh. "How about going with me and holding my hand? I don't know much about social events."

"You don't really want to go, do you?" she asked, looking over her shoulder at him knowingly.

He shook his head. "But it's expected. One of the penalties of being well-off. Socializing."

"Yes, I'll be very proud to go with you."

"Need a dress? I'll buy you one, since it was my idea."

She lowered her eyes. "No, thank you. I…I have one at my apartment, if you'll have someone drive me up there."

"Give Ted the key. He'll pick it up for you," he said, naming his chauffeur, who was also the new yardman.

"All right."

"Is it white?" he asked suddenly.

She glared at him. "No. It's black. Listen here, Everett Culhane, just because I've never—"

He put a finger over her lips, silencing her. "I like you in white," he said simply. "It keeps me in line," he added with a wicked, slow smile.

"You just remember the nice new wife you'll have and the kids running around the house, and that will work very well," she said with a nip in her voice. "Shouldn't we go back? The carpet-layers may have some questions for me."

"Don't you like kids, Jenny?" he asked softly.

"Well, yes."

"Could you manage to have them and a career at the same time?" he asked with apparent indifference.

Her lips pouted softly. "Lots of women do," she said. "It's not the dark ages."

He searched her eyes. "I know that. But there are men who wouldn't want a working wife."

"Cavemen," she agreed.

He chuckled. "A woman like you might make a man nervous in that respect. You're pretty. Suppose some other man snapped you up while you were decorating his house? That would be hell on your husband's nerves."

"I don't want to get married," she informed him.

His eyebrows lifted. "You'd have children out of wedlock?"

"I didn't say that!"

"Yes, you did."

"Everett!" Her hands pushed at his chest. He caught them and lifted them slowly around his neck, tugging so that her body rested against his.

"Ummmm," he murmured on a smile, looking down at the softness of her body. "That feels nice. What were you saying, about children?"

"If…if I wanted them, then I guess I'd get married. But I'd still work. I mean… Everett, don't…" she muttered when he slid his hands down to her waist and urged her closer.

"Okay. You'd still work?"

His hands weren't pushing, but they were doing something crazy to her nerves. They caressed her back lazily, moving up to her hair to untie the ribbon that held it back.

"I'd work when the children started school. That was what I meant… Will you stop that?" she grumbled, reaching back to halt his fingers.

He caught her hands, arching her so that he could look down and see the vivid tautness of her breasts against the thin fabric of her blouse.

"No bra?" he murmured, and the smile got bigger. "My, my, another Freudian slip?"

"Will you stop talking about bras and slips and let go of my hands, Mr. Culhane?" she asked curtly.

"I don't think you really want me to do that, Jenny," he murmured dryly.

"Why?"

"Because if I let go of your hands, I have to put mine somewhere else." He looked down pointedly at her blouse. "And there's really only one place I want to put them right now."

Her chest rose and fell quickly, unsteadily. His closeness and the long abstinence and the sun and warmth of the day were all working on her. Her eyes met his suddenly and the contact was like an electric jolt. All the memories came rushing back, all the old hungers.

"Do you remember that day you fell off the horse?"

he asked in a soft, low tone, while bees buzzed somewhere nearby. "And your blouse came open, and I looked down and you arched your back so that I could see you even better."

Her lips parted and she shook her head nervously.

"Oh, but you did," he breathed. "I'd seen you, watching my mouth, wondering…and that day, it all came to a head. I looked at you and I wanted you. So simply. So hungrily. I barely came to my senses in time, and before I did, I was hugging the life out of you. And you were letting me."

She remembered that, too. It had been so glorious, being held that way.

He let go of her hands all at once and slid his arms around her, half lifting her off her feet. "Hard, Jenny," he whispered, drawing her slowly to him, so that she could feel her breasts flattening against his warm chest. It was like being naked against him.

She caught her breath and moaned. His cheek slid against hers and he buried his face in her throat. His arms tightened convulsively. And he rocked her, and rocked her, and she clung to him while all around them the wind blew and the sun burned, and the world seemed to disappear.

His breath came roughly and his arms trembled. "I don't feel this with other women," he said after a while. "You make me hungry."

"As you keep reminding me," she whispered back, "I'm not on the menu."

"Yes, I know." He brushed his mouth against her throat and then lifted his head and slowly released her. "No more of that," he said on a rueful sigh, "unless you'd like to try making love on horseback. I've got a man coming to see me about a new bull."

Her eyes widened. "Can people really make…" She turned away, shaking her head.

"I don't know," he murmured, chuckling at her shyness. "I've never tried it. But there's always a first time."

"You just keep your hands to yourself," she cautioned as he put her into the saddle and climbed up behind her.

"I'm doing my best, honey," he said dryly. He reached around her to catch the reins and his arm moved lazily across her breasts, feeling the hardened tips. "Oh, Jenny," he breathed shakily, "next time you'd better wear an overcoat."

She wanted to stop him, she really did. But the feel of that muscular forearm was doing terribly exciting things to her. She felt her muscles tauten in a dead giveaway.

She knew it was going to happen even as he let go of the reins and his hands slid around her to lift and cup her breasts. She let him, turning her cheek against his chest with a tiny cry.

"The sweetest torture on earth," he whispered unsteadily. His hands were so tender, so gentle. He made no move to open the blouse, although he must have known that he could, that she would have let him. His lips moved warmly at her temple. "Jenny, you shouldn't let me touch you like this."

"Yes, I know," she whispered huskily. Her hands moved over his to pull them away, but they lingered on his warm brown fingers. Her head moved against his chest weakly.

"Do you want to lie down on the grass with me and make love?" he asked softly. "We could, just for a few minutes. We could kiss and touch each other, and nothing more."

She wanted to. She wanted it more than she wanted to breathe. But it was too soon. She wasn't sure of him. She only knew that he wanted her desperately and that she didn't dare pave the way for him. It was just a game to him. It kept him from getting bored while he found himself a wife. She loved him, but love on one side would never be enough.

"No, Rett," she said, although the words were torn from her. She moved his hands gently down, to her waist, and pressed them there. "No."

He drew away in a long, steady breath. "Levelheaded Jenny," he said finally. "Did you know?"

"Know what?"

"That if I'd gotten you on the grass, nothing would have saved you?"

She smiled ruefully. "It was kind of the other way around." She felt him shudder, and she turned and pressed herself into his arms. "I want you, too. Please don't do this to me. I can't be what you want. Please, let me decorate your house and go away. Don't hurt me anymore, Rett."

He lifted and turned her so that she was lying across the saddle in his arms. He held her close and took the reins in his hand. "I'm going to have to rethink my strategy, I'm afraid." He sighed. "It isn't working."

She looked up. "What do you mean?"

He searched her eyes and bent and kissed her forehead softly. "Never mind, kitten. You're safe now. Just relax. I'll take you home."

She snuggled close and closed her eyes. This was a memory she'd keep as long as she lived, of riding across the meadow in Everett's arms on a lovely autumn morning. His wife would have other memories. But this one would always be her own, in the long, lonely years ahead. Her hand touched his chest lightly, and her heart ached for him. If only he could love her back. But love wasn't a word he trusted anymore, and she couldn't really blame him. He'd been hurt too much. Even by her, when she hadn't meant to. She sighed bitterly. It was all too late. If only it had been different. Tears welled up in her eyes. If only.

CHAPTER ELEVEN

JENNIFER wished for the tenth time that she'd refused Everett's invitation to the exclusive party in Victoria. It seemed that every single, beautiful woman in the world had decided to converge on the spot just to cast her eyes at Everett.

He did look good, Jennifer had to admit. There just wasn't anybody around who came close to matching him. Dressed in an elegant dinner jacket, he looked dark and debonair and very sophisticated. Not to mention sexy. The way the jacket and slacks fit, every muscle in that big body was emphasized in the most masculine way. It was anguish just to look at him; it was even worse to remember how it was to be held and touched by him. Jennifer felt her body tingle from head to toe and the memory of the day before, of his hands smoothing over her body, his voice husky and deep in her ear. And now there he stood making eyes at a gorgeous brunette.

She turned away and tossed down the entire contents of her brandy glass. If she hadn't been so tired from overworking herself, the brandy might not have been as potent. But it was her second glass and, despite the filling buffet, she was feeling the alcohol to a frightening degree. She kept telling herself that she didn't look bad herself, with her blond hair hanging long and loose around the shoulders of her low-cut clinging black dress. She was popular enough. So why didn't Everett dance one dance with her?

By the time she was danced around the room a couple of times by left-footed oilmen and dashing middle-aged married men, she felt like leaping over the balcony. How odd that at any party there were never any handsome, available bachelors.

"Sorry to cut in, but I have to take Jenny home," Everett said suddenly, cutting out a balding man in his fifties who was going over and over the latest political crisis with maddening intricacy.

Jennifer almost threw herself on Everett in gratitude. She mumbled something polite and completely untrue to the stranger, smiled, and stumbled into Everett's arms.

"Careful, honey, or we'll both wind up on the floor." He laughed softly. "Are you all right?"

"I'm just fine." She sighed, snuggling close. Her arms slid around him. "Everett, can I go to sleep now?"

He frowned and pulled her head up. "How much have you had to drink?"

"I lost count." She grinned. Her eyes searched his face blearily. "Gosh, Rett, you're so sexy."

A red stain highlighted his cheekbones. "You're drunk, all right. Come on."

"Where are we going?" she protested. "I want to dance."

"We'll dance in the car."

She frowned. "We can't stand up in there," she said reasonably.

He held her hand, tugging her along. They said good night to a couple she vaguely recognized as their hosts; then he got their coats from the maid and hustled her out into the night.

"Cold out here," she muttered. She nudged herself under his arm and pressed against his side with a sigh. "Better."

"For whom?" he ground out. His chest rose and fell heavily. "I wish I'd let Ted drive us."

"Why?" she murmured, giggling. "Are you afraid to be alone with me? You can trust me, honey," she said, nudging him. "I wouldn't seduce you, honest."

A couple passed them going down the steps, and the elderly woman gave Jennifer a curious look.

"He's afraid of me," Jennifer whispered. "He isn't on the pill, you see…"

"Jenny!" he growled, jerking her close.

"Not here, Rett!" she exclaimed. "My goodness, talk about impatience…!"

He was muttering something about a gag as he half-led, half-dragged her to the car.

"You old stick-in-the-mud, you." She laughed after

he'd put her inside and climbed in next to her. "Did I embarrass you?"

He only glanced at her as he started the Lincoln. "You're going to hate yourself in the morning when I remind you what you've been saying. And I will," he promised darkly. "Ten times a day."

"You look gorgeous when you're mad," she observed. She moved across the seat and nuzzled close again. "I'll sleep with you tonight, if you like," she said gaily.

He stiffened and muttered something under his breath.

"Well, you've been trying to get me into bed with you, haven't you?" she asked. "Propositioning me that last day at the ranch, and then coming after me, and making all sorts of improper remarks…so now I agree, and what do you do? You get all red in the face and start cussing. Just like a man. The minute you catch a girl, you're already in pursuit of someone else, like that brunette you were dancing with," she added, glaring up at him. "Well, just don't expect that what you see is what you get, because I was in the ladies' room with her, and it's padded! I saw!"

He was wavering between anger and laughter. Laughter won. He started, and couldn't seem to stop.

"You won't think it's very funny if you take her out," she kept on, digging her own grave. Everything was fuzzy and pink and very pleasant. She felt so relaxed! "She's even smaller than I am," she muttered. "And her legs are just awful. She pulled up her skirt to fix her stockings…she hardly has any legs, they're so skinny!"

"Meow," he taunted.

She tossed back her long hair, and leaned her head back against the seat. Her coat had come open, revealing the deep neckline of the black dress. "Why won't you make love to me?"

"Because if I did, you'd scream your head off," he said reasonably. "Here, put your tired little head on my shoulder and close your eyes. You're soaked, honey."

She blinked. "I am not. It isn't raining."

He reached out an arm and pulled her against him. "Close your eyes, sweet," he said in a soft, tender tone. "I'll take good care of you."

"Will you sleep with me?" she murmured, resting her head on his shoulder.

"If you want me to."

She smiled and closed her eyes with a long sigh. "That would be lovely," she whispered. And it was the last thing she said.

Morning came with blinding light and some confounded bird twittering his feathered head off outside the window.

"Oh, go away!" she whispered, and held her head. "An axe," she groaned. "There's an axe between my eyes. Bird, shut up!"

Soft laughter rustled her hair. She opened her eyes. Laughter?

Her head turned on the pillow and Everett's eyes

looked back into her own. She gasped and tried to sit up, then groaned with the pain and fell back down again.

"Head hurt? Poor baby."

"You slept with me?" she burst out. She turned her head slowly to look at him. He was fully dressed, except for his shoes and jacket. He even had his shirt on. He was lying on top of the coverlet, and she was under it.

Slowly, carefully, she lifted the cover and looked. Her face flamed scarlet. She was dressed in nothing but a tiny pair of briefs. The rest of her was pink and tingling.

"Rett!" she burst out, horrified.

"I only undressed you," he said, leaning on an elbow to watch her. "Be reasonable, honey. You couldn't sleep in your evening gown. And," he added with a faint grin, "it wasn't my fault that you didn't have anything on under it. You can't imagine how shocked I was."

"That's right, I can't," she agreed, and her eyes accused him.

"I confess I did stare a little," he murmured. His hand brushed the unruly blond hair out of her eyes. "A lot," he corrected. "My God, Jenny," he said on a slow breath, "you are the most glorious sight undressed that I ever saw in my life. I nearly fainted."

"Shame on you!" she said, trying to feel outraged. It was difficult, because she was still tingling from the compliment.

"For what? For appreciating something beautiful?"

He touched her nose with a long, lean finger. "Shame on you, for being embarrassed. I was a perfect gentleman. I didn't even touch you, except to put you under the covers."

"Oh."

"I thought I'd wait until you woke up, and do it then," he added with a grin.

Her fingers grabbed the covers tightly. "Oh, no, you don't!"

He moved closer, his fingers tangling in her blond hair as he loomed above her. "You had a lot to say about that brunette. Or don't you remember?"

She blinked. Brunette? Vaguely she remembered saying something insulting about the woman's body. Then she remembered vividly. Her face flamed.

"Something about how little she was, if I recall," he murmured dryly.

She bit her lower lip and her eyes met his uneasily. "Did I? How strange. Was she short?"

"That wasn't what you meant," he said. One lean hand moved down her shoulder and over the covers below her collarbone. "You meant, here, she was small."

If she looked up, she'd be finished. But she couldn't help it. Her eyes met his and the world seemed to narrow down to the two of them. She loved him so. Would it be wrong to kiss him just once more, to feel that hard, wonderful mouth on her own?

He seemed to read that thought, because his jaw

tautened and his breathing became suddenly ragged. "The hell with being patient," he growled, reaching for the covers. "Come here."

He stripped them away and jerked her into his arms, rolling over with her, so that she was lying on him. Where his shirt was undone, her body pressed nakedly into his hairy chest.

His eyes were blazing as they looked up into hers. He deliberately reached down to yank his shirt away, his eyes on the point where her soft breasts were crushed against his body. Dark and light, she thought shakily, looking at the contrast between his dark skin and her pale flesh.

But still he didn't touch her. His hands moved up into her hair, oddly tender, at variance with the tension she could feel in his body.

"Don't you want…to touch me?" she whispered nervously.

"More than my own life," he confessed. "But I'm not going to. Come down here and kiss me."

"Why not?" she whispered, bending to give him her mouth.

"Because Consuelo's on her way up the stairs with coffee and toast," he breathed. "And she never knocks."

She sat up with a gasp. "Why didn't you say so!"

He laughed softly, triumphantly, his eyes eating her soft body as she climbed out of the bed and searched wildly for a robe.

"Here," he murmured, throwing his long legs over

the bed. He reached under her pillow and got her nightgown. "Come here and I'll stuff you in it."

She didn't even question the impulse that made her obey him instantly. She lifted her arms as he held the nightgown over her head and gasped as he bent first and kissed her rosy breasts briefly, but with a tangible hunger. While she was getting over the shock, he tugged the long cotton gown over her head, lifted her, tossed her into the bed, and pulled the covers over her with a knowing smile.

And Consuelo opened the door before she could get out a word.

"Good morning!" The older woman laughed, handing the tray to Everett. "Also is hair of the dog, in the glass," she added with a wry glance at Jennifer. "To make the señorita's head a little better."

And she was gone as quickly as she'd come. Everett put the tray down beside Jennifer on the bed and poured cream into her coffee.

"Why did you do that?" she whispered, still shaking from the wild little caress.

"I couldn't help myself," he murmured, smiling at her. "I've wanted to, for a long time."

She took the coffee in trembling hands. He steadied them, watching her shaken features.

"It's part of lovemaking," he said softly. "Nothing sordid or shameful. When we make love, that's how I'll rouse you before I take you."

She shuddered, and the coffee cup began to rock

again. Her eyes, meeting his, were wild with mingled fear and hunger.

"Except," he added quietly, "that I won't stop at the waist."

Coffee went everywhere. She cursed and muttered and grumbled and moped. But when she raised her glittering eyes to his the pupils dilated until they were almost black.

He laughed softly, menacingly. "Almost," he said enigmatically. "Almost there." He got up. "I'll get Consuelo to come and help you mop up." He turned with one hand on the doorknob, impossibly attractive, wildly sensuous with his hair ruffled and his shirt open and his bare, muscular chest showing. "The brunette was Jeb Doyle's daughter," he added. "She's looking for a husband. She rides like a man, she loves cattle and kids, she's twenty-eight and she lives about five miles south of here. She may be small, but she's got nice, full hips. Just right for having children. Her name's Sandy."

She was getting madder by the second. He was baiting her! She picked up the coffee cup and, without even thinking, threw it at him.

It shattered against the closed door. He went down the hall laughing like a banshee and she screamed after him. By the time Consuelo got to her, the rest of the coffee and the headache remedy had turned the bedspread a strange shade of tan.

For the next week, she gave Everett the coldest shoulder she could manage. He was gone from the ranch frequently, and she noticed it and remembered what he'd said about the brunette, and wanted desperately to kill him. No, not just kill him. Torture him. Slowly. Over an open fire.

It got worse. He started having supper with Jennifer every night, and the whole time he'd sit there and watch her and make infrequent but agonizing remarks about the brunette.

"Sandy's getting a new colt tomorrow," he mentioned one evening, smiling wistfully. "She asked if I'd come over and look at it for her."

"Can't she see it by herself?" she asked sweetly.

"Conformation is very important in a horse," he said. "I used to breed them years ago, before I got interested in cattle."

"Oh." She concentrated on her food.

"How's the decorating coming?"

"Fine," she said through her teeth. "We're getting the paper up in your bedroom tomorrow. Then there'll only be the other bedrooms to go. You never said how you liked the way the living room and the study came out."

"They're okay," he said. He lifted a forkful of dessert to his mouth and she wanted to jump up and stab him in the lip. Okay! And she'd spent days on the projects, working well into the night alongside the men!

He glanced up at her flushed face. "Wasn't that enthusiastic enough?" He took a sip of coffee. "Damn, Jenny, what a hell of a great job you're doing on the house!" he said with a big, artificial smile. "I'm pleased as punch!"

"I'd like to punch you," she muttered. She slammed down her napkin, slid out of the chair, and stomped out of the room.

Watching her, Everett's eyes narrowed and a faint, predatory smile curved his lips.

The next day, she concentrated on his bedroom. It was difficult to work in there, thinking about whose territory it was. Her eyes kept drifting to the bed where he slept, to the pillow where he laid his dark head. Once she paused beside it and ran her hand lovingly over the cover. Besotted, she told herself curtly. She was besotted, and it was no use. He was going to marry that skinny, flat-chested brunette!

She didn't even stop for lunch, much less supper. The workmen had left long before, and she was working on the last wall, when Everett came into the room and stood watching her with a cup of coffee in his hand.

"Have you given up eating?" he asked.

"Yep."

He cocked an eyebrow. "Want some coffee?"

"Nope."

He chuckled softly. "Bad imitation. You don't even look like Gary Cooper. You're too short."

She glared down at him. Her jeans were covered with glue. So were her fingers, her bare arms, and the front of her white T-shirt. "Did you want something?"

"Yes. To go to bed. I've got to get an early start in the morning. I'm taking Sandy fishing."

She stared into the bucket of glue and wondered how he'd look plastered to the wall. It was tempting, but dangerous.

"I'd like to finish this one wall," she murmured quietly.

"Go ahead. I'm going to have a shower." He stripped off his shirt. She glanced at him, fascinated by the dark perfection of him, by the ripple of muscle, the way the light played on his skin as he started to take off his...*trousers!*

Her eyes jerked back to the glue and her hands trembled. "Everett?" she said in a squeaky voice.

"Well, don't look," he said reasonably. "I can't very well take a bath in my clothes."

"I could have left the room," she said.

"Why? Aren't you curious?" he taunted.

She gritted her teeth. "No!"

"Coward."

She put glue and more glue on a strip of wallpaper until the glue was three times as thick as the paper it was spread on. Not until she heard the shower running did she relax. She put the wallpaper in place and started scrambling down the ladder.

Unfortunately, just because the shower was running, it didn't mean that Everett was in it. She got down and started for the door, and there he stood, with a towel wrapped around his narrow hips and not another stitch on.

"Going somewhere?" he asked.

"Yes. Out of here!" she exclaimed, starting past him.

She never knew exactly how it happened. One minute she was walking toward the door, and the next she was lying flat on the bed with Everett's hard body crushing her into the mattress.

His chest rose and fell slowly, his eyes burned down into hers. Holding her gaze, he eased the towel away and bent to her mouth.

She trembled with kindling passion. It was so incredibly sweet to let her hands run over his hard, warm body, to feel the muscles of his back and arms and shoulders and hips. To let him kiss her softly, with growing intimacy. To know the crush of his body, the blatant force of his hunger for her. To love him with her hands and her mouth.

He lifted his head a minute later and looked into her awed eyes. "You're not so squeaky clean yourself," he said softly. "Why don't you come and take a bath with me?"

Her hands touched his hard arms gently, lovingly. "Because we'd do more than bathe, and you know it," she replied on a soft sigh. "All you have to do is touch me, and you can have anything you want. It's always been like that. The only reason I'm still a virgin is that you haven't insisted."

"Why do you think I haven't?" he prodded.

She shifted. "I don't know. Conscience, maybe?"

He bent and brushed his mouth softly over hers. "Go and put on something soft and pretty. Have a shower. Then come downstairs to the living room and we'll talk."

She swallowed. "I thought you had to get to bed early. To take Sandy fishing," she murmured resentfully.

"Did it ever occur to you that you might be formidable competition for her, if you cared to make the effort?" he asked, watching her. "Or didn't you know how easy it would be to seduce me? And once you did that," he murmured, touching her soft mouth, "I'd probably feel obliged to marry you. Not being on the pill and all," his eyes went back to hers with blazing intensity, "you could get pregnant."

Her breath caught in her throat. She never knew when he was teasing, when he was serious. And now, her mind was whirling.

While she worried over his intentions, he moved away from her and got to his feet, and she stared at him in helpless fascination.

"You see?" he said, his voice deep and full of secrets, "it isn't so shocking, is it?"

She lifted her eyes to his. "You're...very..." She tried to find words.

"So are you, honey," he said. "Take your bath and I'll see you downstairs."

And he walked off, oblivious to her intent stare.

Minutes later, she went nervously down the staircase in a white dress, her hair freshly washed and dried, loose around her shoulders. Something that had been brewing between them for a long time was coming abruptly to a head, and she wasn't quite sure how to face it. She had a terrible feeling that he was going to proposition her again, and that she was going to be stupid enough to accept. She loved him madly, wanted him madly. That Sandy person was after him, and Jennifer was afraid. She couldn't quite accept the idea that he might marry someone else. Despite the pain he'd caused her, she dwelled on the fear of losing him.

He was waiting for her. In beige trousers and a patterned beige shirt, he looked larger than life. All man. Sensual and incredibly attractive, especially when she got close enough to catch the scent of his big body.

"Here," he said, offering her a small brandy.

"Thank you," she said politely. She took it, touching his fingers, looking up into dark, quiet eyes. Her lips parted helplessly.

"Now sit down. I want to ask you something."

She sat on the edge of the sofa, but instead of taking the seat beside her, he knelt on the carpet just in front of her. Because of his height, that put her on an unnerving level with his eyes.

"Afraid of me, even now?" he asked softly.

"Especially now," she whispered, trembling. She put the snifter to one side and her trembling fingers reached out and touched the hard lines of his face. "Everett, I'm…so very much in love with you," she said, her voice breaking. "If you want me to be your mistress… oh!"

She was on the carpet, in his arms, being kissed so hungrily that she couldn't even respond to him. His mouth devoured hers, hurting, bruising, and he trembled all over as if with a fever. His hands trembled as they touched, with expert sureness, every line and curve of her body.

"Say it again," he said roughly, lifting his head just enough to look at her.

Her body ached for his. She leaned toward him helplessly. "I love you," she whispered, pride gone to ashes. "I love you, I love you!"

His head moved down to her bodice, his mouth nudged at the buttons, his hands bit into her back. She reached down blindly to get the fabric out of his way, to give him anything, everything he wanted. There were no more secrets. She belonged to him.

His mouth taught her sensations she'd never dreamed her body would feel. She breathed in gasps as his lips and teeth explored her like some precious delicacy. Her hands held him there, caressed his dark head, loved what he was doing to her.

He raised his head to look at her, smiling faintly at her rapt face, her wide, dark green eyes, her flushed face, the glorious disarray of her hair and her dress.

"I'll remember you like this for the rest of our lives," he said. "The way you look right now, in the first sweet seconds of passion. Do you want me badly?"

"Yes," she confessed. She brought his hand to her body and held it against her taut flesh, brushing his knuckles lazily across it. "Feel?"

His nostrils flared and there was something reckless and unbridled in the eyes that held hers. "For a virgin," he murmured, "you're pretty damned exciting to make love to."

She smiled wildly, hotly. "Teach me."

"Not yet."

"Please."

He shook his head. He sat up, leaning back against the sofa with his long legs stretched out, and looked down at her with a wicked smile. "Fasten your dress. You make me crazy like that."

"I thought that was the whole point of the thing?" she asked unsteadily.

"It was, until you started making declarations of love. I was going to seduce you on the sofa. But now I suppose we'd better do it right."

Her eyes widened in confusion. "I don't understand."

He pulled her up and across his lap. "Oh, the hell with it," he murmured, and opened the top button of her bodice again. "God, I love to look at you!"

She swallowed hard. "Don't you want me?"

"Jenny." He laughed. He turned and brought her hips very gently against his. "See?" he whispered.

She buried her face in his throat and he rocked her softly, tenderly.

"Then, why?" she asked on a moan.

"Because we have to do things in the right order, honey. First we get married, then we have sex, then we make babies."

She stiffened. "What?"

"Didn't you hear me?" He eased her head down on his arm so that he could see her face.

"But, Sandy..." she faltered.

"Sandy is a nice girl," he murmured. "I danced one dance with her, and she went back to her fiancé. He's a nice boy. You'll like him."

"Fiancé!"

He jerked her close and held her hard, roughly. "I love you," he said in a voice that paralyzed her. His eyes blazed with it, burned with it. "Oh, God, I love you, Jenny. Love you, want you, need you, in every single damned way there is! If you want me to get on my knees, I'll do it, I'll do anything to make you forget what I said and did to you that last day you were here." He bent and kissed her hungrily, softly, and lifted his head again, breathing hard. "I knew I loved you then," he said, "when you handed me that check to pay for my bull, and told me the truth. And all I could think of was that I loved you, and that you were out of my reach forever. A career woman, a woman with some money of her own, and I had nothing to offer you, no way to keep you. And I chased you away, because it was torture to look at you and feel that way and have no hope at all."

"Rett!" she burst out. Tears welled up in her eyes and she clung to him. "Oh, Rett, why didn't you tell me? I loved you so much!"

"I didn't know that," he said. His voice shook a little. His arms contracted. "I thought you were playing me along. It wasn't until you left that I realized that you must have cared one hell of a lot, to have done what you did for me." He shifted restlessly, and ground her against him. "Don't you know? Haven't you worked it out yet, why I sold the oil rights? I did it so that I'd have enough money to bring you back."

She caught her breath, and the tears overflowed onto his shirt, his throat.

"I didn't even have the price of a bus ticket." He laughed huskily, his voice tormented with memory. "And I knew that without you, the land wouldn't matter, because I couldn't live. I couldn't stay alive. So I sold the oil rights and I bought a car and I called Sally Wade. And then, I parked across the street to watch for you. And you came out," he said roughly, "laughing and looking so beautiful...holding on to that redheaded ass's arm! I could have broken your neck!"

"He was my friend. Nothing more." She nuzzled her face against him. "I thought you wanted revenge. I didn't realize...!"

"I wouldn't let Consuelo touch your room, did she tell you?" he whispered. "I left it the way it was. For the first week or so...I could still catch the scent of you on the pillow..." His voice broke, and she searched blindly for his mouth, and gave him comfort in the only way she could.

Her fingers touched his face, loved it; her lips told him things, secrets, that even words wouldn't. Gently, tenderly, she drew him up onto the sofa with her, and eased down beside him on it. And with her mouth and her hands and her body, she told him in the sweetest possible way that he'd never be alone as long as she lived.

"We can't," he whispered, trembling.

"Why?" she moaned softly.

"Because I want you in church, Jenny Wren," he whispered, easing her onto her side, soothing her with his hands and his mouth. "I want it all to be just right. I want to hear the words and watch your face when you say them, and tell the whole world that you're my woman. And then," he breathed softly, "then we'll make love and celebrate in the sweetest, most complete way there is. But not like this, darling. Not on a sofa, without the rings or the words or the beauty of taking our vows together." He drew back and looked into her damp eyes. "You'll want that, when you look back on our first time. You'll want it when the children are old enough to be told how we met, how we married. You won't want a tarnished memory to put in your scrapbook."

She kissed him softly. "Thank you."

"I love you," he said, smiling. "I can wait. If," he added with a lift of his eyebrow, "you'll put your clothes back on and stop trying to lead me into a life of sin."

"I haven't taken them off," she protested.

"You have." He got up and looked down at her, with the dress around her waist.

"Well, look at you," she grumbled. His shirt was off and out of his trousers, and his belt was unbuckled.

"You did it," he accused.

She burst out laughing as she buttoned buttons. "I suppose I did. Imagine me, actually trying to seduce you. And after all the times I accused you of it!"

"I don't remember complaining," he remarked.

She got to her feet and went into his arms with a warm sigh. "Me, either. How soon can we get married?"

"How about Friday?"

"Three days?" she groaned.

"You can take cold showers," he promised her. "And finish decorating the house. You're not going to have a lot of time for decorating after we're married."

"I'm not, huh?" she murmured. "What will I be doing?"

"I hoped you might ask," he returned with a smile. He bent his head, lifting her gently in his arms. "This is what you'll be doing." And he kissed her with such tenderness that she felt tears running down her warm cheeks. Since it seemed like such a lovely occupation, she didn't even protest. After all, she'd have plenty of time for decorating when the children started school. Meanwhile, Everett showed promise of being a full-time job.

* * * * *

Choose the romance that suits your reading mood

Home and Family

Harlequin® American Romance®
Lively stories about homes, families and communities like the ones you know. This is romance the all-American way!

Silhouette® Special Edition
A woman in her world—living and loving. Celebrating the magic of creating a family and developing romantic relationships.

Harlequin® Superromance®
Unexpected, exciting and emotional stories about homes, families and communities.

Look for these and many other Harlequin and Silhouette romance books wherever books are sold, including most bookstores, supermarkets, drugstores and discount stores.

SMP60HOMER2

HARLEQUIN®
A Romance FOR EVERY MOOD™